TO HELL AND BACK

Also by Bill Blume

West of Apocalypse

The Cold Shoulder

Secrets Hidden in the Light (Audio Drama)

The Dragon Spy

Gidion's Hunt

Gidion's Blood

The Deadlands: And Other Stories

TO HELL AND BACK

BILL BLUME

Time Killer Publishing

Book Cover by Phillip Hilliker

First Time Killer Publishing paperback edition January 2026

Every book I write is for Sheri,
but this one, more than any other I've done, is for her.

Many beloved furballs have shared our journey together:
Wicket & Mocha,
Tuffy, Fluffy, Scoundrel, Akasha, Lady Macbeth, & Page

Author's Note

For my fellow dog lovers, take heart. The dog doesn't die in the end, and he gets a happy ending.

As for the humans and demons, I make no such promises.

PART I

THE BLOOD REALM

Chapter 1

After four days and nights of traveling the Blood Realm's backcountry, Ty and Dani had reached the wall of Vel with their dog Wicket. They were exorcist's swords and hunting for a demon in Hell.

Long, slender shafts of ivory bone, carved from gigantic ulnae, tibiae, and humeri, formed the forty-foot-tall wall that surrounded the city. Only God and the demons knew what kind of beasts those bones had belonged to.

Ty and Dani had slipped in and out of Vel plenty of times during the past five years to hunt demons that had escaped exorcists in the mortal world. This wasn't even the first time they'd come to claim a demon's head and heart for revenge.

They navigated their way to the center of the city, which sat higher than the rest of Vel. Their fifteen pound silky terrier insisted on stopping for the occasional sniff of local filth staining the ground. They stayed with the darker paths between homes, even though they'd disguised themselves in uniforms and helmets they'd taken from a group of guards they'd killed. The closer they got to the center of the city, the more impressive the structures became, constructed from bones much smaller than those used for the city wall. Going this route forced them to climb stairs assembled from vertebrae three feet in diameter instead of taking the gentle slopes of the major streets. Their light brown furball handled most of the steps, but Dani and Ty sometimes had to lift him up.

The pale shape of a castle grew more defined against the night sky as they ascended the city. The stairs they were climbing led to one of the castle's towers. The round structure was carved out of a single, massive femur and resembled a rook cannibalized from a giant's chessboard. The walls jutting out from the tower were built from thousands of smaller bones.

Ty pulled out the sling they used to carry Wicket when they needed their hands free. "I'll take him."

Dani picked up the little furball and kissed the top of his head. Wicket licked her face. After Ty slipped on the sling so that Wicket could rest against his back, Dani placed him in it.

"You all good?" Ty whispered to his wife.

She kissed him. "I will be once we've killed this bastard."

It was good to see her smile. Four days had passed since the demon Malum had killed Dani's mother and every member of their order in Richmond. They both wanted to end this demon, but she needed this.

About halfway up the wall, Wicket shifted in the sling. Ty stopped climbing until the little terrier had settled down. "No more of that, pal. We gotta move fast."

Dani reached the top of the battlements and waved to Ty that all was clear. The muscles in Ty's arms and legs burned as he clung to the wall. A few minutes behind Dani, he cleared the top. While Ty leaned over the parapet of foot-long, sharp teeth, Wicket climbed out of the sling and jumped off his back to land at Dani's feet.

She scratched Wicket behind his ears as she watched the rest of the castle wall and the courtyard below. "Need a hand?"

"I'm good." Ty pulled himself over the teeth without cutting himself. It helped that the tips of the teeth were dulled.

A small fire burned in a pit at the center of the courtyard below them. At least two dozen demons were gathered down there, positioned at all of the castle's entry points. The portcullis, one of the few metal features of the castle, was down. Some of the demons slept while others kept watch, probably taking turns. Most of them likely weren't used to being awake at this time. That still left too many for Ty and Dani to walk out of here with Malum's head and heart in a bag. They'd been lucky to make it this far without being seen.

Ty and Dani kept low as they walked along the top of the outer wall, which surrounded the castle in the shape of a hexagon. The main structure of the castle was attached to the wall opposite from the portcullis with its outer wall against a cliff overlooking the north side of the city. A few hints of firelight shown in the homes below, with most of the city asleep.

As they neared the roof of the main structure, they saw two figures moving on it. The pair stood at the wall's edge and stared down the cliff.

One guard was a whiter, one of the most common races in the Blood Realm. Bone-white flesh covered their human-like torso, attached to a pair of furry legs that were double-jointed like a goat. Their hands and feet resembled the scaled talons of a dragon.

The other demon was a raven. Black feathers covered the raven, which had a ten-inch long beak. Since the raven didn't have any hands to hold things, they didn't carry any weapons. That didn't leave them without any means of attack. Their birdlike wings were razor-sharp.

If either of the demons turned their way and spotted Ty or Dani, any chance of going undetected vanished.

Dani knelt and patted Wicket's back. The dog looked up at her. She pulled out a dog treat and grinned up at Ty.

She tossed the treat so that it landed on the roof, on the opposite side of the demons. Wicket bolted after the treat and as he passed the demons, they turned to watch him. Their confusion at the appearance of the small dog only lasted a second, but that gave Ty and Dani the opening they needed. Ty went for the raven. His sword missed the bird demon's neck but still caught the back of its head, crushing its skull. The demon collapsed.

Dani, armed with her two short swords, slit open the whiter's throat. The demon gasped, grabbing at the wound with its free hand. He stumbled back. Dani's second strike severed his head and some of his blood-covered fingers. The head, still covered in its helmet, bounced off the edge of the parapet and tumbled down the outer wall of the castle.

Ty cursed as he ran to the edge of the wall, too late to do more than watch the helmet and head strike the edge of a balcony's railing below them. Then the demon's severed head and helmet bounced off to continue their fall along the cliff face.

Wicket ran up beside them as they stared down at the balcony. Fire-light danced through cracks in the leather drapes. The room the porch connected to was Malum's chambers. The noise of that metal helmet bouncing off the balcony wasn't loud enough to alert any of the guards in the castle's courtyard, but if Malum was awake or if the noise woke him, then the guards would swarm them.

Dani let out a long breath when nothing stirred from within Malum's chambers. Her hands shook as she slid her swords into their scabbards on her right and left hips and then made the sign of the cross.

Ty stroked her arm and whispered to her. "Better to lose someone else's head than your own."

She muffled a snort with her hand. "That was really bad."

"Says the woman who laughed at it."

She picked up Wicket to place him in the sling against Ty's back. The furball grumbled his disapproval at returning to the sling so soon.

They considered jumping down to the balcony, and while the drop might be safe enough, they'd make too much noise. They'd pushed their luck enough with the whiter's head. They climbed down the side of the castle.

A huge talon that jutted out of the castle wall formed the balcony below them. The talon's digits reached up with smaller bones connecting their tips to form the railing. That they were descending into the palm of that demonic hand provided a metaphor that distracted Ty as he tried to keep his footing along the wall of bones. As if to echo Ty's thoughts, Wicket growled softly causing his small body to vibrate against Ty's back.

Ty made it down onto the balcony a few seconds before Dani. Wicket stirred within the sling as Dani pulled him out. Dozens of long leather strips formed the curtain into Malum's chamber. Ty peeked through one of the gaps where the strips didn't quite meet.

The demon slept on a circular slab of stone with his sword resting next to him. Malum was a steed, one of the rarest races of demons. His slender head resembled a starved horse's. Dark brown fur covered his body, and a blood red mane ran down the back of his head and neck to spill over the edge of the bed.

Dani drew one of her swords and nodded to Ty that she was ready. Drawing his own sword, he pulled aside the curtain with his free hand. Dani entered, and Ty followed a few steps behind her. He moved slowly to make as little noise as possible as he let the curtain fall back into place. This part was the one reason they'd hesitated to bring Wicket. Silence wasn't their terrier's strong suit, but they weren't about to leave him alone outside the city. Dogs worked better than a compass to navigate the many realms of Hell, which was why every exorcist's sword had a dog.

Dani glared down at the demon as his pointed ears twitched. Ty stopped right behind her as they waited to make sure the sound of their footsteps hadn't awakened him. Once it was clear Malum still slept, Ty walked past Dani to place himself between her and the door to the hallway.

He positioned his foot up against the bottom edge of the door to make sure no one could open it, at least not easily. Part of Ty was shocked they'd made it here, having expected both of them to die long before they got this close.

Dani raised her sword over her head. Ty hadn't bothered to ask if she wanted to deliver the killing strike. Malum had slaughtered their friends, but he'd killed her mother.

She took a deep breath. Her arms tensed as her fingers tightened their grip on the hilt.

Then she swung.

In the brief moment between the start of the swing and the strike of the blade, Malum's red eyes opened.

Malum couldn't grab the sword resting on the stone beside him or roll away. The demon's eyes widened in panic. He couldn't do anything but scream a single word before the green blade of Dani's sword cleaved through his throat and struck the stone beneath him.

"Guards!"

Chapter 2

Dani wiped Malum's blood from her sword using the rag she kept on her belt and slid it into the scabbard on her left hip.

The handle on the door clicked. Ty braced his foot against the bottom of the door. Someone slammed against it, shouting for "Premier Malum!"

Dani pulled out a rectangular-shaped autopsy saw from the sheath on her right thigh to cut open the demon's chest and rip out his heart.

The demons slammed against the door again. Wicket barked at the demons as if he now owned Malum's chambers and the guards were the intruders. Ty kept the door shut, but it nearly shook free of its frame. "I wouldn't recommend savoring the moment," he said over Wicket's barking.

Dani laughed as she sawed into the demon's chest. "Ruin all my fun."

A demon's sword stabbed through a narrow gap in the bones that formed the door. The blade stopped an inch short of Ty's torso. It didn't cut him, but it startled him enough to jump back.

Before Ty could plant his foot against the door again, it burst open.

A whiter with a long brown mane led the charge. Ty knocked their sword aside and then slashed through their chest. The blade caught on the underside of the demon's ribcage, so Ty shoved forward. The whiter, wide-eyed with pain, dropped his sword and grabbed Ty's green blade in a wasted effort to force it back out. Ty shoved the sword straight through the demon and into another whiter behind him. The strike didn't kill the second demon, but it forced him to retreat into the hallway.

Ty kept the impaled demon in the door frame as a barrier to keep the others out. "How's that coming along?"

Dani answered between grunts as she sawed into Malum's chest. "Wishing we got to practice this more."

The impaled demon slashed at Ty's face with their talon hands. The borrowed helmet protected Ty's face from the demon's attack. That made him realize this demon, possibly too proud of his impressive mane, wasn't wearing a helmet like the other guards. Ty head-butted the demon. The helmet had a little padding on the inside, but that didn't stop Ty from seeing stars. The blow knocked the fight out of the impaled demon, though.

Dani's curses shifted into Spanish, which was never a good sign, even if Malum's corpse was the one being called a pendejo.

He heard her draw one of her swords and repeatedly strike the demon's chest.

"Should I be getting worried?" Ty asked as he dodged a sword shoved at him from over the maned demon's shoulder.

"Just softening up this bastard to speed things up," she said between swings. "Don't feel like you need to save any of those demons for me."

"Noted." He cursed as the demons in the hallway got smart and grabbed his improvised barrier under the arms and pulled him off Ty's sword and out into the hallway. Ty kicked the maned demon in the chest, sending the two holding him onto their asses.

Wicket barked more as Ty charged into the hallway. The narrow space didn't do his long sword any favors, but it didn't help the guards either, despite their shorter swords. The demons could only get to him one at a time. He kept all the demons in front of him. If any of the demons came at him from the opposite end of the hallway, he'd be screwed.

"Much better!" Dani shouted as she resumed sawing into the demon.

Ty sliced the head off a whiter, and the demon collapsed to the floor. A raven rushed up behind them. Their wings sliced at Ty, forcing him to retreat. Ty leveled his sword to use it like a spear and ran it through the raven's chest. Unlike the maned whiter, this strike pierced the demon's heart, killing it.

Feet pounded up the stairs behind Ty. He was about to get surrounded. Wicket barked at the incoming demons.

"It's getting a little crowded out here!" Ty held the raven in place as a barrier. The guards couldn't pull him off his sword as easily as the maned demon because of the sharp wings, but they'd get him loose soon enough. The raven wasn't that heavy compared to the whiter.

The blocked demons cursed at him. Ty shoved them back a bit so he could snatch up the shorter sword dropped by the whiter he'd impaled.

He positioned himself in front of the door to Malum's chambers as the demons came up the stairs behind him.

He glanced in at Dani. She'd gotten the chest open and was cutting the heart free. Black blood covered the stone bed and bone floor.

"Any ideas for getting out of here?" Dani asked as she pulled the demon's heart free.

"Other than hacking our way through all of these demons?" Ty parried a swing from the first demon to emerge from the stairs behind him. Then he sliced open the underside of the demon's forearm, causing him to drop his sword. Ty cut the demon's throat next but didn't straight out kill him. He made a more useful barrier while still alive and on his feet.

Another glance into Malum's chambers confirmed Dani was shoving the demon's heart and horse-like head into the leather bag they'd brought for the task. She then shoved the bag into her backpack.

Dead demons normally resurrected within five days, reappearing in their home realm. A priest had blessed the leather bag, which bought them a little more time, giving them seven days. If they could get Malum's head and heart into an Eternal Flame before the demon's remains evaporated and resurrected, then poof! No more Malum—ever.

They'd been hoping to have a half night's head start, but that hope died with Malum's scream. The clock was counting down for them to reach an Eternal Flame.

The demons finally shoved their fallen comrades out of the way to get at Ty. Before the demons could close in on him, though, Dani ran out into the hallway with both of her swords drawn. She and Ty stood back-to-back with Wicket safely between them as he barked his head off.

"Wishing you were still in that cubicle job in California?" Dani asked as she tore into the demons still filling the hallway.

Ty blocked a large whiter's sword and kicked him in the stomach, knocking him back several feet. "You just want me to joke that it was worse than Hell."

She laughed as she parried a demon's attack and slit open the inside of his thigh with her other sword. "Bet you I can clear my side faster than you can yours."

"Hardly fair considering I softened up that side." He stabbed his sword up, below a raven's beak and into its brains.

Much as he wanted to fight his way out of here as fast as possible, Ty paced himself. Their plans for a quick escape had vanished. For now, they needed to clear their way out of this hallway, and then the rest of the castle. Once they'd done that—if they managed that—they could worry about where they might run to next.

This was either going to be a long trip home or a quick and painful death.

Chapter 3

Six Years Earlier

Against his best friend's advice, Ty was going to Richmond for the job interview.

"Do not meet with Maria Cortez," Barry said over the phone while chewing his way through a pretzel stick. *"That lady is the dead end of dead ends for you. Call her back and tell her you're not going."*

"They've paid for my plane ticket." Ty was already riding to LAX in a taxi, which smelled like moldy corn chips. He'd considered asking Barry for a ride but had opted against it. "It's a free trip. Besides I'll be three hours outside of DC. I can finally go see the International Spy Museum."

"Listen, dude. Do you remember Joo-wan? He was killing it, and then he met with Maria Cortez, and no one heard from him again."

Ty considered hanging up his cell phone before Barry could launch into his sermon on how Ty needed to focus on film and TV opportunities, that he could use his skills to make a decent living as a stunt man for films, and that with a face like his, he could even land some decent acting roles if he got the right opportunities. Barry made a living half of the year as a truck driver, and then spent the other half competing in swordfighting tournaments. They'd met years ago at a competition in San Diego. They'd hit it off after the two of them had fought each other in the late rounds of the tournament. Ty had knocked Barry out of the competition and went on to win first place. They realized they lived near each other and became sparring partners when Barry wasn't driving cross-country. There was something hysterical about building a friendship around frequently beating the snot out of each other. He'd noticed lately, though, that their get-togethers had gotten more about grabbing a beer at a bar and less about sparring.

Barry had big dreams about how people could make a living as a swordfighter, and none of those dreams were realistic. Ty had taken enough acting lessons by now to know he had no chance of carving out an acting career for himself. As for stunt work, that offered its own set of challenges and didn't excite him.

"What is it about this Maria Cortez that makes you so sure she's a nutjob?" Ty asked.

The lady had come across stone-cold sober on the phone. She'd called his cell while he was at work at the county Social Services office. He'd been copying information from a mountain of application forms into the computer system. Ty still wasn't sure how she'd gotten his cell number, but the possibility of a job that wouldn't be half as mind-numbing as his current one appealed to him. Sure, the government benefits were nice and getting time off wasn't difficult compared to other jobs, but trying to advance in his current career didn't appeal to him. More pay? Sure, that sounded great. More paperwork, though? He'd rather die slowly, impaled on a pole.

"Every swordfighter I've known who's gone to work with Maria Cortez has vanished like a fart in a tornado. How have you not heard about this lady? Guys at the tournaments talk about her like she's a glorified bogeyman." Barry pounded out the protest between chomping on his pretzels. *"Did she even tell you what the job is?"*

Ty groaned, because his answer wasn't going to help his cause. "No, not exactly." She'd offered to fly him first class and put him up in a five-star hotel while in Richmond. The lady even paid for his side trip up to DC. Only in hindsight did he realize she'd suggested the trip to see the Spy Museum without him mentioning his interest in it. He didn't have a clue how she knew he wanted to go there.

"Right, I'll also bet she didn't mention she works for the Catholic Church."

"Wait." Ty sat up. "What?"

"Maybe it's the Episcopal Church. I don't remember, but she's a religious wacko. I'm telling you. Don't. Go."

"Barry, I can't back out now. I've already committed to it. I'm in a taxi on the way to the airport."

Barry groaned.

Ty offered his most earnest tone, which wasn't that great given his poor acting skills. "Relax. I'll be back in five days."

"You better be. I'm telling you, whatever this lady offers, run in the other direction. Do not pass go or any of that other board game bullshit."

Barry hung up on him to punctuate the point. Was just as well. The taxi pulled into the drop off lane at the airport.

After eight hours of travel, with a layover in Charlotte, Ty landed in Richmond around ten at night. By the time his cab had taken him to the hotel, his nose was dripping like an old sink.

"Allergies?" the front desk clerk said with a sympathetic smile as Ty checked in. "Yeah, Richmond is hell for people with allergies."

Getting to sleep turned out to be miserable, too. The combo of allergies, the fact his body was convinced it was three hours earlier than it was, and the way his conversation with Barry had his brain running in circles made falling asleep take several hours.

The change in time zones also didn't do him any favors in the morning when his phone's alarm blared at him at a quarter to seven. His fogged brain insisted it was too early as he showered and got dressed.

He finally met Maria Cortez in the lobby around eight (five o'clock back home, his brain unkindly reminded him). She stood at the bottom of a tall staircase covered in red and gold carpet. The whole place looked straight out of *Gone with the Wind*. Maria turned out to be a grizzled woman, probably in her fifties, with an honest-to-God eyepatch over her left eye. She parted her black hair, which didn't make it down to her shoulders, on the right to partially obscure the eyepatch. Despite the miles, she wore all the wear and tear with a confidence that turned it into something attractive. She shook his hand the way many of the type-A guys at sword tournaments liked to do, crushing his hand in hers. "Let's grab some breakfast," she said. "There's a café near the office we can go to." As she turned her back to him to lead the way out to the parking lot, he silently cursed as he flexed his fingers, trying to get feeling back into his hand.

They didn't drive far, parking on a cobblestone street next to the café, sitting on a street corner. The entire front wall of the café was made up of tall doors that were all turned open to take advantage of the pleasant spring weather. Ty sucked down his coffee. It tasted stronger than what he preferred, but as tired as he was, he considered that a good thing.

"I imagine you have a lot of questions." Maria sat at one of the tables closest to the sidewalk with people dressed in business suits and hospital scrubs walking by. She crossed her legs and leaned back in her chair, draping her arm over the back of it.

"I'm told you work for the church?" He decided against gambling on whether it was the Catholic or Episcopal Church.

"Heard that, did you?" She cracked an amused grin, as if she'd been privy to his conversation with Barry. "That's only partially true. We're funded by the Church of England, but we don't answer to them."

Taking a chug of his coffee, Ty then asked, "And who is *we*?"

"A fair question, and I'll get to that soon enough." She paused for her own sip of coffee. When she continued, she stared out at the street as cars rumbled across the cobblestones. "I'd like to talk about you a bit first. I notice you've started the transition."

"The what?"

"Oh, you're trying to find a way to make a living off that sword arm of yours that doesn't require a nine-to-five job typing on a keyboard or some other nonsense. You're going the usual route: giving lessons to wannabes drunk on fantasies of medieval knights or *Star Wars*. You know. The usual stuff." She looked at him with a smirk that assured him she already knew the answer to her next question. "You enjoying all that?"

He cleared his throat and sniffed. His sinuses were still killing him.

"I'm paying my bills." He shrugged, trying to mimic her nonchalance by turning his focus out onto the street and the passersby. Didn't keep him from seeing her amused reaction to his answer, that she knew he was full of shit.

Yeah, he'd taken to giving part-time lessons at a local fencing club that included saber fighting. Most of the job seemed more about punishing clients into the realization that they weren't going to turn into Inigo Montoya overnight and that fighting with a sword required both finesse and brutality. Being good with a sword required a killer instinct. Forcing others with limited skills to realize they didn't have that certain something was taking a toll on him.

"Look, Mr. Faison." She leaned forward, crossing her arms on the table. "For some people that's enough, and that's fine." The way she said "fine" left little doubt it was anything but that. "But someone like you…" She shook her head.

He tried to bluff, acting amused and disinterested, but his acting skills failed him again. "You think so?"

The way her expression hardened, that single eye narrowing on him, forced his full focus on her. "I think you're the kind of person who's only ever whole when he's got a sword in his hand and a real fight in front of him."

She leaned back in her chair again, with all the satisfaction of a wild-cat dining on a fresh kill. The silence offered him a chance to respond, but she'd left him speechless. No one had ever peeled him down to his bones like this—not even his parents—not this fast or with such ease.

After giving him his chance to answer and seeing he wasn't able to, Maria sipped her coffee and then continued. "You're twenty-six. You used to finish in the top three at most competitions you entered but you haven't in more than a year. It's not that your skills or body are fading, and it's not because you're distracted by the side work that pays the bills. No, it's because even the competitions are starting to bore you. Those fights aren't real anymore, because all that's at stake there is pride."

"And what? You're offering me a 'real fight'? What is this? Some kind of underground sword fight club, where the loser dies, and the first rule is to not talk about it?"

She shook her head, grinning at his attempt at wit. "This is no game or club. Underground? Somewhat. But what you'll be doing will make a real difference in people's lives. I'm offering you a chance to reclaim that fire that ignited the moment you first touched a sword.

"I'm giving you a chance to find your heart."

Chapter 4

More than half of the night was gone by the time Ty and Dani fought their way out of Malum's castle. The low notes of horns thundered from the gate tower as the guards fell to Ty and Dani's swords. The summons roused the rest of the city's guards and alerted those who were already awake. Ty and Dani would never reach the breach in the city wall that let them slip inside of Vel.

Instead, they retreated into the bowels of the city. Ty would have preferred any other option, if they'd had one, because blood, not water, flowed through the sewers of Vel.

Ty didn't doubt the demons would eventually think to look for them down there. If luck treated them kindly, though, the demons were spread too thin to prevent him and Dani from getting out of the city this way.

Like most mysteries of Hell, the source of the blood flowing through Vel remained hidden from the living. If the demons knew, they weren't sharing. Ty had once joked with his fellow swords in the Richmond branch of the Order that maybe God had slit the Devil's throat, and this level of Hell was where it all spilled out. Dani was the only one to laugh.

Fortunately, they didn't have to walk in the blood. Narrow, raised walking paths ran along the walls. In some places, bones had broken off and narrowed the width of their path to six inches.

Wicket took the lead. While Ty had a decent sense of direction and assumed they could simply follow the flow of the blood, they couldn't afford to waste any time getting out of Vel. Dogs had an innate ability to navigate the realms of Hell to find the rips in reality that connected Hell's realms to each other and with Purgatory.

"He's feeling mighty proud of himself." There was no missing the smile in Dani's voice or the confident trot to Wicket's walk.

"You'd think he was the one who fought off all those demons."

Wicket paused to sniff at the ground.

No torches or lamps burned down here. The only light came from the glow crystals they carried in the mesh pouches on the sleeves of their jackets. The crystals came from a realm of Hell that existed entirely underground, or at least seemed to. Sadly, the crystals only worked within Hell and Purgatory. In the mortal world, they made for some lovely paperweights and little else.

Dani pulled one of her crystals from its pouch to hold it out for a better look at this section of the sewer. Wicket had stopped them where a smaller tunnel intersected this one. "We'll be lucky to get out of the city before sunrise at this rate."

He knew where her mind was, and it wasn't on finding their way out of the city. "Wasn't your fault. The bastard just happened to wake up."

Even in the dim light of the crystal, he didn't miss her scowl. "If I'd swung a second sooner, he'd have never gotten the chance to scream."

He reached back and took her hand in his. "We're gonna finish this."

"I know." She shook her head. "Would've been nice not having to fight our way out of Hell. That's all."

"Yeah, but I wish I could've seen it up close when Malum realized what was coming."

That brought back her smile. "It was satisfying."

They squeezed their hands tighter and then let go. "Well, let's make sure it sticks then," he said.

Wicket kicked up a leg and took care of some business, then continued down the narrow path of white bones.

They journeyed in the dark for what felt like an hour until they came to a split. Voices echoed through the tunnels. Seemed the demons were searching for them down here. Wicket led them down the tunnel the voices didn't come from.

Before Ty could voice his concern that the demons didn't seem to be worried about patrolling this part of the sewers, Dani shushed him.

When she spoke, she lowered her voice. "Point one of your crystals ahead. Don't talk."

Wicket stopped and growled, the token complaint came out as a quiet rumble.

A low gulp came every few seconds from somewhere ahead of them in their tunnel. Nothing stood out until he noticed a bit of debris, something like a five foot long stick floating on the blood. Then a small pop of an air bubble broke the surface, and the realization hit. The "stick" flowed in the opposite direction of the blood.

Ty exchanged a quick glance with his wife. She drew both of her swords. He returned the glow crystal to the mesh pocket on his left sleeve that allowed its glow to help them see without having to hold it and then drew his own sword.

The "stick" floated closer. Wicket kept growling, but he didn't launch into a barking fit. Ty took a deep breath and held it.

The unknown thing pushing against the flow of blood reached them. This close, Ty could see it definitely wasn't a stick. At least ten pinkish bone-like pieces comprised it. Each piece had a spike, some had as many as three, that pushed up a few inches. Two of the thickest spikes, one near the front and the other bringing up the rear, had two black spherical bulbs atop them.

The stick that wasn't a stick moved past Ty. He quietly released the breath he'd been holding and smiled to Dani. She didn't see his expression, though. All her focus stayed on the thing moving by them.

It reached her and continued past.

Then it stopped, no longer pushing against the blood flow nor surrendering to it.

Both black bulbs turned atop their spikes until they pointed directly at Dani.

The rest of the beast erupted from the blood, sending up a red spray in all directions. The thing's ten-foot-long body ended in an armored tail reminiscent of a scorpion, except that had a round mouth at its tip with hundreds of razor sharp teeth. A larger version of that hideous mouth convulsed with a roar at the front end. The "stick" that had been visible formed part of the spine that ran along its back. Half a dozen pairs of spidery legs pushed the torso up out of the blood. The right side had a serrated pincer that repeatedly snapped in a gleeful and hungry fashion. The greater threat rested on its left, a mushroom type bulb burst open and released a dozen whip-like threads.

Dani screamed her war cry as the sewer scorpion lunged towards her. Her swords slashed at two of the creature's whip-like extensions when they shot at her. She didn't cut the whips. Instead, she knocked them off target, causing them to slash at the bone wall behind her. Bits of bone rained down as the the whips jerked away, but they didn't pull back into the mushroom. The other whips thrashed around, kicking up more sprays of blood and creating a shifting shield to deflect any attacks to its left side. The two whips, as they retracted, wrapped around the blades of Dani's sword and jerked. The smooth surface of the blade prevented the whips from getting a decent grip, but the sewer scorpion knocked Dani off-balance.

Ty grabbed Dani by the arm and pulled her back from the brink.

Wicket ran ahead and barked. He sounded like he was telling Ty and Dani to quit fighting the ugly monster and follow him.

"It's after the demon bits in my bag!" Dani raced behind Ty as they followed Wicket.

Blood splattered across the walls and onto all three of them as the monster pursued them. The thickness of the blood flow slowed the beast a bit. Its pincer snapped after Dani's backpack. Its roar warbled and echoed through the sewers.

Dani blocked the pincer with her left sword and then hacked at the offending appendage with her right sword. She couldn't get past the exoskeleton to cut off the limb. The blade made a cracking sound against the pink outer shell.

Ten yards ahead, a metal grate blocked their path of escape. Wicket reached it and barked as if angry that the door didn't have the decency to open for him on its own.

"Dead end!" Ty shouted.

"Get on its other side!" Dani stood her ground and battled the pincer, but when she went still, the sewer scorpion spun around to attack her with its whips. One wrapped around her leg, but the instant it went taught, her sword slashed at the extension and sliced it in half.

The scorpion screamed. The mouth on its tail spit out a black sticky substance that hit Dani's backpack.

Ty leaped across to the narrow platform on the other side. His foot caught the edge and the femur he landed on snapped off. He fell waist-deep into the blood that splashed everywhere.

Dani shouted as the scorpion tail snapped down at him. Ty threw up his sword with one hand gripped around the hilt and the other braced against the flat of the blade. The tail slammed against the sword, but the blade kept the thing's mouth at bay.

The monster jerked away from Ty as the bottom of its tail scraped against the sword, drawing a small bit of pusslike blood.

Ty lunged forward. His sword thrust into its underbelly near the point where the tail met the rest of its body.

A loud yelp erupted from both mouths of the sewer scorpion, and it dove into the blood. Its spine, the only part still visible above the surface of the blood flow, sped away.

Wicket ran past Dani to bark after the retreating beast. Dani leaned back against the wall and sighed, before erupting into laughter. "You all right?"

Ty laughed with her. "I can't begin to tell you how gross I feel at this moment."

She held out a hand to help him back onto the platform.

The sensation of blood soaking his socks and other places he preferred to not think about was a unique experience he prayed to never suffer again. "Suppose we need to figure out a different way to go." He pointed towards the metal grate that barred their path. At least they didn't hear any demons coming their way. Either they hadn't heard the fray or weren't dumb enough to risk running into whatever that monster was.

Dani narrowed her eyes as she studied the grate. "Hon, I think you should take a closer look at that." She pointed towards the edge of the grate along their wall.

He walked over to it and noticed a small gate latch. Hinges were visible on the opposite wall where the grate met it. He flipped up the gate latch and pulled the grate open.

"Are you kidding me?"

Dani snorted. "You were quite heroic, though." She wiped the blood from his cheek and kissed him. "Just no hugging until you've had a bath."

Chapter 5

The tunnel Ty and Dani traveled ended at a cliff with the blood spilling into a red river. The demons hadn't expected them to come this way for good reason. They spent an hour climbing down the fifty yards of jagged rocks. A few ravens passed overhead during their descent. Each time, Ty and Dani hugged the rocks and waited on the ravens to pass. Wicket slept most of the way down in the sling against Ty's back; probably the only reason he didn't bark at the demons flying overhead. Thankfully, the ravens appeared more focused on the riverbank. As soon as they reached the bottom, Ty and Dani ran for cover.

Barren rock littered with massive formations that loomed in a similar fashion to trees dominated the countryside beyond Vel's walls. The "trees" resembled thirty-foot tall people kneeling but without any distinguishing features to assure they were ever actually statues. If someone told Ty they were ancient giants turned to stone by some other creature in Hell, he might have believed them.

Three miles separated them from the cliff to the start of the swamp. They jogged most of the way with the formations obscuring the sky as it began its transition from black to dark orange. It wouldn't get much brighter than that in this realm of Hell. Wicket loved the chance to stretch his legs after his nap. He often ran ahead of them to sniff around and occasionally kick up a leg to mark his territory.

They paused halfway to the swamp. Dani leaned against the kneecap of one of the smaller formations. "Running is rubbish."

Ty caught his breath while walking in a circle. "I'd have thought this fit into your list of reasons to run. You always say you don't believe in running until you've got monsters chasing after you."

She turned her head to stare at him in disbelief and then pointed back the way they'd come. "You see anyone coming?"

"Well, just because we don't see them"— He stopped as her glare darkened into what he affectionately referred to as *The Look*. "I'll shut up now."

"Smart man."

He grinned at her and pointed the way they needed to go. "Why don't we keep walking? We can jog again once we're up for it."

She nodded and started walking with her hands on her hips to keep her back straight. "Been thinking about our plan."

"Uh huh?" His instincts screamed he'd hate her suggestion.

"If we go through the swamp, we can reach the Purgatory Arch in two days. Cuts our time in half."

He took in a deep breath, less because he needed the air and more because he wanted to stall for a counterargument she'd agree with. The arch was a thin place, the link between this level of Hell and Purgatory, and Purgatory offered the only certain path home.

Ty didn't spare on the skepticism when he replied. "You're assuming it'll only take us two days."

"Look, I know my sense of direction might be worthless, but the road we were going to take goes the long way around the swamp. All I'm suggesting is that the shortest path between two points is a straight line." She wiped her forehead with the back of her forearm. "Even you said we needed a big head start to get around the swamp to reach the Purgatory Arch before the demons, and we've lost our head start."

"I know what the map says, but no one in the Order has ever gone through the swamp and lived to tell about it."

"Bullshit!" She managed a laugh, even though she was still somewhat out of breath. "Nelson hid in there for a day once."

He glared over at her. She would invoke that lousy ass—may he rest in peace. She'd gone out with Nelson once during their training academy, right before she and Ty got involved. He and Nelson had taken an instant dislike to each other. That bastard thought he knew everything. Nelson might not have been stupid, but his sword skills were sub-par.

"Nelson," he said the name with all the venom the man deserved, "hid out on the edge of the swamp. He didn't go through it. Even doing that, he nearly got eaten by one of the beasts in there."

She shrugged and grunted in an obvious taunt. "I mean, if you don't think you can do better."

"Don't you try that with me!" In spite of himself, he couldn't repress a grin. Dani could be shameless. "Look, we don't know what kind of conditions we'll face in there. It's a swamp. In Hell. At best, we'll be up to our ankles in blood-soaked muck. Never mind there's no telling what recent tectonic shifts might have changed in this realm. The swamp could be even bigger than we know. Even the demons avoid that place, because most every creature in there wants to eat them, too."

She leaned her head back, taking in a deep breath and then slowly releasing it. "Malum's army knows where we're headed, and they'll send every raven flying there and have them notify any demons they can find along the way to gather at the Purgatory Arch. Cutting through the swamp improves our odds of getting there before they can plant their army between us and the passage to Purgatory."

Dani stared straight ahead. She was breathing hard again, and it had nothing to do with their run from the city.

Ty had put the idea out there after they'd found her mother's body and learned the Order's oversight officers were on their way. No one in the Order knew Malum as well as they did. That's why they were the most qualified to kill the bastard and turn him into ash for eternity, but in the end, they needed to do it. Dani more than Ty.

Wicket, having gotten impatient with the way the two of them were walking and no longer jogging, ran behind them and growled as he turned his body sideways, as if his fifteen-pound body could force them to move. Dani snatched him up and hugged him to her. Wicket licked her nose until she put him down.

Their actions had killed the only blood relative Dani considered family and dozens more. Once the Order realized Ty and Dani had unintentionally made Malum's rampage possible, they'd be forced to run for the rest of their lives, assuming they even survived this fool's quest. If the Order's oversight officers caught them, then they'd most likely end up in some remote prison in Europe for God only knew how many years, separated from each other and from Wicket. A part of him feared if Dani went into that cell without first destroying Malum, she'd never come out of it alive. She had to know she did everything she could to make this right. Truth be told, he did, too. Most of all, he needed Dani. If she wasn't there to meet him at the end of his sentence, then getting out of his own cell wouldn't matter.

No matter how badly they wanted to end Malum, desire alone didn't translate into reality. Dani was right. Beating Malum's army to the Purgatory Arch had never been likely. That meant taking any short cut they might find.

"All right. Let's do it."

He just hoped this risk wouldn't kill them sooner than later.

Interlude 1

Char stormed through the front gates of Premier Malum's castle. Red marred the skies with the start of day. Black smoke wafted from the demon corpses left behind by the exorcists and filled the air with the stench of brimstone.

"Pile them over there." The command came from a whiter dressed in a dragon-skin bandolier and a leather kilt over the top half of his goat-like legs. When Zhor realized Char had arrived, he fell in beside him.

"How bad is it?" Char waited to ask the question until they were inside the castle and out of earshot of most of the guards.

"We're standing in a fucking piss storm from a swarm of angels." Zhor laughed without any humor to it. "Two exorcists got in and out of the castle. They killed Malum and more than thirty guards."

They climbed the main stairs from the Great Hall to the residences. The odor of brimstone stank worse in here than in the courtyard.

"How bad is it with Malum?" Char asked as they neared the door to Malum's bedchambers.

"The exorcists made off with his head and heart."

Fire and ash! Char had warned Malum about this. He told them the exorcists wouldn't take his murderous romp without retaliation. Malum had assured him the Order of the Emerald Blades would be too busy punishing their own and cleaning up the mess he'd left behind.

Two other demons stood by Malum's bed. They avoided standing in the pool of black blood next to it.

Nera, her arms crossed, looked up at Char. She was a rare breed of demon, a fallen mortal. Char's name would fit her better with her charcoal-black, burned skin. He knew nothing of her mortal life and cared little for most of what it might have been, but he'd often wondered what damned her. Whatever had thrown her down with the foragers of the dead, she gave no sign of regret except for her unwillingness to speak of it. That she kept the origins of her damnation hidden always forced Char to question her loyalty, no matter how much her actions declared her devotion to him.

The voice of the raven next to Nera came out in a warped fashion as Kene forced her avian vocal chords and beak into forming words in the more common demon tongue. "My squadron is searching the city and the surrounding countryside. It's possible they're still hiding in the city."

Char stroked the fur of his wolf-like snout as he considered this. He'd already been hunting the countryside outside the city's walls, which delayed him getting here. "No, they'll be out of the city by now. Do we know which exorcists did this?"

"The guards say it was a man and woman who did this," Kene said. "The woman had long, black hair and fought with two short swords. The man had black hair and a beard. He used a single sword."

Char ground his teeth together. "The wife and husband."

"If those two have already made it out of the city, then Malum is as good as rot for worms." Zhor absently ran a hand through his brown mohawk to clear his view when it fell in front of his left eye.

Char stayed silent for a moment as he worked through their options. The exorcists would have less than seven days now to get Malum's head and heart to an Eternal Flame. Normally, they'd only have five days, but exorcists had ways of preserving the remains longer than that. If Char stopped these humans from getting to the mortal realm before those seven days were up, then Malum's head and heart would evaporate, restoring him here in the Blood Realm.

"Kene, send your ravens to the Purgatory Arch, and have a few go to the outpost near the Fakri Artery. I want every demon assembled at the arch before the next daybreak. Once you've dispatched your ravens, rejoin the three of us in the courtyard."

"You mean every warrior?" Kene cocked her head to the side.

"No, every demon, even if they don't have a sword or know how to fight. Those humans will be forced to assume they're all warriors. Put a large enough obstacle in their path, and they'll either lose time trying to contrive a way past all of us or attempt a different route to a Purgatory Arch in another realm. All we have to do is delay them seven days, and Malum will resurrect."

"Assuming he does?" Nera still had her arms crossed. "You know it doesn't always work. When it's a demon's time to end..." She shrugged, the gesture filled with her indifference for Malum's survival.

Char glared at Nera, but when he spoke, he turned to Kene. "Go and assemble those demons at the Purgatory Arch."

Kene nodded before turning to walk out onto the balcony and then leaped into the sky.

"Zhor, I want half the city guard sent down the Arch Highway. If the exorcists are using it, then we'll drive them into the warriors waiting for them at the Arch." He canted his head towards the door. "Go."

Char walked closer to Malum's body. His orange taloned feet made a slurping sound as they stepped into the pool of blood on the floor.

The body had started to rot instead of evaporating like the other bodies dragged out into the courtyard. That confirmed the exorcists had his head and heart. They'd be keeping both in something blessed by a priest to prevent them from evaporating. Char and the other demons would need to wear gloves to handle whatever the humans were using to carry Malum's head and heart.

He placed a hand on Malum's shoulder as if he could silently will a promise from his thoughts to his leader's shattered essence. Then he looked up at Nera. "See that our dovras are saddled. You, Zhor, and I are going hunting for these exorcists."

Nera arched a lavender eyebrow, the most she'd moved since he entered the room. "I thought that's what the guards were doing?"

"The guards are making certain the exorcists can't use the road from here to the Arch, but I doubt they will. The Arch Highway leaves them too out in the open." He growled as he considered this, once again stroking his dark brown snout with his fur-covered hand. "These exorcists got out of the city. I'll find their trail and track them. You, Zhor, Kene, and I will find them and end them."

When Nera didn't answer, he looked up to find her staring at him in disbelief.

"What?" He bit out the word.

"You're making enough of an effort so that everyone will see it, but if you let these exorcists destroy Malum, then all that was his becomes yours. You'll be the new—"

He choked off Nera's words as he grabbed her by the throat and slammed her down onto the stone bed. "I have given my oath to Malum, and I will honor that! You might not have been born a demon, but even you should know by now that an oath made to another demon is unbreakable."

When he released her, she coughed and rolled onto her side away from Malum's body. Some of Malum's blood clung to the tips of her lavender hair

"That's," she coughed again. "That's a funny notion. An oath to a demon who gained his power from the oaths he broke."

"Malum is no oathbreaker. He chose his words well. The line between honoring his oaths and betraying his allies might have been thinner than a single ray of light in the dark, but he never broke his oaths." He leaned in closer to her. His snout brushed against her cheek as his hot breath caressed her burned flesh. "He always kept his oath to me, so I will not break mine to him. And you will honor yours to me."

As her coughing subsided, she grinned at him. "I always have," she whispered as she reached up to his throat and ran her fingers through his fur. "I always shall."

His forked tongue slid out from between his jaws and tasted the back of her hand before he pulled away from her. "Get our dovras saddled. We leave as soon as they're ready."

She answered her assent with only her eyes. Then she rolled off the bed and walked out, headed for the stables.

Char turned to Malum. "I know you would prefer I save these exorcists to kill yourself, but this one time, I think it best to save you from your passions."

He placed his hand on Malum's shoulder one more time before he turned and walked out.

Chapter 6

The tall trees that defined the border of the swamp swayed in a lazy dance. Their long, thin red leaves drifted back and forth. The lack of wind made that all the more disconcerting. The trees moved themselves.

Wicket sniffed at the muddy ground ahead of them, clearly not interested in stepping into the muck despite marking it as his territory.

"Doesn't meet with your approval, Captain Prissy Paws?" Ty said.

"Poor boy isn't going to like this either." Dani pulled out the sling from one of the pouches on her backpack, so they could carry Wicket through the swamp. This was another downside to going this way to the Purgatory Arch.

Some exorcist's swords preferred to get more intimidating dogs like German shepherds or Dobermans. Rumor had it an exorcist's sword in Berlin had adopted a two hundred pound Russian bear dog. Didn't matter how big the dog was, though. They couldn't do any lasting damage to a demon. The only thing that consistently made a deadly wound to a demon was transcendental steel, found only in the spiritual realms. Exorcist's swords really needed dogs for their noses. Silky terriers might not be as renowned for their sniffers as some of those other breeds, but Wicket had pulled through for Ty and Dani every time. Unfortunately, he couldn't lead them anywhere riding in a sling.

"It's going to get dark soon." Ty still wasn't thrilled with this idea, even if he'd already agreed to it. "Won't take much for us to get turned around in there, no matter how hard we try to go straight through it."

They poured some water from Ty's bottle into its cap for Wicket to lap up. The little terrier drank most of the water, and once Wicket finished, Ty poured the leftover water back into the bottle and put it in his pack. Water was too precious in the Blood Realm to waste any of it.

Ty pointed to Dani's backpack. "You want me to take that?" Wicket weighed about fifteen pounds, roughly the same as Malum's head and heart combined. They each already had plenty to carry with their swords and other gear.

"No, I'll hold onto them." Dani didn't meet his gaze as she offered Wicket's sling to him.

Once he had the sling wrapped over his shoulder, Ty whistled Wicket over to him, scooped him up, and slid him into it. The dog squirmed around for a good minute before getting settled against his chest. No sooner had Wicket gotten comfortable than his body vibrated with a loud growl.

Dani grabbed Ty by the arm and pulled him towards the swamp. "Ravens!" Three small shapes flew in a triangular formation across the dark red sky.

They ran through the swaying leaves of the red trees. The ravens kept flying in the same direction and didn't swoop down. If they'd seen Ty and Dani, they weren't trying to attack and they weren't changing direction.

"I can't tell if they spotted us," Ty said as Wicket continued to growl.

"All the more reason to get moving." Dani took the lead. Their crystals, resting in their shoulder pouches, glowed brightly within the shadows of the trees. The thick tree foliage above hid them from the ravens.

He glanced down at his boots. Ten feet into this swamp, and the muck already reached up past his ankles. Their boots went up to just below their knees. He hoped that would be enough. He'd already had to walk waist-deep in blood. He didn't care to endure the muddy version of that.

Chapter 7

Dim rays of light cut through the narrow gaps of the trees in the swamp. Their glow crystals provided more light by comparison.

For hours, they trudged around the animated trees and through the mud, their legs dipping deep enough to engulf their calves. Ty hoped they wouldn't get any deeper into the muck, but their luck ran out at midday when they reached a pond of bright red blood.

"I don't see a way around it." Dani had already ventured ten feet into the pond and was already up to her kneecaps. The pond stretched out in all directions except for the way they'd come.

"What about Wicket?" The drowsing terrier's big, black eyes blinked open at the mention of his name. "If the blood gets too deep, we'll be forced to go around it anyway."

Dani shrugged in her way that made it clear she didn't see any other option. "We need a walking stick. At least that'll let us find the deep places before we step into them."

"On it." Ty stomped through the mud to a leaf-barren, white tree with narrow, gnarled branches that reached out in all directions. When he found a branch that was somewhat straight, he drew his sword and sliced it off.

"This should do the trick." He tossed the stick over to Dani.

As she caught it, Dani's eyes widened, and she shouted Ty's name.

The warning came too late to spare him from something slamming against the back of his head. He dropped to his knees as everything blinked black for a split second.

Dani appeared in front of him. She swung with both of her swords, slashing at the tree next to Ty. The tree groaned and creaked as its trunk twisted like a rung towel, its branches spinning.

Wicket barked as something wrapped around the dog and Ty's chest. Dani reached for Ty, but with her hands wrapped around her swords' hilts, she couldn't grab him.

One of the long red leaves from the swaying trees jerked Ty back towards the trunk . His feet dragged through the mud, unable to get any leverage to fight the pull of the swaying tree. He reached for his sword, but another long, red leaf wrapped around his right wrist, stopping him short of grabbing the hilt.

"Dani!" Ty shrieked as he struggled. Another red leaf wrapped around his torso.

Wicket barked and squirmed within the sling. He bit into the thin leaf which shredded itself as it attempted to pull taut around them.

Then Dani lunged towards them. Her swords sawed through the leaves attacking Ty enough to free his arm. The trees tried to grab her, too.

Able to move his arm again, Ty drew his sword from his left hip and helped Dani slash through the swaying tree's leaves and branches.

"Let's grab that stick and go!" Ty ran towards the pond. Dani snatched up the stick he'd cut off the tree and placed herself between the tree and Ty as they ran deeper into the blood.

The red leaves swatted at them, a hundred whips, cracking in the air and spraying them with mud.

Wicket barked and wriggled within the sling. Ty held the dog in place with his free hand, worried he might fall out.

Ty realized he was shaking once they were deep enough into the blood to where it reached up past their knees.

Dani, her swords back in their scabbards, pulled him to her. He could tell by the way she held him that if Wicket wasn't between them, she'd have crushed him in a hug.

"Let me check your head."

He didn't resist as she turned him around. "Don't see any blood or swelling. You feeling dizzy? Your vision clear?"

"I'm good on both." He sheathed his sword.

She made him count backwards by fives from a hundred to five. He passed that test without any trouble.

They divided their attention among all the nearby trees. The closest one, a massive black tree trunk, reached above all the other trees in the swamp. Its branches didn't start until well past the other surrounding trees and ended in large bulbs with red spikes protruding from them.

Ty hoped that giant wouldn't attack them, too. He assumed that wasn't likely, as long as they didn't try to cut into it the way he had that other tree. If anything, the other trees seemed scared of it. He realized their swaying leaned away from the giant's branches anytime Big Black and Spiky drew close, as if expecting to get chewed up by their larger sibling.

"Wait, is that big one spinning in place or is it just me?" Unlike the white tree, this one's trunk didn't twist up like a towel getting rung out.

"The whole tree is turning." Dani poked at the floor of the pond with the walking stick as she led them through the bright red blood. "Its roots must be shifting beneath the ground. You feel it vibrating?"

He cursed under his breath. Now that she'd pointed it out, he couldn't not notice the way the ground quivered. Only now did it strike Ty that the space between the giant tree and the smaller ones formed a circle.

"We need to get away from these trees," Ty hugged Wicket closer to his chest as the ground shook beneath them and formed ripples in the surface of the blood river.

"The smaller trees are getting more agitated, too." Dani stopped and poked at the ground around her. "Stay close. The ground drops off to our right and left."

The more Dani led them through the pond, the more the path forced them towards a copse of the smaller, white trees with long red leaves.

"Hopefully, these aren't pissed at me for hacking off part of their friend back there." Ty held his sword ready.

Dani shifted the walking stick to her left hand and drew the sword from her left hip with her dominant right hand. She grinned over her shoulder at him. "I'll beat them up, if they try to mess with you."

As Dani said that, one of the white trees lunged at them. A wave of red leaves crashed down on her.

Ty rushed towards her, but the tree moved too fast for him to cut at the leaves. He grabbed the end of the stick.

"Hold on!" Ty yelled over Dani's curses. The leaves shook around her with each swing of her sword, but the amount of leaves wrapped around her was so thick that Ty couldn't see her sword or any of her body.

Ty's feet dragged through the muddy bottom of the river as he struggled against the tree's pull on Dani.

A shadow swooped down at them. Ty ducked as four of the giant tree's red spiked bulbs crashed into the trunk of the smaller tree attacking Dani.

The long, red leaves grabbed at the spiked bulbs, trying to rip them out of its trunk. Blood splattered out of the smaller tree's white bark as three more of the spiked bulbs smashed into it.

The smaller tree groaned but didn't give up its hold on Dani, not yet. Ty pulled on the stick. More of the leaves enveloping Dani split off from her to focus on the larger tree's attack.

The ground shook as something splashed through the surface of the river. Something long and slender slapped against the blood, splashing up around Ty. Wicket barked and squirreled around within the sling, frustrated by being unable to get free to do anything.

Ty first thought that snakes were flinging themselves at each other through the lake, but then he realized the smaller and larger trees' roots had joined the struggle. Each root was scaled like a reptile and the smaller tree's roots even ended in round mouths with hundreds of tiny teeth shifting within the small maws.

The bigger tree won, though. The small tree's trunk had pulled up out of the ground enough for the bottom of the trunk to become visible, revealing where its white bark broke off to expose the same slimy, scaled flesh to match its roots.

"Dani, you gotta get free of that tree now!"

Her legs were still wrapped in the long leaves, as tightly as a mummy.

The larger tree yanked the small one free of the ground in a spray of blood and mud. Dani released the stick and drew her second sword. Her blades slashed through the remaining leaves as the small, white tree launched into the sky.

Dani flipped through the air and landed feet first into the pond with a splash that sent up a spray of blood. Ty turned his back to Dani and hunched over to protect Wicket from the blood raining on them.

Above them, the giant tree flung the smaller one up into the air above its trunk. A snakelike head snapped out of the top of the trunk and chomped down on the smaller tree before yanking itself and its prize back down into the massive, black trunk.

Dani sheathed her swords as Ty ran towards her.

"You all right?" he asked.

She placed a hand on his upper arm and leaned into him as she struggled to catch her breath. After her breathing calmed, she nodded. "You remember that time you asked me why I don't like camping?" She patted his arm affectionately and then rested her head against his chest.

"Point made."

"Damn right."

Wicket poked his head up out of the sling and licked a spot on her nose that wasn't covered in blood.

Dani laughed as she pulled away from Wicket's kisses and patted his head. She met Ty's gaze and smiled at him, but then her eyes widened in panic. She stepped back and pulled off her backpack to check the leather bag with Malum's head and heart. She opened the bag and checked inside. She sighed in relief and tied the bag again.

"All there?" Ty asked.

She nodded. Her body shook as Ty hugged her. He suspected she was less shaken by how close she'd come to dying and more so by the thought she could have lost Malum's remains in the struggle.

"Let's get moving," she said. "You take the lead for a while."

He kissed her, and then poked at the bottom of the lake with the stick and led them towards the same copse of trees they'd been heading towards before the attack. He kept his sword ready, but he noticed the trees leaned away from them now. Apparently, they weren't interested in risking a bite of human when taking a swing at them might place them in the big one's sights.

Ty and Dani made it past the smaller trees and stayed to the middle of the pond for a while. The angle of the sunlight cutting through the branches and leaves above suggested the sun would soon set. He hoped the swamp might sleep once night fell, but he doubted it.

Interlude 2

Char knelt close to the ground. His black nose twitched as he breathed in deep. He didn't miss any details: not the small herd of fat, stub-nosed pallards that passed this way a day ago, nor the snake that burrowed further into the land moments ago in fear of the demons walking on its surface. Even the week-old urine of a passing bat stained the dirt trail. All those things existed within this realm.

Three scents did not.

Char didn't let his companions' impatience ruin his focus as his nose inhaled all around him. Even as he followed the stench of the two humans and their furry abomination, he heard the rumble in the back of Zhor's throat and the subtle shift of Kene's wings as they overlapped in a way reminiscent of someone crossing their arms. Only Nera stayed motionless.

He followed the scents of the humans to the edge of the swamp and went to the right about twenty yards before turning back.

"Your scouts were right," Char said to Kene who nodded her acceptance of the compliment. "The exorcists went into the swamp. They brought a hound with them, too."

Zhor snorted and pointed to the darkening sky. "Between the carnivorous trees, locusts, and all the other beasts, those mortals are as good as dead. Might as well ride back to Vel."

"No, we're going in after them."

When none of them responded, Char turned to look at them.

Zhor leaned back in the saddle of his large dovra. The tall-legged reptile's long, flat jaw snapped in response to its rider's irritation. "Odds favor they're dead already, and if they aren't, then they won't make it through the night when the beasts wake. I'd prefer not to suffer the same fate."

"No." Char mounted his own dovra, sleek with dark grey scales like armor. "Malum underestimated these exorcists. We shall not."

"You're right." Nera's voice sounded raspier than usual. "Malum underestimated them. He made his bed, and now he can rot on it."

Char glared at her. The only thing that betrayed how much he unnerved her was the way her dark green dovra danced in place, eager to run.

Kene spread out her wings. "I cannot help you in there. It's too dark and dense with trees for me to fly, and none of your dovras will accommodate a second rider. I can't even see anything from above the swamp with all the tree cover."

Char stared off at his own thoughts as he considered that. Once he made up his mind, he focused on Kene. "Fly to the far end of the swamp, the point closest to the Purgatory Arch. I want a regiment waiting to greet these humans and their hound."

Kene nodded and then leaped into the air, disappearing over the edge of the treetops.

Zhor cursed under his breath. Char ignored it and said, "The three of us are going in after them."

"And if we refuse?" Zhor's words sounded more like a threat than a question.

"You may do as you like, but your choice will not be forgotten when weighed against your vows to me."

Nera tapped the side of her dovra with her foot. The large reptile walked over to the line of red, long-leaved trees. Her eyes slid over to Char. "You know where we're going, so you first."

Char's dovra sauntered through the wall of red leaves. Its webbed feet sank into the mud with an offensive sucking sound that accompanied each step.

"Malum better reward us like kings for this," Zhor grumbled as he followed them into the swamp.

Chapter 8

At nightfall, Dani found a small island within the swamp. Two small trees with thin, dark red trunks and bright red leaves sprouted from the middle of the island. The ground was damp but not muddy like most of the swampland.

Wicket happily ran around the small bit of land once freed from the sling. He also took advantage of the taller of the two trees for kicking up a leg. Ty stood ready to snatch up their dog if the tree took offense at being used as a urinal. Either the trees were sleeping or weren't as animated as the earlier ones they'd dealt with. Regardless, Ty opted not to lower his guard.

Once Wicket finished his business, Ty took small bites from a stick of beef jerky. After this sad meal, they'd each have one more stick of beef jerky left. That would leave them with protein bars and a pair of oranges.

"Think we should sleep?" he asked between bites. They'd been going for an entire night and day. He'd reached that point where his eyes hurt from being open too long.

"I wish." Dani hugged her legs to her chest and rested her forehead against her knees.

Ty sat next to her and rubbed her back with his hand. "Yeah, I know." He wished they could curl up in their bed in their loft apartment, not that they'd likely ever get to see their apartment again. Getting through Purgatory to the mortal plane wouldn't be the end of the race.

They still had to toss Malum's head and heart into an Eternal Flame. The only one in Richmond rested beneath a church a few blocks from Hollywood Cemetery, where their passage through Purgatory would deposit them. That's when the Order would turn into the bigger problem. Even if the Order hadn't yet placed the blame for the slaughter of the Richmond branch on Ty and Dani's heads, they'd insist on interrogating them about what happened. That wouldn't end well. Thinking about that distant problem of eluding the Order hurt Ty's head, especially when getting out of the Blood Realm offered trouble enough.

He looked at the backpack resting on the ground by Dani's left hip. The dark spit from the sewer scorpion still covered part of it. He ran a finger over the black splotch. Even hours later, it felt wet and sticky. It stank, too—even by Hell standards. The stench had assaulted his nostrils ever since the fight in the sewer. How could Dani stand carrying it?

"Any idea how close we are to the Purgatory Arch?" Dani didn't raise her head, which muffled her voice against her thighs.

"No, but I feel like we've made good time."

One of Dani's brown eyes peeked out from her legs. "Really?"

Ty shrugged. Truthfully, he had no damn clue, but he wasn't about to say it out loud. As best he could tell, they'd kept a straight path through the swamp. That the blood had never gotten deeper than mid-thigh had helped.

Wicket derailed their conversation, kicking up bits of dirt with his hind legs while he growled. The dog focused on the direction they'd come from. Ty stood and held up his glow crystal.

"What is it?" Dani stood next to him.

"Not sure. Maybe Wicket saw a tree moving."

Dani took in a sharp breath and jumped to her feet. "Grab Wicket!"

That's when Ty spotted the spine of the sewer scorpion moving through the blood, same as it had beneath Vel.

"It followed us?"

Dani grabbed the walking stick. "I don't think it's the same one, because there's at least five of them now."

Chapter 9

Ty scooped up Wicket, who yelped in mid-bark, and slipped him into the sling against his chest.

"Are there any more the way we're headed?" Ty drew his sword.

"Not that I can see."

"Dani, dip your backpack in the blood. I think that scorpion marked your bag while we were in the sewer so he could track us."

Dani cursed. She sheathed her sword and tossed the walking stick to Ty to free up her hands. She jerked the backpack off and dunked it in the blood deep enough to cover all of the black, scorpion spit. With any luck, that would mask the scent of the sewer scorpion's mark. As soon as she had the backpack on again, Ty threw the walking stick to her.

Blood splashed into the air around them as they ran through the pond.

Ty glanced behind him, but with their glow crystals positioned on the front of their jackets' sleeves, he could only see about a dozen feet behind them. The only good news was that it meant the scorpions weren't that close yet, but there was no telling how fast they were moving now that he and Dani had reentered the pond.

Wicket squirmed within the sling, determined to position himself so that he could see around Ty's torso. He scrambled up enough to look over Ty's shoulder and barked in a rage that confirmed the scorpions were still there and probably getting closer.

Wicket's grip on Ty's shoulder wasn't strong enough to keep him from dropping away from Ty's chest as the bottom of the pond startled them by dropping at least half a foot deeper, bringing the bloodline halfway up Ty's thighs. Wicket yelped. Ty grabbed the dog in a tight hug, careful not to cut him on his sword, and saved the dog from falling into the blood.

"Not a good idea, furball." Ty forced him back into the sling.

"Remember what I said about there not being any ahead of us?" Dani's tone made the reason for the question obvious.

"How many?"

"Two."

Ty stopped and turned to let his crystal illuminate the swamp behind them. He could see four of the five they'd originally spotted. They were less than thirty feet away and moving fast.

"Suggestions?"

"Skewer the two ahead of us and then run like hell!" Dani didn't wait for him to offer an opinion. She charged as fast as she could at the nearer of the two.

Ty followed her lead and went for the other one. This one had the mushroom stalk on its right side, and as soon as Ty neared it, the scorpion turned that side towards him and unleashed its tendrils to whip and grab at him. Ty trudged through the river of blood to his right, trying to get around the scorpion to the side with its pincer, but the monster turned much faster than he could.

Dani faced a similar problem, unable to get on the safer side of her scorpion.

They spun in circles with Ty and Dani slashing at the tendrils. The other scorpions were getting close. Much more of this pointless dancing, and they were going to die here.

Their rotations placed the pincer side of Dani's scorpion right behind Ty. He slashed at the latest thrust of tendrils from his scorpion, then spun around and thrust his sword into the blood and up into the belly of Dani's scorpion. Black blood spilled out onto the red river. The scorpion thrashed and screamed.

Ty turned to his scorpion as the beast lunged towards him. Its tendrils didn't attack him, though. The scorpion shoved him aside and descended on its wounded sibling.

"Run for it!" he shouted as the rest of the scorpions piled onto the other two.

Dani sprinted through the blood. Ty placed himself behind her. He glanced back at the frenzied scorpions. More black scorpion ichor rained down on the crimson pond, and not all of it belonged to the one Ty had skewered.

Dani laughed. "Guess we don't smell as good as the local livestock."

"Not to those things, at least."

Wicket continued to bark, but the dog's fury had shifted into a more token warning for any other creatures that might try to take a bite out of them.

Any notions Ty had about sleeping in this swamp died along with the scorpion eaten alive by its siblings.

Chapter 10

Dani made a habit of dipping the backpack with Malum's head and heart into the blood. Whether that kept the scorpions off their scent or if they were sated from feasting on one of their own was hard to say. Regardless of the reason, their absence satisfied Ty.

They left the pond of blood for the mud. In some ways, the bloody soil made their trek worse, because the constant effort to lift their feet out of the muck and plunging them back into the same mess exhausted them.

"I need a break." Ty leaned against a tree trunk and sighed in relief when the branches and roots didn't attack him. The tree looked dead with its leaves missing.

Dani joined him. She leaned her back against the tree and closed her eyes for a moment. "I keep telling myself not to think about how long we've been awake."

"How's that working for you?"

"Lousy, because it reminds me how long we've been awake." When she opened her eyes, she leaned closer for a quick kiss, pausing afterwards to glance down at Wicket. The terrier slumbered within the sling. "Don't suppose there's room for me in that thing, too."

"Sure, we can take turns."

Dani yawned, speaking again near the end of it. "I think there might be some problems with that plan." She snuck another look at the sleeping dog before canting her head to the side for them to keep moving.

A few hours later, they neared a split tree with half of the trunk fallen to the ground and hollowed out. The branches reached out like skeletal hands. Ty pointed to it. "You notice the trees?" Like the tree they'd rested against earlier, this one lacked any leaves.

Dani glanced at the fallen tree. "Been a while since I saw any that looked alive."

All three moons glowed above them, partially visible through the barren branches.

"I can't tell what's killing them." Ty had noticed several fallen trees with their mud-covered roots twisting outward like exposed pipes from a section of a wall without a building.

"Fine by me if we don't find out."

Not long after that, the moons vanished and the dark orange sky of day appeared between the spiderweb formations of empty branches. Something in Ty's brain panicked at the realization he was seeing a second day dawn without ever having slept between.

They paused on a small hill more solid than mud. Wicket happily ran around in circles, pausing to sniff and take care of his business.

"Looks like we're nearing the end of the dead trees," Dani said. Red leaves swayed in the distance.

Wicket dug into the wet ground, pausing for a few sniffs. Lord only knew what small creature he was burrowing after. Ty hoped he wouldn't draw out something determined to kill all of them.

Then he heard something else. He stood and walked to the edge of the island in the mud. "Dani, make him stop for a moment."

"Come here, baby." Dani kissed the dog on the head as she lifted him up. The terrier grumbled a protest but then licked her face.

Ty used his hand to blot out the brightening sky to peer through the tangle of dead trees. "Can't see anything, but..." He shrugged.

"No, I hear it, too." Dani handed Wicket to Ty, helping him slip the dog into the sling. The dog smelled of freshly turned dirt from his digging.

"We need cover." He pointed towards another fallen tree. So much mud still clung to the tree's exposed roots, that it provided a good hiding place.

Ty peeked through a small opening in the tangle of roots. Dani found another gap a little lower. Wicket growled softly in a token protest. Dani rested a hand on the dog's back, which silenced him.

"That works on you, too," she whispered with a sly grin.

"I'd dispute that if it wasn't true."

That's when the three riders came into view. They started as silhouettes moving among the dead trees. Ty recognized the lead rider, the one with the wolf head. They'd met Char the first time they encountered Malum. The demon's amber eyes glowed in the dim daylight. The loose ground didn't hold the impressions of their feet, but if Char's sense of smell was as keen as an actual wolf's, then they were screwed.

As the demons passed the fallen tree, Ty got a better look at the other two. The whiter with the mohawk didn't look familiar, but those bone-white beasts with their goat legs and reptilian talon hands didn't exactly stand out in Hell.

The woman with the charred skin, though... Ty had never encountered a fallen human. The Order spoke of them, but most exorcists considered them myths. He looked forward to sharing that in their next debrief. That thought twisted the knife of regret deeper into his heart.

There wouldn't be a debrief, not after this quest and certainly never again. At best, the Order would interrogate him and Dani before tossing them in cells to rot.

Of course, that assumed he and Dani didn't get killed here and now. He'd hoped all the beasts with a taste for demons would deter Malum's servants from following them into the swamp.

The large trunk concealed Ty and Dani as the demons passed. Ty leaned lower to look through the thin gap between the bottom of the fallen tree trunk and the ground. The long legs of the reptilian beasts the demons rode clopped through the mud with greater ease than they had walking through it. Better for them, if these demons got ahead of them, then maybe they could take a different path to get out of here.

Char's beast stopped, bringing the other two to a halt.

The wolf's nostrils sucked in the air in rapid, beating breaths. He growled as he turned in his saddle to point at Ty and Dani's hiding place.

"There!"

Chapter 11

Char's dovra turned and charged.

Ty and Dani drew their swords as they scrambled from their hiding place. If they didn't move fast, they'd end up trapped against the tree trunk. Mud kicked up in the air as Ty and Dani ran out into the open.

Instead of going around the fallen tree, Char launched his beast onto the trunk and then the dovra kicked off it, flying over Ty and Dani to land in their path of retreat. The demon drew his sword as he spun his mount around to face them.

The whiter and his mount scrambled around the fallen tree, taking the long way around its tangled top of limbs. The fallen human and her dovra leaped on top of the tree trunk and stayed there to guard the high ground.

"Zhor! Nera! Hold!" Char's voice echoed through the swamp as he raised a hand to stop the whiter from drawing closer once he rounded the tree and then towards the woman whose dovra perched on the tree trunk.

Char snarled as he pointed his sword at Dani. "I call Malum my Premier and my friend, but I will grant you that he wronged you both."

"He murdered my mother and slaughtered children in their beds!" Dani adjusted her grip on her swords, ready for the demon's charge. "'Wronged' doesn't cover what that bastard did."

"Human death means nothing to us when your souls receive chance after chance at a fresh journey across the mortal plane." His lips curled back, revealing the long rows of pointed teeth in his snout. "Keep in mind how little value I place on your lives as I make this offer. If you surrender Malum's head and heart to me, I will let you leave Hell unharmed. Refuse my offer, and we'll cut you down here."

Dani laughed. "Not a chance in Hell."

Char growled and spurred his dovra into a charge.

Ty and Dani moved so the dovra would pass between them, but then Nera's dovra landed behind them. The large beast kicked up a spray of bloody mud at Ty's back. Wicket squirmed within the sling, growling and barking.

The dovra's maw opened as wide as a crocodile's and then snapped at Ty's right arm. Ty slammed his sword into the side of the beast's head. The metal blade sparked against the armor-like scales. No chance of drawing blood, but the force of the blow knocked it stupid for a moment.

Nera attacked with her sword. She moved fast, each swing an efficient movement that kept Ty off-balance and pushed him back. More importantly, it pushed him away from Dani, keeping them from working together.

The dovra growled as it got its senses back. Wicket barked his retort.

The whiter with the mohawk charged past them both towards Dani. Char abandoned his dovra to fight Dani on foot.

Nera kept pushing Ty away from his wife. Her dovra snapped at him again, drawing more protests from Wicket. Ty ducked beneath Nera's swing and slashed at the dovra's belly. Sparks flew off the beast's armored hide, but Ty cut his true target, the belt that held the saddle in place.

The dovra turned to pursue him.

"Come on!" Ty shouted more at the beast than its rider. The dovra's jaw flew open for another bite at him. Ty shoved the point of his sword at the roof of its mouth. The beast reared before the blade could pierce up into its brain.

Nera panicked as the saddle slid down the dovra's back and sent her tumbling into the mud. The beast screamed in confusion as it spun around and slapped at Ty with its long tail.

The thick whip crushed into Ty's side. The attack knocked him off his feet. Wicket yelped as Ty crashed against the prone tree trunk they'd used for cover. Thankfully his back suffered most of the impact. If his front side had crashed into it, that would have killed Wicket for certain. The trunk vibrated with a strange hum.

Wicket's angry barks drowned out the noise from the tree as he squirmed within the sling. At least the little furball was unharmed.

The growl that followed didn't come from Wicket, though. Ty brought his sword up to block Nera's attack. She swung again. Ty dodged the blade, and it slammed into the tree trunk.

Ty backed away to put more space between him and Nera. She glanced over her shoulder at Dani and the other two demons fighting her. Ty grinned at the sight of his wife holding her own against both of them. She'd used the same trick of slashing the saddle harness to knock the whiter off of his dovra.

Ty's joy didn't last long.

"Focus!" The fallen demon hissed at him in a whisper before she swung her sword overhead at him.

He dodged the swing, knocking her sword off course as he retreated, putting even more distance between him and Dani.

"You won't make it through the Purgatory Arch in this realm." She pressed her attack, but she made no effort to hide the intended path of her swings, making it all too easy for Ty to block her or step out of the way.

"We made it this far." Ty kept his voice to a whisper, too. If he was guessing right, then she pushed him away from the others to keep them from hearing her.

"There's already an entire regiment and more waiting for you, hundreds of demons. If you don't die here, you will end there." She drew back a moment, to catch her breath and pointed meaningfully towards Wicket with her sword. "You must gate to another realm and take a different Purgatory Arch."

She pressed in with another attack that pushed him to his left towards the tree trunk.

"Why would you help us?"

She grinned as she canted her head towards the others. "I'm sworn to Char, not Malum."

"That won't do you much good if Dani and I die here."

Nera rushed at him, her sword flashing with practiced swings that prompted them to pivot, placing Dani and the other demons behind him.

She shifted her eyes towards the east. "Your best chance is that way. You'd best run fast."

Nera glanced past him, looking for something. What that might be, Ty couldn't say, but then she slammed her sword hard into the tree trunk. The bark shattered apart revealing its hollowed out insides that were anything but empty. Insects, each larger than Ty's fists, writhed within the tree. The buzz of the insects turned angry, and they erupted into the open air, pushing Ty and the demon apart.

"Locusts!" Nera shouted the warning to Char.

These locusts' bodies resembled grasshoppers, except for their heads. A single compound eye rested atop a stalk between the antennae, and the rest of the head resembled some bizarre beak that split open into five parts with a foot-long stinger sticking out the middle of it.

One bug circled towards Ty. He swung with his sword. The blade didn't cut it but swatted the insect away like a baseball.

"Dani!" He forced his way through the swarm of armored bugs to get to his wife. One bug slammed into Ty's back but didn't pierce his jacket. Another insect narrowly missed Wicket. He felt the dog's panicked barks, more than he heard it, drowned out by the collective buzz of the locusts.

He wrapped his left arm around Wicket's body, hugging him close. His right arm swung his sword at the swarm, trying to clear a path through them to where Dani was. The swarm thickened in this direction. Ty wondered if that might be because Char and Zhor were that way, that the bugs preferred items from the local menu, like most of the creatures they'd encountered. He hoped so, because he didn't want to think these things were swarming after Dani, although Malum's remains in her bag might also attract the swarm.

Ty screamed to Dani. The distance between them felt like miles.

Most of the swarm broke away, heading towards the living trees he'd seen in the direction of the Purgatory Arch. The bugs latched onto the long, dangling leaves and chewed their way up. Others leaped onto the tree trunks and stabbed their stingers into them.

The metallic clang of his sword striking another blade caught him short. The other weapon was Dani's.

She grabbed him by the arm. "Come on!"

"No, this way!" He pulled her in the direction Nera had suggested. Part of him considered himself a damn fool to put his trust in a demon. That same mistake had landed them in this mess.

To Ty's relief, Dani's pack bounced against her back without any bugs latched onto it for a sample of Malum's head and heart.

Ty hoped the swarm would last long enough to conceal the way they were going. Char and Zhor howled and screamed as they battled against the insects buzzing through the air around them. Ty had a bad feeling that if Char and his companions caught their trail again before they got out of this blood swamp, they were dead.

Chapter 12

Six Years Earlier

Maria Cortez drove her red Mini Cooper up to the front gates of Hollywood Cemetery. A security guard nodded and waved to her from his post as she drove by.

Ty had never found a cemetery frightening, not even as a kid. Maybe if he'd visited one at night, he'd have gotten it. Still, something about this daytime guided tour with Maria made the experience unexpectedly disturbing. She hadn't mentioned when they left the café that they'd be coming here.

The cemetery looked huge, with roads curving and interconnecting through the hilly terrain. Gravestones, some almost two hundred years old and in disrepair, were clustered so close as to be claustrophobic.

She drove to the far end of the property and parked in front of a small mausoleum. The road formed a perfect circle in front of the white brick building with an obelisk of the same bricks standing in a grassy island in the center of the asphalt circle.

Maria climbed out of her car. "This part of the cemetery belongs to my organization."

"I really hope this isn't the retirement community for your employees."

She grinned at him with a pair of sunglasses hiding her one good eye and most of her eyepatch but didn't confirm or deny what he'd suggested.

"So let me guess. This is the point where you tell me there's no turning back if I go inside?" He couldn't resist the sarcasm. When they left the café, Maria said that she planned to show him something that would help him make his decision.

"Not at all. I've had some people over the years who've walked away after this point. I gladly let them leave, but I know a sure thing when I see it."

What bothered him most was how certain she sounded.

"First," she said, pointing to the mausoleum, "I'd ask you to walk around it, to get a feel for how small it is."

"All right," he said more under his breath to himself. Her wording seemed odd. Most people would have probably said "how big," not "how small."

He walked up to the front of the building. It stood more than ten feet tall, with four pillars supporting the roof that angled down to the right and left sides of the building. Someone had engraved an infinity symbol on the black steel door. The sides and roof of the building went into the hill behind it, reminding him of the hobbit houses in *Lord of the Rings*.

"Here lies Bilbo Baggins," he muttered to himself in a creepy voice as he circled the building, which meant also circling the hill the building jutted into.

The hill wasn't much taller than the mausoleum, and no headstones touched the hill, even though the rest of the cemetery used every bit of available space to give as many people as possible their final dirt nap.

Maria was sitting on the hood of her car with her arms crossed when Ty finished circling the hill and the building.

"Okay." He shrugged, still unclear what the point of this was.

She gestured towards the mausoleum. "About how far in would you say it goes? Counting the hill."

He turned to look at it again and shrugged. "Maybe forty feet, at most."

She nodded, lips pursed in a way that suggested she found his answer acceptable. "A little less than that, but close enough."

Maria stood and walked over to the front door and reached into her jacket pocket. She pulled out a key as big as her hand. Ty noticed the key also had the infinity symbol engraved into the fat end of it. She unlocked the door and pulled it open with a loud, metallic creak.

The interior stayed dark until they stepped inside and Maria pulled the door shut. Then she flipped a switch, and two gas-fueled lamps attached to the far wall ignited. The lamps were stuck into the wall next to the most disturbing arch Ty had ever seen in his life.

While all the surfaces inside the mausoleum were made out of the same white brick as the exterior, the arch that formed a doorway on the far wall and led into a dark grey, brick corridor was made out of something far different.

"Are those?"

"Human skulls?" Maria said with a hint of pride. "Most of them."

Other bones formed the arch. Some looked like femurs, humeri, and ribs. At first, Ty thought that was what she had meant by "Most of them." Then he saw the skulls at the base on each side. He knelt next to the skull at the very bottom of the arch on the right side. "Wolf skull?"

She shook her head and grinned, as if savoring a private joke and enjoying his failure to understand the punch line.

The skull directly above the "not wolf" skull seemed more human but deformed. Only, if it was deformed, the mirror skull on the left side looked almost identical, as if they were supposed to look like this.

Another odd thing about the deformed, "not wolf" skulls—they looked burned, almost turned black.

Then he stared into the tunnel. It had to be some kind of optical illusion, because the tunnel appeared to go much further than the hill allowed.

Maria stepped over to the arch and pulled out a flashlight. "Shall we?"

Ty shifted his eyes from her to the tunnel and back to her. "Shall we what?"

"Take a walk," she said, as if that was obvious. She stepped through the arch and kept walking.

Ty watched her get farther and farther away. She eventually stopped, and he assumed she'd hit the end, but then she turned on her flashlight. The light revealed even more of the brick passage.

When she continued to walk on without him, he ran after her to catch up. He kept expecting the path to reach a dead end, but it kept going. Eventually, he stopped to look back at the distant outline of the arch and the glow of the gaslights.

"That isn't," he stopped and struggled to find his voice again. "I mean, there's no way."

Maria had stopped and watched him, her flashlight pointing in the direction they'd come from. The flashlight had dimmed, as if the batteries were about to die.

"Yes?" she asked.

"The hill?" He looked up and down the passage. "It wasn't this big. We didn't go down at all, so—how—there's no way. How are we still under the hill?"

"Well, for starters, we're not under the hill," Maria said. "We haven't been under the hill since we went through the arch."

He struggled to breathe. "No, that's crazy. I mean—I went around the hill." He pointed down, insisting the hill had to be right where they stood. "It wasn't this big."

"I know," she said in the voice a teacher might adopt to introduce algebra to a kindergartner. "When we crossed the arch, we entered Purgatory."

Ty stayed silent, too busy trying to figure out when she drugged him and why he didn't feel drugged. His brain puzzled out all the ways an architect might create this illusion. Bricks angled to push in or some other nonsense. He couldn't accept this.

"Those skulls and bones that make up the arch aren't randomly placed there. It's an intricate combination that forms an entrance into the realm of the dead, starting with Purgatory." She pointed her half-dimmed flashlight ahead again. "People like to think Purgatory is rolling hills or a desolate plain, but the reality is that it's not all that different from where our bodies are laid to rest."

"No way," but he couldn't think of an explanation to argue that denial. "This is some Lion, Witch, and the Wardrobe type shit." His normally deep voice went up with his building panic.

Maria laughed, and the way she acted so relaxed about all of this only made it seem more insane.

"Well, where do you think C.S. Lewis got the idea?"

"Are you telling me that C.S. Lewis worked for you guys? And who the hell are you people?"

She pointed towards the arch, directing him to follow her back to it. "No, he wasn't, but one of our members got a little too drunk at a pub while sitting near him." She stopped when she realized Ty hadn't moved to follow her. "We really should go back. If we go far enough, the flashlight will stop working, and lingering there wouldn't be safe, especially unarmed. I just find most of my recruitment prospects don't react well to seeing me belt on my sword."

His brain took a few seconds to process what she'd said. Then he stared down the tunnel into the darkness. "What's in there that you need a sword?"

Chapter 13

Ty and Dani stopped on the edge of the blood swamp. The wind had picked up, whistling a taunt at them as it added to the unnatural creak of the swaying trees.

Dani sat on a patch of solid ground holding onto Wicket as she stared straight ahead at nothing. The silky terrier licked at her cheek, eventually coaxing a small smile from her. "You want to abandon the quickest way out of here on the word of a demon." The words didn't hold any heat to them, but Ty didn't miss the implied accusation.

The debate over what to do next had pushed him to pace across the small strip of dry land within the blood swamp. She hated when he paced, but it helped him think and stay awake.

"They've moved faster than we expected. We've got hundreds of demons at the gate waiting for us." He'd already made this point. The previous time he'd said it, Dani had let the detail fly past unaddressed. This time, she rolled her eyes in his direction.

"She claims."

Ty focused his attention on Wicket. He preferred that to the look on Dani's face that demanded why he wanted to fuck up all of their plans.

"We lost our full night's head start!" As soon as the shout came out of him, he regretted it and took a breath to calm himself before he continued. "Sorry. Look, cutting through the swamp was a good call, but only because it kept us from getting hacked up on the road to the arch. There's no advantage that can help us get past all of those demons."

"Don't you think I know that!" Now, she avoided looking at him, resting her chin on Wicket's back as she hugged him to her chest.

Ty cursed under his breath at himself. He hadn't mentioned the loss of their head start as an accusation, but she was still beating herself up over Malum waking before she could kill him or prevent him from shouting for his guards. The lack of sleep was also getting to them. Thinking literally hurt his head.

The tension between them must have gotten to Wicket, because he squirmed out of Dani's grip and ran in a circle between his two humans, barking a few times before he dug at the ground.

Ty stopped his pacing and knelt in front of Dani. "We need Wicket to find us a new path." He said the words with all the caution he'd use if approaching an angry tiger.

She tapped at the face of the watch on her right wrist as it counted down the hours remaining for them to end Malum for good. "A path that can get us home in five days or less?"

The thin places that offered a path to Purgatory were fixed, but the Hell gates that led to other dimensions within Hell sometimes moved. Some collapsed to open in other places or vanished altogether. They were nearing nightfall again, reinforcing that time was working against them. Dani would never forgive herself if she failed to avenge her mother, and Ty would hate himself for failing his wife, if this decision sabotaged their chances of ending Malum for good.

Wicket dug at the ground, growling in anticipation of whatever he hoped to find, seemingly oblivious to the debate brewing over his ability to guide them. That he could find them a way home went without question. He'd understand the command to guide them, but they couldn't convey a time frame to him.

The wind shifted, pushing the stench of the blood swamp towards them. Ty had grown numb to the odor of blood and mud while they were knee deep in it, but now that they'd neared the borders of the blood swamp, the more frequent absence of the stink made it all too noticeable when it returned.

Ty stepped into the mud and walked to the row of swaying trees. He pushed the long red leaves aside, moving slow enough to avoid antagonizing the trees, for a glance beyond. The grey and cracked land outside the swamp resembled over-baked cement. The land turned uneven, forming a maze of canyons. If they committed to this path, then they'd have to move fast and find a way out of this dimension before the demons caught up to them. As soon as Char reached the Purgatory Arch and realized they'd given up on it, he'd dispatch his ravens to find them.

So long as they remained in the Blood Realm, the chances increased that the demons would catch up to them. They'd been going non-stop for almost two full days. That had kept them alive, but they couldn't maintain this pace much longer.

Dani walked up behind him and slipped her arms around his waist. "We give it two days." The whispered words conveyed how weary she was. She rested her head against the back of his shoulder. Despite how muggy the blood swamp was, her warmth comforted him, prompting him to lean his head back against hers. What he wouldn't give to lay here with her and close their eyes for a few hours.

He cleared his throat and lowered his voice as he asked, "And after two days?"

"If we aren't convinced we'll get home in time to burn Malum, we turn back."

That sounded like a horrible idea. Doing that meant running head-long into any demons on their trail. Taking this alternate route created a slim chance they might draw Char and his soldiers away from the Purgatory Arch, assuming the demons believed he and Dani had given up on that route. Ty wouldn't place any bets on those odds. Never mind that turning back might not be an option. The way the gates in Hell worked, they could find their return route cut off by a collapsed or relocated gate.

"Well?" Dani asked.

He'd waited too long to answer, and she suspected his opinion.

He placed a hand over her right hand, which was resting over his belt buckle. "All right. Two days."

She kissed the back of his neck and then released her grip on him to put on her backpack with Malum's remains in it.

This wouldn't go well. Unless they ended up in a dimension they knew, they wouldn't be able to tell how close they were to another Purgatory Arch. Dani might balk if they ended up anywhere uncharted, possibly even before two days had passed. Ty knew that, but with the closest way out cut off and an army of demons on the hunt for them, all they had left to choose from were the best of bad ideas.

Chapter 14

They emerged from the blood-soaked muck of the swamp. As soon as Ty set Wicket on the dry ground, he ran in a happy circle and yapped at them.

Dani knelt next to their dog and brought him to a halt with a scratch to his chin that drew his big eyes to meet hers. "Wicket, seek gate."

Wicket darted into the canyon. They raced after him. The uneven terrain didn't challenge the little four-legged furball. He leaped along the grey piles of rocks and sloping ground that soon placed them within the canyon's towering walls.

If they fell behind, Wicket would stop and spin in circles until they caught up to him. That happened frequently, because they weren't as well-rested as their dog.

As muggy as the swamp had been, this terrain was barren and lifeless. Even some of the larger rocks crumbled to dust when they placed their weight on them. Dani grabbed Ty's arm in time to spare him from sliding down a steep hill when the boulder he leaped onto shattered.

Wicket barked at them to keep moving.

"There's no cover here." Dani pointed up at the rocky walls which all sloped up and away from the bottom of the canyon. As uneven as the formations were, nothing jutted out enough to shield them from the view of any ravens that might pass overhead. Nor had they seen any caves. They'd reached plenty of splits in the canyon that forced them to choose which way to go. Thank goodness Wicket's nose made those decisions for them. As much as Ty prided himself on his sense of direction, he was hopelessly lost.

The reddish-orange sky of the approaching sunset pressed down on them like a hot and heavy blanket, giving the canyon a claustrophobic quality. More than once, Ty looked at the path that had led them here. Bits of dark red dirt, the bloody swamp mud that covered their boots, was flaking off to leave a clear trail for anyone to follow them.

"You know anything about these canyons?" Ty asked. He'd studied the maps of the Blood Realm many times. They'd also made their fair share of trips here to hunt down demons guilty of possession, but he didn't recall anything about this region.

"Not much." She stopped and called for Wicket to come to them. The dog grumbled as he trotted back to them, impatient to keep moving.

Ty handed her their water bottle. She took a small sip and groaned as she pulled it away from her lips. He knew how she felt. The comfort of the water against his chapped lips made him wish he could upend the bottle on his sweat-covered face.

"Let's pray the next gate leads somewhere with water." Dani shook her head as she paused to take a deep breath and then stand straight. "I don't think we've got enough left to last more than a day."

That assumed they could even find a gate in that time.

"Wish he could tell us how close the gate is." Wicket had given up on them moving at the pace he wanted. He'd hopped onto a boulder three times as big as him and rested his head on his front paws. His big black eyes shifted between his two humans with the obvious question of how long they were going to wait here. Ty offered the dog some water, but he wasn't interested.

Dani scrubbed her face in her hands as if the friction would rouse her. "We need to keep moving."

He knew what she meant. As soon as they'd stopped, the ground pulled on him with the magnetic promise of sleep. Staying upright and all the thinking required to navigate the difficult terrain kept them awake, but even that was losing its effect.

Ty prayed they might find the gate before nightfall, but during the next few hours, as the sky darkened, he abandoned that hope. They slowed their pace as even Wicket's passion to keep moving had ebbed into a steady trot.

"Haven't seen any ravens," Ty said. "You?"

"No."

She looked over her shoulder at him. Her eyes were red from exhaustion and wide with panic. "Much longer, and we're gonna have to risk some sleep."

"I know."

As tired as they both were, they'd never manage to take turns sleeping. Once they stayed still long enough, they'd both pass out, and stopping was inevitable. Wicket wouldn't keep going forever, and they couldn't push on while he slept in the sling. Only he knew the way to go.

"Before I forget," Ty said as he recalled their encounter with Char, "'*Not a chance in Hell?*' Really?"

Dani snorted. "Oh, please. You'd have been disappointed if I hadn't said it."

"Those would have been terrible last words."

"Then you had incentive for us to live. You're welcome."

"Smart-ass."

"You've never complained about my ass before."

"That is true."

She reached over, taking his hand into hers, fingers twining in a way that they didn't do as often as they had when they'd first fallen in love.

They walked that way until the ground became too uneven again, forcing them to travel one behind the other.

The sky turned black, and even though they stopped for Wicket to eat a small can of dog food and some water, he surprised them both by pushing on for the next gate despite the dark. Just enough moonlight shone to help them see and keep up with their furry guide.

That's when the hissing started.

Infrequent whispers came from all directions, but it built up in a hurry. Wicket growled and barked in protest with a strong "Stay off my lawn!" quality to his tone.

Ty and Dani stopped as Wicket ran a circle around them, barking a warning. Something moved along the ground all around them.

Dani grabbed a small rock and threw it off to their left. When the rock hit the ground, a loud series of hisses followed along with a flare of bright red light. The bright light rippled along the spine of several two-foot-long lizards. The lizards stalked towards them from all directions, and the red glow appeared along their backs. The nearest one was ten feet away. Wicket lunged at it with a loud bark and a snap of his teeth. The lizard, its glow flaring to a blinding extreme, scrambled back as Wicket stood his ground. Then another lizard decided to test their resolve and Wicket raced over to push that one away.

Ty drew his sword. "I'm gonna remind you of these ugly bastards the next time you try to talk me into getting a bearded dragon for a pet."

Dani answered with a deadpan stare that had her unspoken "Really?" written into it. She took a step away from him and drew both of her swords from the scabbards on her hips.

"How many do you think there are?" she asked, giving her swords a relaxed spin.

"Maybe a hundred."

If they attacked one at a time, Dani and Ty could kill them all without too much trouble, but the way the lizards' collective glow intensified, Ty could tell they didn't have long before the entire lounge rushed them.

Wicket placed himself behind them and spun in place. He did the same thing when he wanted to herd them into a particular room of their home, usually to bed when he decided they'd stayed up too late.

Then Wicket sprinted past them and in the direction he'd been herding them. He reached the nearest lizard and leaped. Three of the lizards snapped at him, but he flew past them and landed on a boulder with two of the lizards on top. His landing sent one of the lizards tumbling over the side. The other hissed at Wicket, its body coiling more like a snake, preparing to strike. Wicket barked his own threat. They lunged at one another at the same time. The lizard's maw snapped at empty air as Wicket slipped around on its left. The canine's teeth latched onto the back of the lizard's neck and flung it off the boulder with a spray of glowing red blood raining down on its siblings below.

"Move!" Dani shouted.

She swiped at the lizards as they rushed in on her side. Ty obeyed and leaped over the lizards to land on the boulder with Wicket. "Your turn!"

Ty slashed at a group of the lizards trying to climb up after him and Wicket. Dani leaped onto the rock behind him with a lizard biting into her right boot. Ty slashed at the lizard, cutting it in half. The mouth clung to her boot, though. Neither of them bothered to pull it off. Instead they followed Wicket as he leaped off the other side of the boulder onto one higher up without any lizards on it. The lizards hissed as their backs glowed brighter with their anger at being denied their meals.

Once they made it off the other boulder, Wicket sprinted for the dark.

Dani and Ty struggled to keep up with their dog. The lizards raced after them and weren't struggling to match their pace. Dani covered their retreat, slicing at any lizards that got too close. The one that had bitten into her boot still hadn't come loose, even though it had stopped bleeding. Then he realized why it hadn't fallen off. It wasn't dead yet.

"Dani, that lizard on you is growing back its hind end."

She cursed as she slashed at it again but missed. The lounge of lizards chasing them was going too fast for her to slow down enough for a decent swing. If it managed to grow back its hind legs, the damn thing would probably scramble up and bite her somewhere less protected than her boots.

"Switch!" she shouted.

He stopped to let her pass. As she went by, she threw him her left sword. He snatched it out of the air and went to work. Lizards leaped up at him, but they couldn't coordinate their attacks to get past his sword swings.

More lizards slipped out of cracks in the canyon's walls and scrambled down to join the pursuit. The one that had been latched onto Dani's leg flew past with a distressed squawk.

A glance over his shoulder let him see that even the ones he'd sliced in half were growing back.

"These things are like fucking hydras!" he shouted to Dani.

His heart felt fit to explode. The exhaustion of the past few days threatened to rip him apart from the inside and let the lizards do the same to the outside.

Wicket barked in a series of excited yips.

"Gate!" Dani shouted.

"Thank God!"

The gate resembled a rip in reality, like a piece of paper torn up the middle and peeled back on both sides. Tiny lightning bolts of yellow light danced up and down the edges of the tear. The image of the other side twisted within the rip as if being puréed in a blender, obscuring what awaited them.

The good news: they'd reached the gate before the lizards caught up to them.

The bad news: the lizards probably wouldn't stop chasing them after they went through the gate.

Wicket went first, pausing only a second before running into the gate to make sure Dani and Ty were still following. Dani followed Wicket with Ty right behind her.

PART II

LOST AT SEA

Chapter 15

The swirling interior of the gate yanked Ty into its embrace. Three seconds passed. The first: the fiery panic of his body coming apart. The second: the truest nothing that nothing can be while still holding the barest minimum of self awareness, with an absence of anything to stimulate any of the five senses. The third: all of reality shoved back into place, but somewhere new.

The strangest part was that despite all that happened between entry and exit, Ty left the gate exactly as he entered. Reality's invisible stage-hands hit pause with him in mid-run, moved him somewhere else, and then pressed "play."

Ty never understood how Wicket or any other dog agreed to enter these gates after taking their first one. Possibly dogs saw reality simple enough not to register the horror of it.

What he expected on the other side wasn't what he got. After the heat of the Blood Realm, the cold mist of this new place sent a shiver through him.

They weren't on any ground, though. They'd emerged onto the wooden deck of what could pass for some old 18th century pirate ship, near the elevated rear of it. The ship's sails were all raised and flapping in a tattered mess above them. The ship didn't rock, and it most certainly wasn't floating in a body of water.

An endless assortment of derelict ships floated in the misty void around them. Thick yellow bridges connected all of the ships in the fashion of a spider web. The floating armada included some more modern vessels, including private yachts and battleships.

"We are definitely off the map." Ty realized the three of them had stopped near the captain's wheel.

Dani looked ready to say something smart, but then she grabbed at his arm and pulled him into a run as the lizards emerged from the Hell gate.

They sprinted for the front of the ship.

"We're going to run out of ship real fast!" Dani said over her shoulder.

Wicket, for his part, didn't require being told to flee from the lizards pursuing them. He went straight to the farthest point of the ship and barked for his humans to follow. Unintelligible voices called from below decks—inhuman voices.

They reached the far end of the ship. Dani pointed to a narrow bridge as long as a football field that protruded from the pirate ship and connected to a 35-foot-long speedboat.

"I'll go first." Dani stepped onto the bridge. It didn't wobble, and while being a foot wide wasn't too intimidating, the mist surrounding them left the uncomfortable impression that what awaited them, if they fell, wouldn't be an ocean or land. Rumor suggested some parts of Hell were bottomless. Until this moment, Ty hadn't given those rumors any credence. After all, unless someone fell and came back to tell the tale, then how did anyone know a hole was truly bottomless and not just really deep? Only, as he stepped onto the bridge behind Dani and Wicket, he felt that certainty in the very core of his soul that one step too far right or left would send him into endless space.

He wouldn't describe the bridge as flat, not exactly. It resembled a six-sided spike driven into the two connecting ships. The rope-like material gave their boots more traction. Sadly, that helped the lizards, too.

"Are they still following?" Dani's voice echoed to him.

He paused in his scrambling shuffle along the bridge to get a look back at the pirate ship. Vertigo hit him hard, drawing a curse out of him. He wasn't normally scared of heights, but the way these ships were arranged—floating above, across, and below one another—wasn't natural. Coupled with the sensation of traversing a bottomless void, the simple act of shifting in place turned into something far more dangerous while going across these ropes. He cursed as he turned to see the lizards leaping onto the rope after them.

"We've got about a thirty-yard head start, but they're moving faster than us."

"Of course they are."

Wicket growled his own complaint. Hard to tell whether Wicket directed it at the lizards or the rope bridge.

They'd made it at least three-quarters of the distance from the pirate ship to the speedboat when Ty heard the skittering of the lizards' feet getting close. He forced himself into one of those dizzying turns again to attack.

"See if you can cut this thing once you get to the boat!"

He still had his sword and one of Dani's. That turned out to be a good thing, because these lizards didn't feel the need to limit themselves to the topmost side of the rope. They skittered across all three sides of the rope's upper half. He purposefully slapped at them with the flats of the swords, sweeping the lizards off into the foggy abyss.

Wicket barked somewhere ahead, probably having reached the speedboat by now.

"Ty, hurry! I can't cut this thing with you on it!"

"Start sawing through it as much as you safely can." She wasn't going to cut it in a single swing. Cutting this taut rope at the speedboat's end should fling the lizards into the abyss. The problem? These ropes appeared to hold the ships in place. Three other ropes stabbed into the speedboat, but nothing guaranteed the boat wouldn't plummet once Dani severed this one.

The flow of lizards increased. They must have drawn out hundreds of these bastards before they left the Blood Realm. A few leaped at him, but Ty hit them away before they could get their teeth into him. One or two slipped past Ty, but judging from his wife's curses and the lizards' plummeting squawks, they weren't making it onto the speedboat.

The rope shivered with Dani's repeated strikes. "All right. That's as much as I can do with you on it."

"Make sure you grab onto something as soon as you cut." Ty swatted off as many of the lizards as he could and then scrambled the rest of the way to the speedboat, leaping past Dani into the seating area of the boat. She swatted at the lizards as much as she swung at the rope. Ty hit off a few that got past her, and Wicket pinned one down that made it onto the floor of the boat's seating area. Ty tossed that one overboard.

"Hang on!" Dani warned him as she took one more two-handed swing at the frayed rope. Ty shoved his sword into its scabbard and scooped up Wicket while wrapping his other arm, still holding onto Dani's borrowed sword, around the back of a seat.

The rope snapped away with a whip-like crack and the fading cries of despair from the lizards as they fell into the void.

Ty and Dani clung to the seats. His wife kept her eyes shut in anticipation of their own fall.

A fall that never happened.

Dani opened her eyes and shifted them back and forth before settling onto Ty. "Well?"

Still clinging to the seat, Ty stomped his foot a few times on the floor of the boat's seating compartment.

"Stop that!" Dani stared at him like he'd lost his mind.

"Just making sure before we move around, you know."

"Yes, well let's not tempt fate."

He snorted. "You mean like going into Hell on a mad quest to kill a demon?"

She laughed with him, relaxing her grip on the seat. Wicket, tired of being held in place, squirmed his way free from Ty's arm with a series of grumbles.

Dani looked over the edge of the boat. "Well, looks like you're getting your way, because I don't see how we'd backtrack to that ship with the gate on it, not since I cut off our only way to it."

At least six more rope spikes burrowed into the pirate ship, but no obvious paths for them to get to it were visible.

Wicket, now free to roam about their limited space, hopped onto the front seat Dani was holding onto and curled up on it.

"I think our dog has the right idea." Dani plopped onto the rear seat, which was more like a sofa compared to the two front seats.

Ty stretched out on the floor of the boat. "I agree."

Dani chuckled as she reclined across the back seat and then muttered. "Aren't you glad you traded in your chances at Hollywood stardom for this?"

He considered pointing out that his odds of making it big in film or TV had sucked, but then his better sense asserted itself. Ty reached over and held her hand. "Second best decision I ever made."

"Second best?"

"Well, second only to marrying you."

"Ditto."

They let go of their hands a moment later and mumbled their endearments before sleep claimed them.

Chapter 16

Six Years Earlier

Since Maria Cortez had called him a sure thing, Ty expected his training to go quickly, but after spring shifted into summer, he'd yet to prove to his trainers he was ready to step foot into Hell or take part in an exorcism. Just as irksome, he still didn't fully understand what the Order had hired him to do.

Sure they'd given him classes and reading material. They'd actually required him to read *Dante's Inferno*, and that was some seriously mind-numbing shit. The most interesting stuff had been about how exorcisms really work, and every time he asked when he'd get to see one of those, they insisted he shouldn't be in a hurry to do it.

By all rights, his sword fighting training should have been the easiest part of all, but that had gone worse than anything else. The head trainer, a grizzled cuss named Zuma, had threatened to throw him off the roof of the building. Given the bastard looked half of Ty's size, the threat shouldn't have carried any weight, but Ty wore four months of bruises to prove the old man had plenty of bite to back his bark.

After a particularly brutal day of training, Ty had soaked in the claw-footed tub in his apartment with the water as hot as he could stand it. As his muscles started to numb from the heat, he got a text message from a number he didn't recognize to get his ass to the training room.

With a groan, Ty dragged himself out of the water and headed to work. While this kind of middle-of-the evening summons for an impromptu training session wasn't the norm, it wasn't unheard of. Considering another ass whooping loomed, he saw little point in spiffing up and made a token effort at being presentable. He regretted that decision as soon as he reached the training room.

The Order of the Emerald Blades occupied the entire twelfth floor of the Rigney Building and served as the Order's main office for the East Coast of the U.S. The space included a large, square training room. The wooden floor contained an elaborate design of circles, squares, and rectangles that divided the room into a variety of dueling spaces. A wooden rack ran along the opposite wall from where he entered and contained a number of swords to practice with, half wooden and the others dull metal blades. None of the metal swords included the strange green metal that their "real weapons" contained.

At this time of night, the room contained a scant amount of track lighting along the edges of the room. Only one other person waited there. The woman's back was turned to him as she plucked a wooden sword from the rack. Before she looked over her shoulder at him, his stomach dropped in his gut as if he'd swallowed a boulder.

Dani Cortez ranked as his training group's undisputed star pupil. The first time they'd sparred, he'd gotten distracted by how beautiful she was. She resembled a walking katana: sharp, sleek, and deadly. This week, she'd dyed her hair a deep red, but in their first spar, her hair had been his favorite color, royal blue. She'd pounded the shit out of him in seconds and planted him on the mat with a hit to his ankle.

No one Ty had ever met fought with a sword half as well as Dani, not even their grumpy curmudgeon of an instructor. Ty wasn't the only person in their group who found Dani distracting, but thus far, she'd not returned the interest with any of them. People in Dani's world only existed as targets.

He'd never been alone in a room with Dani until now. He'd thrown on a tattered, faded red zip-up hoodie with the washed-one-too-many-times remnants of a mustard yellow film logo on the back. He'd not bothered with a hair brush, having run his fingers through the disheveled mess. Worst of all, he'd skipped brushing his teeth, and he'd eaten a spicy chicken curry for dinner. The one time he'd eaten onion rings at lunch, Dani had ended up standing next to him as they assembled and asked what foul thing he'd eaten. He'd not eaten onions at lunch ever since.

"Are we the first ones here?" He kept his breath a good ten feet away from Dani.

Her eyes narrowed on him. "I was the first one here. You're the last one, and you're late."

He silently cursed himself for being late, which delayed him from making the obvious realization.

"Wait." He glanced around the dimly lighted room. "No one else is coming?"

"No. It's just us." She looked away from him to study the wooden sword she'd selected, as if disgusted by the sight of him.

"I overheard Zuma tell my mother that he expects you to quit within the next two weeks."

When she looked up for his response, he turned away. To make it look less like he was avoiding her eyes, he walked over to the sword rack and sifted through the options while avoiding breathing in Dani's direction.

"I hadn't made any decision like that." He'd been thinking about it, though. The night before, he'd gotten as far as pulling up his contacts list to find his friend Barry's phone number. His thumb had hovered over the ten digits before swiping the contacts app shut.

"Good," Dani said, "because it would be a pretty fucking stupid decision."

He forgot about the practice swords and turned to face her. "I'm getting my ass handed to me every day." He left out the punishment he'd suffered from that asshole Nelson the day before. "Getting myself killed in Hell with a demon's talon ripping open my throat doesn't sound like the smartest career move."

She closed the distance between them and grabbed him by the arm. "Yeah, a demon would rip you apart, but that's got nothing to do with how good a fighter the demon might be."

"Is this supposed to be the argument for me to stay, because it's sounding like the opposite?" His voice cracked at the feel of her hand on his arm. Even through the thin cotton of his hoodie's sleeve, her hand's touch made him dizzy from being this close to her. Short of her hitting him in a spar, she'd never touched him until now.

"I've seen your form, the way you move. Nelson should have never beaten you yesterday, and you know it."

"Yeah, but he did. Thanks for the reminder."

She let him go and threw up her hands. "Don't you get it? The only piece you're missing is the killer instinct."

"I can assure you that you're the first person in years to ever accuse me of not being aggressive enough in a fight." Hell, he'd been reprimanded for being too vicious in a tournament two years ago.

"The only advantage that Nelson has is that he's not fighting by any rules. You still act as if a headshot is off-limits." She stabbed the point of the practice sword on the floor. "We need to fix that."

"Wait." His stupid brain finally connected the dots. "You sent that text to me?"

He'd assumed Zuma sent it.

"I pulled your number off of my mom's phone." Her head shook in a sassy sort of challenge, daring him to ask why she'd done it.

"What exactly are you offering here? To train me?"

"Someone needs to kick your ass into gear, because I'll be damned if I'm gonna let Zuma prove my mom wrong about you."

That last part doused Ty's hopes—hopes he hadn't even realized he'd entertained. For a moment, he'd assumed she wanted to keep him around for herself.

They started their private lessons that night. At first, Dani only focused on getting him to go in for the kill. That took more than two weeks, and Ty assumed that after that point, she'd lose interest. That he'd stayed longer than Zuma predicted proved the old man wrong and her mother right: mission accomplished. Only, their practice fights didn't end there. If anything, they grew more intense. She got him to turn off the restraints he'd trained into himself for all those years of competitions.

Even when he'd turned the corner and crushed his academy-mates in their daily training sessions, Ty kept fighting at night with Dani. When they reached a point where their fights were no longer a sure thing for Dani, Ty repaid the favor by teaching her some of the finesse to his style of fighting.

The nights passed by until three months had gone by with them practicing together in private each night. Dani grew colder and angrier near the end of that time, and one night, she stood him up. He texted her from the floor of the training room and didn't get an answer. He considered going to her home, but the fact she lived with her mom, the big boss, doused any chance of that.

The next morning, that fucking shit Nelson had gloated about taking the Order's "princess" to dinner. They'd gone on a date! And she hadn't told him.

Ty and Dani met to train that night. A part of him couldn't stand his relief that Dani hadn't stood him up again.

"How was your date with Nelson?" The way he asked the question came out wrong. He'd intended to sound friendly and casual. Only, the words came out pissed—exactly how he felt. The idea of her with that asshole made him want to puke.

She kept her profile to him as she stretched her way through her warm-up exercises. That didn't hide her grin. "We went dancing after dinner." When she stopped stretching, she looked right at him and said, "You got a problem with that?"

"Guy seems like an absolute dick, but if you had fun, then great." He snatched his practice sword from the rack.

Her grin increased at that. "You ready?"

She rushed him, wielding a practice sword in each hand. He slammed his wooden blade into her left sword and then followed through to strike her right sword. Her momentum sent her past him.

They rushed at each other. Ty aimed his sword just below her throat.

Dani ducked beneath the attack. She dropped into a slide across the smooth, wooden floor. She came up once she was clear and spun around, attempting to sweep his legs out from under him. Ty moved too fast for her, though.

Their wooden swords cracked against each other as they rushed one another again. Her two swords forced him to speed up his countermoves, lest one defense leave him open to an attack from her other sword.

She tired him out, and when he left his stomach exposed, she slammed both of her swords into his abdomen like a pair of baseball bats.

He dropped to his knees and gasped. Each breath shot fissures of fiery pain through his torso.

Dani spun the sword in her right hand as she stood back to wait for him. "Want to go again?"

He glared up at her as he bit out his answer. "Oh, yeah."

Ty leaped up after her. Their swords cracked at a furious pace. They didn't stop with the swords. Fists swung. Legs kicked. She'd trained him to do this, to embrace that willingness to abandon the rules and put all of his body into making the kill. In the end, the swords simply provided extra appendages.

This time, he caught her off guard, dropping his sword as he ducked under her attempt to swing both swords at him at once. The move left her right side exposed. He slipped around her attack, grabbed her by the back and flung her across the room. She shrieked as she skidded along the slick floor. As soon as she came to a stop, he planted the tip of his sword in the center of her back. The move didn't injure, but it made the point.

She growled as she swatted the sword away and got to her feet. "Again!"

They went at it for an hour until they were both a sweaty, smelly mess. They'd taken off their shirts with Dani down to her sports bra and Ty to his bruises.

They fell into a wrestling match, and the feel of her skin against his completely undid him. She tackled him to the floor and planted the edge of one of her swords to his throat as she straddled him.

"You done playing?" Her question held the hint of a laugh to it, but with a sharp threat behind the words.

"Are you?"

The humor vanished from her face as she leaned in close to him. "I haven't been playing since the first night we did this. When are you going to make the damn move!"

He grabbed the sword at his throat, ripped it from her grip, and flung it into the rack along the wall. He flipped her onto her back. For a long moment, their eyes held one another, a different sort of duel taking place without swords or fists or words.

When he saw the opening there, her invitation for him to strike, he kissed her. She rolled him onto his back and kissed him again. They'd dropped their swords and if they hadn't known the risk of someone walking in on them, their clothes would have joined their weapons.

When she came up for air, they both laughed.

"For the record," Dani said as she ran her thumb along his jawline, "last night was the worst fucking date of my life."

"Good."

"Because the entire time, I wanted to be with you."

"Even better."

They got to their feet, threw their gear onto the rack, and grabbed their discarded shirts. They almost ran to Ty's car, which he drove as fast as possible to his apartment. They stumbled through his apartment's door and stripped each other, leaving a trail of clothes on the floor as they raced for the bed.

They made love twice that night. As Dani pointed out, "Making up for lost time."

Ty feared the excitement would fade in the weeks and months that followed. Their nightly spars didn't end, but they did go on more legitimate dates some nights. The desire to be together never vanished. The fury to their spars never abated. Even the sex got better as they felt out one another, discovering all the things that made their climax take longer or sometimes faster. Time together turned into the most addictive drug Ty had ever tasted, and they surrendered to the need in every way.

Within six months, they'd married.

After their training ended, the Order tried in vain to partner them with others to go on missions to Hell. Ty and Dani eventually started going to exorcisms together, too, which wasn't the norm. The Order considered one sword enough. They simply refused to let anyone or anything separate them.

Even on their worst days, no matter how much they might have fucked up something or pissed off one another, nothing changed the God-given fact they were designed to be together.

Interlude 3

Flocks of ravens swam through the sky, watching for any sign of movement near the Purgatory Arch. Char rode his dovra down the hill into the arch's valley doing his best not to show how badly he hurt from his wounds. At least a hundred demons armed with swords surrounded the arch, which pleased him.

Skulls and other bones formed the arch with a pair of green metal doors set within the frame. The arch itself took advantage of the natural thin place that existed there to keep Purgatory accessible from the Blood Realm. Without the arrangement of skulls and other bones around the doors, the path to Purgatory wouldn't always work, like some temperamental child.

A raven broke from the flying demons' formation and flew down to land and walk at Char's side. Char pointed towards the small army assembled around the arch. "Well done, Kene. Any sign of the exorcists?"

"Not yet." Kene glanced back at their two other companions on their dovras. Nera rode in the rear. She'd wisely held her tongue since they'd lost the exorcists in the swamp. She'd suffered only two stings from the locusts, to her right shoulder and her left leg. The insects preferred the taste of true demon blood. They'd draped Zhor's body over his saddle. His white flesh had turned more grey in death as smoke wafted from his body, the regeneration process working its magic. With any luck, he'd return to full health in less than four days, but that process sometimes failed. Just as bad, Zhor wouldn't be restored in time to help track down the humans.

Kene looked from Zhor's body to Char. "What happened in the swamp?"

"Locusts." Char growled, partly from the pain of his injuries but also from the frustration of having failed to catch the humans. "They cut us off from our prey about half a day's ride from the arch."

Starting to fall behind, Kene flapped her wings to fly alongside Char's dovra. "My scouts have spotted the city guard on the road. They'll be here within a day."

Char looked over his shoulder at the swamp. Were the humans hiding in the trees? If they were, he hadn't caught their scent. The arch here provided the only direct route to Purgatory from the Blood Realm. With any luck, the number of demons already assembled had scared the humans into waiting while they planned how to get past Malum's army.

"Night isn't far off," Char said. "Keep your ravens patrolling through the night and widen their search along the borders of the swamp." Many of the whiters assembled here wore their helmets. Normally, he would have approved of that. "Send word to all our demons encamped here: no helmets. I don't want these damn humans slipping past us in a stolen set of armor."

Kene nodded and then flew ahead to deliver Char's orders.

Nera spurred her dovra ahead to ride next to Char. "You didn't mention you need a healer."

Char snarled, his teeth bared, partially in pain. "I am more than well enough to fight."

She lowered her voice. "Save your pride. That exorcist with the two swords held her own against both you and Zhor. She might not have delivered that wound to your side, but you can bet all the souls you own that she'll take advantage of that injury if you face her with it."

A locust had burrowed its stinger into his left side and dug in with its legs. Nera had helped him rip it out and even dig free the part of the stinger that broke off in him.

"You've lived among us for half a century, and you still think too much like a human. If I show any weakness before these demons, I will lose my sway over them."

"Better to show weakness for a moment than to stay weakened and be defeated."

Char growled. She wasn't wrong, but neither was he. He'd tend to the wound, but he'd do it himself.

The next morning arrived without word of the exorcists. Char's mood fouled as he questioned whether the humans would risk a run for the Purgatory Arch.

Char emerged from his tent and grabbed the nearest demon by the arm. "Bring me a gate map."

Nera stirred from her slumber as he reentered the tent. The space provided enough room to also act as a command post.

"Feeling better?" Nera purred as she asked the question. Despite his decision to tend to his wound himself, she'd aided him. Sealing his wound shut with a sword heated in a fire.

He ignored the question, given she knew the answer before she'd asked.

"Find Kene and bring her here. We need to figure out our next move."

She didn't move right away, but she nodded her assent. Getting up, she dressed. That she took her time didn't go unnoticed, though Char couldn't decide if she was teasing him or defying him.

By the time Nera returned with Kene, Char had unfurled his gate maps on a low table in the center of the tent.

"I suspect these exorcists intend to reach another Purgatory Arch." Char slid his pointed nails across the map.

Kene grunted as she knelt across from Char. "They still have almost five days until Malum's heart and head evaporate and his body reforms. It seems perfectly reasonable they're licking their wounds, hoping to come at this arch when they're fresh."

Nera remained standing with her arms crossed. "I agree."

Char growled up at Nera. "These humans didn't race through the blood swamp to sit and wait while our forces here double." He pointed to the canyons. "There's a gate here that would have been within their reach."

Kene leaned over the map for a better look. "The gate to the Triangle Realm?"

"That gate has been there for less than a year." Nera shook her head. "How could they possibly know about it?"

Char kept his focus on the map, checking the other gates. "They had their hound with them."

"The one the man carried with him like a babe?" Nera didn't hide her ridicule for the hunters' choice of guide dogs.

"A small one," Char said, as he marked two other nearby gates on the map, "but a hound nonetheless."

"So, what?" Nera didn't bother taming the taunt to her words. "You want to disperse the forces you've gathered here to send them chasing into random gates on the thin chance you'll catch up to them and in the process leave this Purgatory Arch undefended? What's to stop them from circling back?"

Char stood, leaning over the table to growl into Nera's face. She didn't flinch, though. She knew damn well he could make good on his threats, but he'd long ago discovered she enjoyed the rake of his claws as much as his kiss.

"Kene, dispatch your best scouts to the gates I've marked."

The raven stood. She didn't speak it, but Char could see in the raven's large eyes that she agreed with Nera.

"Find out which one they've taken," he said.

"If they've taken any of them," Nera muttered.

Char slapped her, sending her spinning to the ground. He snarled and then pointed to Kene. "Dispatch your ravens now!"

Kene nodded her bow and marched out through the tent's flaps.

"My patience for your games grows thin."

Nera licked the blood from a split to the corner of her mouth. She glared up at him, but that didn't stop her lips from curling into a smile.

Char stabbed his finger in the direction of the tent flap. "Get out."

She did as told, leaving the tent without another word and looking as satisfied as a cat after feasting on its prey.

Chapter 17

A sad truth of dog ownership Ty had learned very quickly with Wicket was that no matter how many times that furball got in his face with his wet nose to wake him up—it worked.

He groaned as he weakly shielded his face with his arms. "All right, I'm awake."

Dani cracked open an eye from where she lounged on the back seat of the speedboat with her arms and legs contorted in a way that his coffee-deprived brain refused to process. He supposed she'd ended up like that to avoid rolling off onto him.

"Middle of Hell," she muttered as she closed her eyes again, "and he still thinks he needs Daddy to take him for a morning walk."

Ty sat up and rubbed the sleepies from his eyes. "Hang on, buddy."

Wicket hopped back onto the seat he'd used for his bed. Ty looked at his wrist watch and the countdown he'd started after they got out of Malum's castle. They'd slept a good ten hours, which meant they had roughly four-and-a-half days left. He forced himself to stand and picked up Wicket to set him onto the long rear of the boat then climbed over Dani without stepping on her to join him. Wicket promptly kicked up a leg to do his business and the byproduct ran off the edge of the boat into oblivion. Ty supposed someone might be getting a Wicket shower far below, but he decided against thinking through that one too long.

Wicket then jumped down onto the seats, hopping on Dani along the way.

"Thank you so much for that, Wicket," she said as she sat up.

Ty dropped into the rear seat beside her. "I really needed that sleep."

"Same, so why do I still feel like a tank ran me over?"

He stood and stretched again. "You really want the answer?"

Her glare conveyed a decisive "No."

Offering her a hand, he pulled her to her feet. She then walked over to the remnants of the rope bridge she'd hacked off. "There's no going back this way, not that I'd really want to deal with those lizards again." She scowled at the bite marks to her boot. "So I guess we better make 'Plan B' work."

Ty avoided looking at her, having expected her to say something like that. He didn't want to think about four-and-a-half days from now if they hadn't made it to the Eternal Flame in time to burn Malum's head and heart. All they'd risked to get this far would be wasted.

He couldn't let that happen. He couldn't let her down. This whole stupid mess was his idea, and while Dani did her best to cover it, he felt the tension in the air around her. The fear of failing her mother, even more than they already had, cut into her spirit. He'd never seen Dani break—close to it, for sure—but she'd never broken in all of their years together.

"You ready?" he asked.

She nodded. "We're lucky Char and his goons haven't found us yet."

"Not much chance of him getting to us with that bridge taken out." He glanced around them. "Haven't seen any ravens, local or otherwise. Maybe they can't fly in this realm's pea soup."

"That's a point in our favor, if they can't." The way she offered that cheery thought made it clear how unlikely she considered it.

"After you, my dear," he said.

She grinned at him. "So chivalrous."

Then she leaned over to Wicket and scratched behind his ear. When she stopped, their dog hopped up onto all fours, sensing they wanted to go.

"All right, Wicket. Seek Purgatory."

Chapter 18

Wicket led them to ship after ship. The rope bridges connecting the vessels never got any less dizzying and nausea-inducing.

If this particular dimension of Hell had any logic to it, they couldn't suss it. In terms of size, most of the ships resembled the pirate ship they'd come across when they first arrived.

"Oh my God," Ty whispered in awe, when they came to another wooden ship that looked like an artifact of the 18th Century. "Now that one is a beauty. Looks a lot like the HMS Endeavour."

"Oh, great." Dani shrugged in that way that made it clear she had no clue what he was talking about.

"The Endeavour is the ship Captain Cook sailed across the globe in the 1700s."

"I'm very happy for him."

Ty groaned in disgust. "Really? Do you have any idea how amazing this is?"

"It's another ship in Hell." She climbed the rope bridge towards it. "Even worse, it's one of those that's probably going to have more of those voices coming from inside of it."

He couldn't argue with her about that. All of the bigger ships had voices coming from below decks. The voices varied, some deep and others shrill, but they all sounded hungry. Some went on about the scent of life on their ship's decks. Others took a more conniving tactic, screaming for help. One even went on shouting "Save me!" At least Ty assumed that was one of the monsters and not an actual victim. How anyone could wander into such a place as this baffled him. Of course, Ty and Dani being here proved it wasn't impossible.

No sooner had Dani set foot on the deck than a voice from below called to them.

"Come down and let us taste you, living things!"

Whatever they were, the rules of their existence somehow trapped them below decks.

Maybe.

Exorcist's swords didn't spend most of their time in Hell. The majority of their work took place in the mortal world. Supposedly, possession hadn't been that common a thing until the past century. More often than not, demons possessed an object and not a person. A priest could free a person or a thing from the demon, but then an exorcist's sword needed to strike down the demon with their unique blades.

Some demons became an ongoing problem. Possession disobeyed the natural laws of a soul's journey, and some demons reached poltergeist levels of troublesomeness. If exorcist's swords couldn't cut them down in the mortal world, then they hunted for them in Hell.

The demons of the Blood Realm had grown into a bigger issue, especially during Ty and Dani's years on the job. When they met Malum, he'd talked a good game and sounded more interested in dialing back things within the Blood Realm to restore demons to their roles as guides for the recently deceased, leading them to Purgatory at their predestined time. They hadn't bought all of Malum's sales pitch, but they'd needed his help to get the demon they were after at the time.

"Join us! Join us!"

"I'd give real money if they'd shut up," Dani said as Wicket led them across the deck of the Endeavour to the next rope bridge.

A loud boom sounded from above. Wicket yelped. Both Ty and Dani jumped in place, feeling the noise all the way into their chests. The ship shimmied beneath their feet.

"What was that?" Dani stared up into the foggy realm trying to see what, if anything, might have changed.

"Sounded like thunder." He mimicked Dani, looking up in the direction the noise had come from.

Then Dani shouted. "Run! Wicket, go! Go!"

Ty didn't question. His wife didn't panic without reason, so he sprinted after her and their dog.

Wicket hopped onto the next rope bridge. Dani shouted after the terrier to keep running. The bridge connected to a small sailboat.

Another clap of thunder shook the realm. This time, distant screams and wails accompanied the thunder. Something moved out the corner of Ty's vision as he leaped onto the sailboat. He glanced over his shoulder. A massive shadow plummeted from above, a large wooden warship. The falling vessel smashed into the Endeavour, sending up the loudest peel of thunder yet.

The collision yanked on all the ropes holding to the Endeavour. The sailboat they were on tilted against the strain. Dani and Ty fell to their knees as Wicket crouched against the deck of the sailboat.

They stared at each other, waiting because they weren't sure it was safe to move. Then a loud snap jolted the sailboat. Ty looked back at the Endeavour. The rope bridges connected to it were ripping under the combined strain of the two ships.

"The Kraken comes for us all!" A voice from within the sailboat screamed as another of the Endeavour's rope bridges snapped. The sailboat jolted beneath their feet, making it tilt even more.

"Keep going!" Ty shouted. "Wicket, seek Purgatory! Go!"

Wicket launched onto his paws and skittered up the next rope bridge. Another snap sounded, much sooner than the first two. A vibration ran through the bridge leading from the sailboat to a large hovercraft that had at least thirteen rope bridges stabbing into it. Their current bridge, one of the longest they'd crossed, forced them to run uphill.

More than halfway to the hovercraft, the struggle to keep going took its toll. All that necessary gear they carried on them weighed down more than ever. Sword, scabbard, food, water, and all the other equipment needed for traversing the realms of the dead felt twice as heavy with their lives at stake. Wicket even lost a bit of his momentum as he neared the end of the bridge. That he'd reached it offered them the only hope they had that they might make it, too.

A loud groan shook the entire realm. The strain on the remaining ropes connected to the Endeavour and the ship that had smashed into it generated a series of low notes, like someone strumming a gigantic bass guitar.

"Almost," Dani said, pausing to catch her breath, "there!"

Thunderous snaps went off one after the other, the last of the Endeavour's rope bridges giving way. They were a few feet from the hovercraft. So close!

Then the bridge fell away from beneath their feet.

Chapter 19

Dani, a few steps from the hovercraft, leaped for it. She grabbed onto the side of the ship.

Ty tried the same, but a good ten feet separated him from the finish line. His fingertips slid across the inflated skirt of the hovercraft's underside but couldn't get a grip on it.

He fell.

The drop proved slower than expected, possibly some strange aspect of the atmosphere to this realm, but he still plummeted fast enough that it wouldn't save him when he landed. Vertigo assaulted him as he fell, making it impossible to make sense of anything.

He caught a glimpse of a large ship rushing up at him. The massive, dark grey deck was split in half with the front of the ship at a different angle than the mostly detached rear of the vessel.

Then the rope bridge he'd fallen from swung back at him. The sailboat, still attached to the hovercraft's rope bridge, acted as a pendulum, swinging his way.

He grabbed the rope in a bear hug as it reached him. The impact knocked the breath out of him, his chest taking the brunt of the impact. He clung to it, fighting the nausea as the realm shifted all around him while the sailboat continued to swing back and forth.

Despite his best efforts, he couldn't climb the rope bridge or prevent himself from sliding down it. He heard the voice of whatever being was in the sailboat screaming. Just before his feet were about to connect with the sailboat, the rope bridge snapped free of the hovercraft above.

He plummeted again, but only for a few seconds. The sailboat smashed into the deck of an aircraft carrier. The sailboat's debris slid away, carried by its own momentum and the tilt of the larger ship's deck. The sailboat and whatever creatures were inside went screaming off the far edge of the aircraft carrier's deck. Ty slid for a bit, but he'd let go of the rope bridge. The deck felt like asphalt and the friction of that hard surface brought him to a halt in the middle of the deck.

Finally still and without the wind of his own motion to drown out everything else, he heard more thunder. Now the sounds retreated below as the Endeavour and the ship that had collided with it continued their endless descent.

"Ty!"

He smiled to himself, hearing Dani call to him and answered by shouting her name.

Her voice, a whisper on the foggy air, reached him. "Are you all right?"

"Yes!" He decided to leave out that he'd gotten the mother of all road rashes. He looked at his right leg. The denim pants covering his thigh were shredded. The exposed skin didn't look much better, but he knew it could have been worse. He was pretty certain he hadn't broken anything. His successful attempt to stand on the slanted deck proved that.

He limped his way to the highest point of the deck. Staring down into the divide between the front and the rear of the massive ship, he saw the exposed insides of the hangar deck below him. The hangar on the opposite half of the ship contained a pile of propeller fighter planes smashed up against each other. Shadows hid most of the interiors of the other decks below the hangar. Rope bridges stabbed through the aircraft carrier, treating it like a giant pin cushion. Three of the rope bridges ran through the interior of the ship, coming out the exposed interior on one side before plunging into the interior of the ship's other half. He'd kill himself trying to jump onto the three bridges from this height.

"Which way does Wicket want to go?" he shouted up to Dani. A long pause answered, during which Ty suspected she directed the terrier to indicate which way led to the Purgatory Arch.

Dani shouted down to him. "He wants to go up!"

"Of course he does," Ty muttered to himself. Wicket had taken them up the entire way, so not that shocking. He'd wanted to make sure, though, before deciding his next move.

"You stay there!" Ty shouted. "Let me see if there's a way to reach you!" He needed to repeat that a few times. They could hear each other, but understanding their words didn't come as easily at this distance.

His current position placed him near the highest point of the ship. He studied the network of rope bridges that connected to the aircraft carrier. The good news? He saw a way to reconnect with Dani on the hovercraft by taking three rope bridges.

The bad news? The first rope bridge he needed to take started on the far end of the aircraft carrier.

"I see a way to get to you!" he shouted up to her.

"The trawler and the motorboat?" She identified the same ships he'd seen to reconnect with her on the hovercraft.

"Show-off!" He laughed, but only for a few seconds, as he accepted the reality of what he had to do. "I'll have to go down through the lower decks!"

The pause in her reply let him know she'd understood what he meant. Going inside the ship, one this big? He'd definitely run into some of their chatty friends along the way.

"Are you sure?" she shouted to him.

"Yeah!" He waited a moment and then added, "You give me two hours! If I haven't reached the bridge to the trawler by that point, then you go on without me!"

"Bullshit!"

That made him laugh some more. No, he hadn't really expected her to agree to that, but he had to try. "You are a stubborn cow!"

"And you love me that way, you stubborn mule!"

"I'll see you on the other side!" He wished he could have concealed from his voice how poor he considered his chances of pulling this off, but his acting skills hadn't improved since Dani's mom had recruited him.

Chapter 20

Ty drew his sword as he searched for the best way to get down into the lower levels. He suspected it would have been easier for him if he'd landed on the side of the aircraft carrier that had the island—at least that's what he thought they called the tower-like structure near the middle of the ship. Of course, if he'd landed on that side of the ship, he wouldn't have had to worry about going down into it.

Even though he needed to hurry, he couldn't bring himself to step inside this metal corpse without first thinking it through. Unlike the other ships, he hadn't heard any voices from below. The silence continued, even as he finally descended a set of stairs going down the outside of the ship and leading to a door for the hangar.

Light spilled into the hangar from where the ship had split in half. Despite the dark at the far end, Ty saw a pile of fighter planes down there. He wondered if the ship he stood inside was the actual ship, something lost at sea. Perhaps all these vessels embodied the soul of a ship. After all, sailors often referred to their ships by assigning them a gender, not referring to them as an "it." Maybe what endowed a ship with the ability to find a place in the afterlife owed itself to how well loved it was in life by the people who lived aboard it. That sounded beautiful save for the place the ship's soul apparently ended up in Hell.

He slipped his glow crystals into the mesh pockets on his sleeves. He wouldn't need them for most of the hangar, but once he got into the lower decks, that would change.

Before he searched for a way to keep going down, he walked up to the split. He wanted to make certain he couldn't jump for it from the hangar deck.

The closest rope bridge that could take him to the other side of the ship jutted out two decks below him. He got lucky surviving the fall onto this ship. Pressing his luck with another long drop sounded beyond stupid. Even worse, if he missed, he'd land in a mess of sharp, jagged metal. No coming back from that.

He considered dropping down to the next floor to avoid going into the dark of the interior, but the aircraft carrier had been torn in two at an angle. The hangar deck's floor stuck out at least four feet more than the deck below it. He also wasn't confident in being able to hold onto the edge of the floor without slicing up his hands on the metal.

Going through the inside of the ship offered his only option.

More than a little over halfway between the split in the ship and the far end with its pile of planes, Ty found a set of stairs not blocked off in the middle of the deck. Someone had blocked the other stairs with all manner of debris. At first, he assumed the occupants had done it to keep out the light, but as he considered that the only way he'd found into the ship was so far back, he suspected something worse. The occupants seemed aware that the only way from one side of the ship to the other meant going below decks. The other ships he and Dani had traversed didn't require that, and perhaps that's why the occupants on those ships had called out to them. They had no other way to lure prey. Whoever or whatever lived below in this aircraft carrier knew anyone fool enough to do what Ty was doing would have to enter the lower decks. That's why they were silent, and that's why they were funneling him into this path, one that forced him to travel a long way in the dark, trying to find his way to the rope bridges connecting the two ends of the aircraft carrier

Ty knelt at the top of the steps. His grip tightened on the hilt of his sword. Nothing moved that he could see. No sounds reached him. The scents on the air all felt right: metal, oil, and even a hint of sea air. From here, the idea that he stood alone aboard this ghost ship sounded plausible, but the best lies usually resembled truth.

He expected a hand to reach out and grab one of his legs as he went down the stairs. His heavy boots landed all too loudly. He might as well shout to the lower deck dwellers and announce himself.

As soon as he got to the bottom of the stairs, he coveted Dani's shorter swords. The walls silently threatened to crush him, given how cramped they were. Long swords and narrow corridors mixed poorly.

The room he found himself in was littered with piles of bullets. He assumed he'd found some kind of ammunition storage room but with everything scattered about. He hoped this ship didn't carry any missiles. He could imagine himself knocking over one and blowing himself to smithereens. Stepping on the bullets scattered on the floor caused him to lose his balance more than once, dropping him to one knee.

He found another set of stairs leading down to the next deck. He remembered that the rope bridge had connected two decks below the hangar. Nothing had threatened him on this deck, not yet. His glow crystals helped to see, but some of the light from outside also made it in here from the opening he'd used. He wondered if the natural light deterred any creatures from coming up here.

He ruled out attempting a jump from this deck to the rope bridge. His look from the hangar had offered enough deterrent. No, the best option meant going down another deck. Other stairs closer to the split might lead below, but he had no guarantee they weren't sealed or blocked like the others he'd seen on the hangar deck. He could get lost in the dark trying to find them, too. The light from the hangar didn't reach beyond this room, not that he could see.

The scent that reminded him of the ocean grew stronger as he took the steps down to the next deck. Only that didn't describe the odor right. The briny stench resembled raw fish that had spoiled.

Down here, only his glow crystals provided any light. They didn't reach far. Tiny specks floated around Ty, contaminating the air. They looked like bits of plankton beneath the ocean's surface.

The steps he descended stopped in front of a wall. He struggled to maintain his sense of direction. The split in the middle of the ship waited somewhere beyond this wall, but with no door here, he needed to find a path to keep going straight. He searched along the wall for a way to go and spotted the faint outline of a door to his left.

He turned his back to the wall to move along it so nothing could attack him from behind. Rectangular metal racks dangled from chains to form three-story types of bunk beds in more than a dozen rows. He'd found the crew quarters, or at least one of them. The long rows vanished into the dark as if this room went on forever, much like the realm this ship haunted.

Clicking sounds came from the dark. The first impression hearkened to a rickety wooden set of stairs shifting beneath feet, but as the strange noise continued, sometimes closer or farther, it reminded him of a playing card flapping in the spokes of a bike but running in slow motion.

His glow crystals revealed hints of movement at the edge of the light. Chains rattled in the dark, possibly something climbing on or off one of those chain-link bunk beds.

The clicking increased as he drew closer to the door he'd seen along the wall at his back. Whatever creatures made that noise were closing in on him. Several of the "voices" clicked in a staccato manner that suggested amusement. Were they laughing because they knew something worse awaited him behind that door?

He adjusted his grip on his sword and glared into the dark towards the laughter. That only drew more snickers.

He found the door shut with a wheel positioned in the middle of it. He grabbed the wheel with his free hand and pulled. The door didn't budge. He tried to turn it, first left and then right. More clicking laughter from his unseen companions warned him they'd known this would happen. Maybe he needed to use both hands, and they expected it would leave him without a weapon in his hands.

He gripped the wheel with both hands, while still holding his sword in his right hand. Even then, the wheel refused to turn.

A singsong voice called to him from the darkness. "Wrong door."

Ty cursed, giving up on the door. He raised his sword to the ready.

Another voice, deeper and raspier, mimicked the first monster's singsong manner. "It wants to play."

The last one to talk emerged from the direction of the stairs and into the faint glow of Ty's crystals. The demon's skin had a metal sheen to its fish-like head. Two large bulbous eyes were positioned to look left and right, with a third, smaller human eye centered on the forehead. The large mouth split almost the entire head with at least two dozen long, slender fangs formed from translucent bones that crisscrossed up and down. Its teeth stuck out in all directions and prevented the mouth from fully closing. That didn't stop the demon from snapping his maw open and nearly closed, anticipating its first bite of "Ty tartare."

From the neck down, the fish demon mostly resembled the shape of a man. It wore a World War II style uniform with a pale blue, button down, work shirt and dark blue jeans with a pair of black shoes. The arms, though, didn't look any more human than the head. The double-jointed arms each pointed down with a claw that resembled a pair of scissors made out of eighteen-inch-long, jagged hand saws. The creature raised both claws and snapped them as they pointed towards Ty.

More of the fish demon's kind emerged from between the rows of beds. The chains rattled as some of them bumped into the suspended bunks.

He counted at least sixteen of them. Half of the demons blocked his way back to the stairs on his left. Odds favored more of them waited in the dark.

Only two, that Ty could see, occupied the row farthest to his right. He charged at that pair. The closer of the two snapped at Ty with its claws. He swatted the claws away with his sword and kicked the demon in the stomach as hard as he could, knocking it into its partner. Both spilled to the floor in a tangled heap.

Ty swiped with his sword through the space between two suspended bunks at more demons on the neighboring row. The monsters snapped at him but retreated from his attack. He doubted the sword would cut the demons, though. His long weapon required more room to strike fast and hard enough to inflict any damage. These demons didn't seem to realize that yet, but the longer this took, the less likely that advantage would last. Even worse, more of them appeared along the row he'd chosen.

The pair on the floor struggled with each other, trying to get up. Ty didn't give them the chance. He stepped on the torso of the demon on top and charged at the demons blocking the path ahead of him.

Ty shoved forward with his sword, using it like a spear. The blade ran through the closest fish demon's chest.

A demon on the neighboring aisle leaned over to snap at Ty with its left claw. Ty grabbed the edge of the bunk separating them and slammed the bed frame into that one's head. Then he kicked at the demon he'd speared, jerking his sword free in a spray of dark blue fish blood that defied gravity to float through the air. The injured creature collapsed to its knees with a loud, pained series of clicks from the gill slits along its throat.

More demons ran up behind him, but the pair still on their backs created an obstacle for them. Too late, Ty realized he should have stabbed the pair with his sword to wound them and keep them there as a barrier. Instead, the newcomers helped them to their feet.

Ty spotted more fish demons ahead of him. He charged with his sword again. The closest creature retreated from Ty's attack and slammed against a wall of lockers.

While the demons ahead of him backed away, Ty dropped onto the nearest bunk and rolled over to the neighboring aisle. A fresh set of fish demons rushed at him from both directions as soon as he got to his feet.

Ty turned his back to two of them that were closer than the others and swung his sword underarm at them. The blade ran through the stomach of the nearer demon, shoving them against the one behind them. Ahead of him, another demon snapped a claw at Ty's throat. He knocked the attack off-course with his forearm and then kicked at the monster's kneecap, drawing a satisfying crack. The tussle caused Ty's sword to shift in the stomach of the demon behind him. Its claws scraped against the blade, struggling to get a grip strong enough to pull it out.

Claws snapped at Ty's legs from the aisle he'd abandoned. He grabbed the middle bunk and shoved it into those demons, striking their chests and heads.

Then he dove the opposite way to roll across another bed frame and over to another aisle free of attackers. The fish demons had flooded the two far-right rows, expecting to trap him.

Loud, angry clicks chased him as he used the many rows of bunks to put space between him and them. None of the fish demons tried to mimic his trick for rolling across the beds. Possibly their claws made it too difficult to perform the same maneuver. Given how his sword complicated the move for him, he could appreciate that.

Some of the demons ran to the far ends of the aisles. Another group raced for the stairs he'd used to get down here. The stairs also continued down to the deck below, but the demons blocked both of those escape routes.

He needed a way out, but he settled on "bed-rolling" to the left side of the room. If he didn't find a way out over there, he'd need to fight his way back to the stairs. The fish demons seemed aware of that. More of them crowded around the stairs.

They hadn't given up on getting to him, though. With the demons no longer hiding in the shadows, he counted close to forty of them. These cramped quarters sucked for using his sword, but the narrow spaces also limited how many of these bastards could snap at him with those long claws.

Ty needed to take out dozens of these things to survive. Killing him only required one of them finding the right opening.

The bed-rolling tactic ended against a rack full of pea coats. A lone fish demon, moving faster than the rest of its friends, raced down the aisle at Ty. Ty grabbed one of the pea coats and flung it at the demon's face. The demon grabbed the coat out of the air with its claws and tossed it aside.

Ty swung overhead, as much as the deck's low ceiling allowed, at the fish demon's face. The demon caught the sword in one of their claws and slammed it to Ty's left, into the wall of pea coats. The demon's other claw grabbed Ty's right thigh.

Pain seared into Ty's leg as the jagged blades of that claw bit through his jeans and deep into his flesh. Ty screamed as he struggled to hold onto his sword with his left hand and swung at one of the demon's large eyes with his right fist. The demon flinched to avoid the attack but its claws didn't abandon their grip on his sword or leg. The one biting into his thigh dug in all the harder. More of these monsters scrambled in behind this one. None had come up behind Ty yet.

Doing all he could think to, Ty grabbed one of the gills along the demon's throat and ripped it open.

The demon shrieked a flurry of clicks as it stumbled back into its comrades running up behind him.

Ty screamed as he struggled to ignore the pain in his leg and stumbled the other way. A small corner of his mind noticed his blood ran down his leg instead of floating into the air like the demons' blood.

The glow of Ty's crystal revealed a small set of doors in the corner of the room. One stood open, leading in the direction he needed to go to reach the middle of the ship. He ran for the opening as fast as his wounded legs could manage.

Angry clicking sounds echoed throughout the dark space. The two-legged beasts sounded like they were arguing over who to blame for leaving this path open to him. Even the ones crowded around the stairs abandoned their post to pursue him into the next room.

Long rows of tables filled the next room with chairs placed around them in what he assumed was the messroom. He cursed himself halfway into the room. He'd been so focused on keeping ahead of these damn monsters that he'd missed his chance to seal the door behind him.

From the waist up, this room provided a large open space. The ceiling might be low, but he'd gained plenty of room to swing his sword like a baseball bat and hack away at these bastards. Unfortunately, the space didn't limit how many demons could attack him at once.

Ty decided against standing his ground and limped as fast as he could for a set of stairs on the far side of the room. The demons poured in through the narrow door like an ocean wave. They scrambled over the chairs and table tops, determined to reach him. One got ahead of the others. Ty cleaved open their stomach as they leaped off a table at him.

The stairs he reached led up and down, but a table blocked the path up. Maybe he could move it to get out that way, but if it didn't budge, he'd be trapped. That meant going down.

Ty grabbed one of the chairs and flung it at another group rushing towards him. Two of the demons got tangled up by the chair and spilled to the floor, taking out a few more of them.

The stairs from the messroom led into a narrow set of crew quarters. He couldn't outrun these things, especially not with the wounds to his right thigh. Each step burned through his leg. Back into cramped spaces, he couldn't do much more than swat at the closest demon's claws and try to spear them. At least they could only attack him one at a time now, and none appeared ahead of him. Each time he knocked down one of these freaks, he gained a few more seconds and space to reach another set of steps leading to the deck above. This path wasn't blocked yet. He didn't try for the stairs right away, though. He needed to make sure they didn't get a bite out of him before he reached the next level.

Ty spotted a locker door hanging wide open. As soon as the locker was between him and the nearest demon, Ty thrust his sword at the demon's stomach to put it off-balance. Then he grabbed the locker door and slammed it as hard as he could into the demon's face. The demon stumbled into the others behind them.

Ty scrambled up the stairs. Claws snapped behind him but missed his ankles.

The stairs led him up into another messroom, connected to the one he'd initially retreated into. He realized they were connected when he heard loud, excited clicks coming from the doors along the far end of the room and more of these damn monsters raced in after him from this deck while the ones from the deck below rushed up the stairs he'd just ascended.

One of the demons pointed to Ty's left at a door. Ty might not understand the languages these creatures clicked to one another, but he recognized the sound of a hunter panicking that their prey had a path of escape.

Ty sprinted for the closed door and grabbed hold of the wheel at its center. The metal screamed as he forced the wheel to turn. When the latches along the door's sides released, he flung the door open and faint light appeared from within the door. Screams of clicks went up through the room at his back as those rays of light cut into the dark space behind him. Ty scrambled through the door and then yanked it shut.

The closed door silenced the clicks and shrieks of the fish demons. He didn't wait to see if any of them could pursue him into the hallway the door had led him into. Judging from their reaction to the light, he liked his odds for the moment.

He spotted stairs leading to the deck below. He held his sword ready, but none of the fish demons appeared from that direction. He'd reached the split in the aircraft carrier.

Ty limped his way down the narrow corridor into the dull but welcome light of the outside. The edge where the ship split in half still offered a less than welcoming sight if he should step wrong. A rope bridge cut into the deck below this, but only required a small step from this deck to get on it.

Halfway to where he needed to go, Ty collapsed to the floor, laughing to himself. The blood from his leg had left a trail of bloody dots and red footprints.

What chance existed that none of these monsters waited aboard the other half of the ship?

He jerked off his jacket and cut off a strip of his shirt to use as a makeshift bandage for his leg. From this far down, the hovercraft was reduced to a blurred silhouette. He considered yelling up to Dani, but he doubted she'd hear him, given she barely had from the top deck. His only chance to hear her voice again meant surviving whatever waited for him on the other side of this ship.

Interlude 4

Char leaned down to sniff the dark red, dried mud sprinkled onto the table in his tent.

The stench of the Blood Swamp lingered on it, but it didn't mask the stink of humanity that tainted it. "The male." Char snarled with disgust. "Where did you find it?"

Kene stood across the table from Char with her wings crossed in front of her. "The canyon, along the trail to the Triangle Realm's gate."

Char's eyes shifted up to stare along his snout at the raven. "Are you certain they took the gate?"

Kene shook her head. "No footprints. The terrain leading to the gate is hard rock, and my ravens can't sniff out a trail the way you can. They found a lot of blood leading up to the gate, though."

Off to the side of the tent, Nera rolled her eyes. "That could be anything. Was it human blood?"

That drew another shake of the head out of Kene. "Glow lizards."

Char growled as he considered that. "Did your ravens check the other side of the gate?"

"Yes, but they didn't get very far. The air in the Triangle Realm," Kene hesitated, twisting her head about as if to look around for the right word, "is fouled. We cannot fly in it. They attempted to question some of the Mulsari."

Nera snorted and stepped out of Char's reach as she muttered. "I'll bet that went well."

Kene shrugged in a manner suggesting she had no counterargument. "The Mulsari ate one of my ravens."

Char glanced out the open flaps of his tent at the army of demons camped in the midday light. They'd assembled close to two hundred demons by this point. Even he recognized it as overkill for two humans.

"No Purgatory Arches occupy the Triangle Realm." Char didn't say this so much to Kene and Nera as much as he was thinking aloud. He scratched at the underside of his snout. He rifled through the stack of maps on his table and pulled out the one for the Triangle Realm. Calling it a map wasn't exactly the most accurate description for it. The paths there altered more frequently than one might change their clothes. He tapped at three places on the map. "These are the most likely gates for them to take."

Nera approached the edge of the table. "Plenty of gates there lead to realms with Purgatory Arches. Why these three?"

"Even if they take any of the others, they'll never reach a Purgatory Arch in the three-and-a-half days they have left before Malum revives."

Kene tilted her head far to the left, almost at a ninety degree angle. "What are you thinking?"

Nera seemed to grasp Char's thoughts and spoke before he could answer. "Our demons will never catch up to those exorcists in those three realms, not before they reach a Purgatory Arch."

"Not on foot." Char felt his plan coming together. This strategy would work. It had to. "Kene, divide your ravens into three groups. Send them," Char paused to place the Blood Realm map on top, "to here and here."

"They can reach the Purgatory Arches in the Fire Realm and the Ruins Realm within a day, if they leave now."

Kene tilted her head again. "What about the Abyss Realm?"

Nera snorted. "Even if they fly non-stop, there's no path through the Hell gates short enough for them to beat the exorcists there."

Char's lips curled back in a toothy smile as he looked up at Kene. "There is if you cut through Purgatory."

"Cut through Purgatory?" Kene said, with obvious revulsion in her voice. "What you're suggesting is costly."

"Exactly, which is why these humans won't anticipate it." Char fell silent as he considered this, then nodded to himself that the plan worked. "Also, I need your fastest raven for an errand into the mortal world."

When Char didn't elaborate on what the errand was, Kene exchanged a look with Nera, but she didn't know Char's reason for the request either. Char returned his attention to the maps.

"These exorcists will be exhausted in order to reach any of these Purgatory Arches in time," Char said. "Offer to grant them safe passage to the mortal realm, if they agree to hand over Malum's head and heart."

"They won't accept," Nera said. "They made that clear enough in the swamp."

"And if by some miracle they do accept the offer?" Kene kept her distance, probably expecting her question to anger Char.

"If they do," Char paused to snarl, "kill them after they hand over Malum."

"There's no guarantee they won't slip past us, especially in the Fire Realm."

"I'm aware." Char snapped out the words as if to bite down on them. "Your ravens aren't my only solution to stop these exorcists. Mark me. They will die before they ever reach an Eternal Flame to destroy Malum."

Chapter 21

Ty crossed the rope bridge to the far side of the aircraft carrier. The good news? He'd gotten across the rope bridge without any problems. The bad news? He ended up on the same deck he'd left. That probably increased his odds of encountering more fish demons, assuming he could even get into this side of the ship.

He looked up at the distant hovercraft where Dani and Wicket waited. How long would they stay there if he didn't make it? Without Wicket, he couldn't guess which way they'd go to reach a Purgatory Arch. No, that thinking went to a pointless place, because Dani would come after him long before that. As much as he wished she was with him to cover his back, he didn't want her and Wicket walking into this giant can of killer sardines.

A long room that ran the width of the ship made up most of the deck at the end of the rope bridge. The fish demons had blocked every set of stairs that led up from there. He should have known, because that would have been too helpful, considering the stairs led up to another room open to the air and would have meant no threat of more fish demons. That didn't make sense, though. If the demons couldn't come out into the open air, then how had they blocked the stairs? He tried to force the debris aside without success.

On the left side of the ship, he came to his last option, a door leading inside. He put all of his strength into the effort to turn the door's wheel to open it. The wheel surrendered to his desperation with a loud creak of scraping metal.

Pulling the door open produced more metallic screams. Given all of the noise, he abandoned any hopes of getting into this side of the ship unnoticed.

Before he went through the door, he removed his glow crystal from the pouch on his sleeve and raised it for a better look. The door led into a long room, too long for his crystal and the outside light to illuminate. He spotted stairs to the right that led up and down.

He left the door to the outside sitting open, hoping it would deter any creatures from coming in here. More debris blocked the stairs that went up. No shock there. Down remained an option, but he wanted to avoid going deeper into this hell ship.

Ty listened before he pushed any further. No clicking noises like he'd heard from the other fish demons. Did the things on this side of the ship know what happened on the opposite side? The Order had never encountered any telepathic or hive mind creatures in Hell, but assuming that wasn't a potential threat here seemed unwise.

For that matter, maybe this side of the ship had completely different demons. He didn't dare to hope there were none.

He returned his crystal to its pouch on his shoulder, drew his sword, and entered the room. After he'd made it halfway into the open space, footsteps pounded behind him. He turned, expecting an attack. Instead, a shadow moved in front of the open door. The door slammed shut, leaving only the glow of his crystal to light the space. One of the fish demons stood by the door. Smoke wafted off of it, along with the stench of burned, spoiled fish. The demon clicked at him and snapped its two claws in a threatening gesture.

Ty rushed the demon. Panicked clicks went up as Ty's sword cleaved through the space the demon had stood. The demon retreated to the center of the room. Ty pursued it, determined to kill it.

Then the far door and the two doors to his right swung open. Demons stalked into the room.

Cursing himself, Ty turned to run for the door he'd used to get in here, but more monsters ran up the stairs to block that route.

Turning in a circle, Ty realized he'd trapped himself in the middle of at least thirty demons.

Chapter 22

The demons had surrounded Ty in a room with no tables or beds, nothing to provide a makeshift barrier or additional weapons. The demons stayed silent, not so much as a single click. A few worked their jaws, the long transparent teeth slipping up and down in slow anticipation of eating him.

The Order trained their exorcist's swords for this sort of thing, but most of the training involved using some common fucking sense to avoid landing in a shit scene like this.

Little late for that.

Long before he joined the Order, Ty had learned the only strategy he had left to play, but it all depended on how coordinated these fish demons were. If they all came at him at once, they'd kill him in seconds.

A single demon stepped forward from the others. It laughed in that clicking manner and snapped its long claws in anticipation.

When the demon rushed at Ty, two more joined him from different directions.

Ty closed the space between him and the closest one. He swatted the demon's attacking claw aside and slipped around the demon to grab it by the shirt and flung it at the other two. That knocked down one but the other avoided the collision.

This part would either save or doom Ty.

The demon's claws snapped at him as it lunged forward. Ty slipped between the two claws and ran through the demon's stomach with his sword. Loud, agonized clicks deafened Ty and fueled his attack as the dark blood of this beast floated up in the thin space between them.

The point wasn't to kill it. No, he needed to make it an example. When Ty ripped his sword's blade free of the fish demon's torso, he followed it up with a strike that severed one of the demon's legs and sent it toppling to the floor.

The other two scrambled to their feet, but Ty got to them first. One lost a head. The other retreated without one of its arms.

Two more examples to make these demons think twice before coming at him for a bite.

"Come on, you ugly shits!" Ty pointed his sword at the ones still standing and slowly turned in place so they got a good look at him. Dark blue blood dripped up off the edge of his blade and formed a circle of drops in the air around him. "Who's next?"

Even if they didn't understand the words, they recognized the tone of the threat.

Ty didn't give them a chance to find their courage. He went for the nearest demon. It croaked in panic, because the cluster of demons around him left no retreat from Ty's sword.

Each demon that came too close lost a piece of itself to his sword. He defended the circle of space they'd given him when they initially surrounded him. The more damage he inflicted, the less eager any of them were to invade his space, giving him the chance to pick them off one or two at a time.

Unfortunately, he needed to take out these demons faster than this. Too many held back and thought through his strategy. If Ty could reach a door, he could use it as a choke point to pick off these things one at a time.

He feinted the way he'd entered this room and then lunged the opposite way. He collided with a pack of five demons who'd wisely hung back. When his sword came at them, Ty only caught one unprepared. The green blade sliced open its torso, sending up a spray of dark blue blood.

The others weren't cowed by the fate of their fallen comrade. Instead, one punched Ty with the blunt end of a claw. Another trapped Ty's right arm in the vice of its claw, digging through the leather jacket and drawing blood.

Forced to swing his sword with only his left arm, Ty couldn't get enough strength into the attack to hack off the limb biting into his right arm. He drew the demon's blood, but that only made the claw bite in harder.

Ty screamed as he flung his whole body at the demons, hoping to throw them off-balance, but the only one who went down was him. The demons pushed him onto his back and clicked with glee.

He kicked with his free leg as the fish heads leaned in to feast but couldn't break free of the demons restraining him.

Ty's screams drowned out even the clicks of the demons around him. Only at the last second did he hear Wicket's bark. Then the closest fish head launched off from its neck and floated up towards the ceiling.

The rest of the demons went still. Their grip on Ty's arm and legs lessened, distracted by the unexplained attack from behind them.

Another demon lost its head in a spray of blood. The demons retreated from Ty. The pair of swords attacking them came from a fresh pair of arms belonging to one very pissed off wife.

"On your feet!" Dani scattered the demons to reclaim the circle Ty had lost. Wicket weaved a dizzying pattern through the legs of the fish demons, tripping some to the floor while others got distracted and failed to see Dani's swords coming for them.

"Come on!" Dani unleashed a fury of damage. She'd never suffered from a lack of killer instinct, a fact these creatures learned in gallons of dark blood and dozens of dismembered limbs. If a target got too close for her swords, she answered with her fists, elbows, and knees.

Ty staggered to his feet, trying to ignore the bloody wounds to his arm and legs. His sword shook in his hands as he stumbled towards the now open door he'd been trying to reach before the demons tackled him.

"Wicket!" Dani called to their dog as she slammed the hilt of a sword on the top of a kneeling fish demon's head. "Seek Purgatory!"

Ty understood the command wasn't just for their dog. She was ordering his sorry ass to follow their dog as she defended their backs.

Wicket ran past Ty, leaping over the bottom lip of the doorway into the adjoining room. Ty stumbled after the terrier into another wide open space.

A pair of demons appeared from the shadows of the room.

Ty roared against the pain ripping through his wounds as he charged at the creatures. Wicket tripped up the demons before Ty's first swing ripped open the stomach of one of them. The second demon fell as Ty buried his sword into the base of their neck. Blood bubbled out of the wound like a lava lamp as Ty ripped the blade free.

"Let's move!" Dani ran through the door and grabbed him by the uninjured arm to hurry him towards the next door before the demons in the other room could pursue them.

Wicket barked for them to hurry as he leaped over into the next space. This one had a table and hammocks, creating a narrow space.

Metallic thunder deafened Ty as Dani swung the door shut behind them.

"Stairs!" Dani pointed with her sword to the far end of the room.

Ty stumbled behind Wicket for their exit, a pair of stairs leading up to the next level.

The door at their backs squealed as the demons pulled it open. Fear-fueled adrenaline made Ty's pain a distant memory as he sprinted up the stairs.

Dani stayed a step behind him as Wicket led the way through the ship. They navigated the path down narrow corridors, turning corners, taking doors, and scrambling up stairs. Ty avoided tripping over more than one fish demon's corpse as he ducked beneath small pools of floating blood. No doubt, Dani had taken out a good many of them on her way through here to find him.

Their flight through the ship left Ty dizzy. As they raced up the stairs into the open air of the hangar deck, the demons' clicked at them. One punctuated their rage at being denied their meal by shouting at them from the safety of the lower deck's darkness.

"Run, you scourges! When false night comes, we'll chase you down!"

They didn't linger for a hug until they'd reached the top deck.

Wicket led them up a bridge to the connecting motorboat. Ty dropped into one of the seats. Dani found a first aid kit on the boat and sanitized his wounds, which hurt as much as being bitten.

"You are so damn stubborn," Ty said through a pained laugh.

"And you love me that way," she said without her usual bravado as she bandaged his arm.

Chapter 23

Ty's body ached as they followed Wicket up the rope bridges. They were racing a clock with no clear idea how far they had to go, so Ty worked through the pain. Wicket would definitely lead them to the nearest Purgatory Arch, but if reaching it took more than three days, then all this had been for nothing. All the apologies and hugs in the world weren't going to make things right for Dani at that point.

Dani paused halfway along a rope bridge that connected a ferry carrying a large load of cars and a small warship with oddly defined lines to its hull's shape, giving its surface corners instead of a smooth curve. "Is it my imagination or are these rope bridges getting stickier?" She lifted one of her feet off the rope bridge, producing a gloopy sound as the sole of her boot peeled apart from the bridge.

"I noticed that, too." Ty left out that it aggravated the wound to his right thigh. The bridges also carried more of a stench to them, reminding him of the fish section of the grocery store, which he still preferred compared to the fish demons' body odor.

Then the bridge shivered. A loud shriek thundered all around them, coming from somewhere in the grey fog above.

Dani dropped to one knee and placed a hand on Wicket's back to keep him steady, even though the dog had already stopped and crouched onto his tummy. "What the fuck is that?"

"I don't know," Ty said as he stared up into the mist, "but it sounds like some kaiju's older, meaner cousin."

"Naturally, it's coming from the direction Wicket is taking us." Dani stroked their dog's fur as if to apologize for suggesting she blamed him.

Ty couldn't discern any shapes in the grey vagueness above. He knew his bones quaked when he felt that roar, though. "I suppose there's always the chance that we'll reach the next gate before Godzilla gets a chance to stomp on us."

Dani snorted. Yeah, Ty considered that a fool's bet, too.

They continued up the bridges and said little more. The thunderous shrieks grew more frequent and louder.

"Did you see that?" Dani pointed to the far left.

Ty saw more of the same: grey fog with the lines of the rope bridges connecting more ships.

"See what?"

"That bridge just appeared," she said. "I swear I saw it shoot through that submarine over there."

Ty stared a little longer. One of the rope bridges connected to the submarine appeared to shimmy, but while that might have been his imagination, he trusted Dani's eyes more than his.

The farther they climbed, the more certain Ty became of something dark taking shape in the mist. The closer they got, the larger it grew with its movements gaining more definition. A shadowy form shifted behind a Viking ship with a single square-shaped sail and a dragon's head carved into the prow of the vessel.

The loudest shriek yet again shook everything and set the grey mist to swirling. The orange and yellow sail on the Viking ship fluttered.

"Duck!" Dani dropped to her knees and grabbed Wicket to her chest.

Ty knelt and hugged the rope bridge. Another wooden ship passed overhead and plummeted to their right.

Wind whipped around them. Wicket yelped. A new rope bridge had formed, passing between Ty and Dani and a mere foot above the bridge they were on now. Ty's gaze followed the path of the new bridge to his right where it split through the hull of an 18th century multi-decked Spanish galleon, the ship that had passed over their heads.

More bridges, fresh ones, cut into it from all directions. The ship's descent halted, causing the new bridge between Ty and Dani to wobble with a deep, comical "boing."

As silence reasserted itself, Ty realized the ship hadn't been falling straight down. It had passed them at an angle, as if something had flung it at them.

"Did that?"—

Before Ty could finish his question, Dani shouted. "Run!" She wasn't focused on the galleon. Her gaze followed the new rope bridge to where it originated. Something crawled down it towards them.

They resembled large spiders with obscenely long legs of varying lengths. Each one looked as big as Ty was. Only, they weren't spiders. Each one had six legs, and their outer shells resembled the mottled orange and white of a crustacean.

Another shriek from above shook the realm, stopping Dani, Wicket, and Ty in mid-sprint. Another shadow emerged from the void above. A catamaran plummeted from ahead of them and passed over their heads. Its two sails fluttered with all the force of a hurricane at its back, causing it to spin in its fall.

Out of the corner of Ty's eye, he saw four of the spider crabs crawl on top of each other. At first, they appeared to attack one another, but they stopped moving when they formed some conjoined position that left their bellies exposed. Yellowish bile burst out of their stomachs and launched in two directions. One end thrust towards the Viking ship and cut straight through its hull and out the other side. The other end of the yellow line of bile snapped through the catamaran at the same time as two other newly formed bridges sliced through it from other directions in the grey mists.

"That is nasty!" Dani sprinted for the Viking vessel.

Ty fought down the burning pain in his right thigh as he chased after Dani. "Yeah, I was a lot happier not knowing these things were made out of spider crab vomit."

"And I was just fine not saying what it is out loud. Ew!"

"Sorry."

Wicket barked as he bounded up the rope bridge and leaped onto the deck of the Viking ship.

Dani stopped and looked past Ty in the direction they'd come from. She drew both of her swords. More spider crabs skittered across the bridges, pursuing them.

Wicket waited to see Ty reach the deck of the Viking ship, barking his approval and impatience, and then scrambled for the next bridge.

Ty considered stopping to hack at the rope bridge, but the spider crabs could create a new one. That only left the options of running or fighting. One thing slowed down the spider crabs. Every time a new ship launched in their direction, the spider crabs stopped to hit it with their "bile bridges." Not all of the spider crabs would stop, but enough of them did to slow down the ones that didn't.

The spider crabs were thirty yards behind them. Ty struggled to keep up with Dani and Wicket. The claw bite to his thigh screamed for him to stop putting weight on it.

They leaped onto the deck of a 16th century Dutch cargo ship with four tall masts of tattered sails and the figure of a swan on the rear of the ship, above the rudder. Fish demons shouted curses at them from below decks as Ty and Dani scrambled across the ship.

The mist ahead cleared when they neared the next rope bridge. An angry shriek shook the ship and set the demons to screaming proclamations of doom. None of that slowed down the spider crabs, though.

Ty started to shout for Wicket and Dani to hurry, but instead they came to a stop as something massive burst through the grey mist. A huge cruise ship emerged, flying towards them. The ship had two red towers atop it with a white, mouse ears symbol on each of them.

All the spider crabs stopped. They hopped onto one another and released a massive bridge at the approaching cruise ship. No way they'd stop it from crashing into the Dutch ship, though.

Wicket led them up a bridge to another sailing cargo ship. The three of them jumped onto the ship's deck as the cruise ship smashed into the Dutch vessel, severing the bile bridge that had connected to the cargo ship.

Half of the bridge now dangled from the cargo ship they were on. Five spider crabs clung to the thick thread. Their unequally long legs struggled to climb the thread at that angle, but then they shot out snake-like tongues to wrap around the thread and keep them from falling off as they climbed. This close, Ty realized each one must be three times his size.

Wicket barked incessantly, but the little terrier wasn't focused on the spider crabs or his humans. Instead, he barked at something that now dominated the sky before them, the monster that guarded the way out of this realm.

Before Ty or Dani could say or do anything, one of the fish demons below decks cried out.

"The Kraken comes!"

Chapter 24

The massive beast descended into a gap within the network of rope bridges and the ships suspended by them. In terms of size, the comparison to Godzilla hit the mark. Even without stretching out its tentacles, its height rivaled a skyscraper's. A spear-shaped body with an arrowhead tip made up the majority of its mass. A set of large red, diamond-shaped eyes ringed the torso near the bottom where dozens of tentacles danced.

A hundred or more Hell gates surrounded the Kraken like a cage it carried with it. The rips in reality twinkled as reality swam within each one. The Kraken's tentacles reached into some of the gates as if to dig around for something. One tentacle dragged out a fishing trawler and then flung it towards the sailing cargo ship Ty and Dani were on. The ship missed, groaning as it passed overhead.

"We're lucky that thing's aim sucks," Dani said.

"Considering we're ants compared to it, it's getting too close for my tastes."

The Kraken shrieked its rage, shaking the entire realm. The source of the Kraken's voice came from a huge, birdlike beak that pulsed out beneath the swarm of tentacles.

Then the Kraken's tentacles all pulled in from the gates and moved in unison to "swim" up. As its body ascended, sacs below its ring of diamond-shaped eyes spit out a dark gaseous substance. The inky mess spread through the grey mist. The deck of the ancient cargo ship shook as cheers from the crew of fish demons thundered below decks.

Amid the shouts of the excited demons, Ty recognized a single phrase: "false night." One of the demons on the aircraft carrier had promised to chase them down when that happened.

"Wicket, Purgatory Arch! Run!"

The darkness enveloped the cargo ship. It didn't black out everything, just made everything darker.

Wicket ran up the next rope bridge with Dani and Ty right behind him. They couldn't see what ship this next bridge led to. The bridge vanished into the gloomy void.

The fish demons' shouts and clicks echoed through the inky fog. Ty couldn't tell what sounds came from behind or ahead. Then the Kraken's shrieks drowned out all of it.

Ty felt the demons draw close. The rope bridge quivered beneath their combined weight.

He spun around with his sword and met the first of the demons. The monster's claws snapped around the blade, stopping Ty's swing from hitting its head. Using the demon's grip on his sword, Ty jerked it towards him and then kicked it in the stomach. The strike sent the demon spilling into another demon behind it. They tumbled off the bridge and into the emptiness.

Ty attacked the next demon, dispatching it in two swings of his sword, sending it diving after the previous two. The rope bridge limited their numbers, but that comfort only lasted a few seconds before he heard Dani's swords mimicking his work. They were surrounded. She cursed. Wicket barked, running back and forth between both sides of the fight. He zipped between the legs of a demon, putting it off balance for Ty to knock it off the rope bridge. Then the dog ran to Dani to do more of the same for her.

A large shadow thrust out of the darkness from behind the demons coming towards Ty. Demons either dove off into the void or were knocked off as one of the Kraken's tentacles swept across the length of the rope bridge.

Ty dropped onto his stomach. "Get down!"

The tentacle passed over Ty. Wicket yelped. The force of the wind from the fast-moving swing would have knocked Ty off into the void, but the stickiness of the relatively new bridge helped him keep a grip on it. More fish demons from Dani's side of the bridge cried out as the Kraken knocked them off.

Ty confirmed no demons were coming at him and then checked if Dani and Wicket were safe. He only saw Dani hunched over, still on the bridge.

"Where's Wicket?"

Dani leaned back and Wicket's floppy-eared head popped out from beneath her. He barked at the demons still standing on Dani's side of the bridge.

"Come on!" Dani leaped to her feet and charged at them. Ty and Wicket raced after her. Her swords hacked through the dumbstruck monsters. She screamed as her swords batted demons off the rope bridge and sliced them into pieces. The monsters and their limbs spilled into the empty space.

The Kraken had taken out most of the fish demons at their back, at least for as far as Ty could see. Sadly that didn't go far, and plenty of clicking sounds warned him that more remained there.

Silhouettes of two ships passed by them. A yacht flew twenty feet over their heads, and a small sailboat whisked by beneath their feet.

The Kraken threw more vessels in their direction. Ty wondered what made it so determined. Maybe it disliked the smell of the living or considered them pests, like a line of ants crawling across a kitchen counter. Each time one of those ships or the Kraken got close, Ty expected to die, tossed into the void until he crashed into something too hard and fast to survive.

Against the Kraken, their swords offered no defense.

Loud clicks and excited shrieks warned that more demons were catching up behind them. Dani cursed at the ones ahead of them, egging them on, but Ty heard the growing fear and doubt in her voice.

Then it all went silent as a large shadow fell over them.

"The Kraken!" one of the demons standing closest to Ty shouted and dove off the side of the bridge.

Ty took a step towards the approaching shadow. The Kraken loomed there, descending through the false night. Its sphere of Hell gates made the dark mist glow, like city lights reflecting against a low ceiling of nighttime clouds.

The Kraken held a flat green vessel with "China Shipping Line" in bold white letters on its side that must have been as long as four football fields combined. Tall stacks of tractor trailer-sized containers filled the deck. As the Kraken raised the ship in its grip, containers tumbled off of its side.

Then the Kraken flung the ship and its cargo at them.

Chapter 25

The cargo container ship plunged down through the dark mist. As soon as the ship left the Kraken's grip, Ty knew the ship would pass way over them.

Sadly, the hundreds of containers raining off of it would not miss.

Most of the demons dove into the misty abyss, hoping to avoid the storm of large, metal containers hurtling towards them. A pale blue container smashed through the bottom of the 16th century cargo ship behind them.

Wicket growled his displeasure as the bridge wobbled beneath them.

"I agree, pal." Ty's stomach protested being jerked back and forth.

The shower of containers didn't end. As soon as the rope bridge steadied enough, Wicket scrambled. Dani and Ty struggled to keep up with him.

Clicking noises came from behind them. Three of the fish demons still pursued them.

More cargo containers rained around them. A dark green container passed so close that the wind of its passing knocked Ty off-balance. He steadied himself by grabbing onto the steep rope bridge.

The fish demons pursued them despite the storm of raining cargo containers.

The dark mist brightened with the lights of the Hell gates as the Kraken swam towards them.

"Wicket!" Dani's shout brought Ty up short.

At first, he feared their dog had fallen off the bridge, but instead, he'd come to a sudden halt. Dani had nearly tripped on him.

"What's going on?" Ty turned and readied his sword for the demons, even as the Kraken's tentacles swam in the air around them, swatting at the falling cargo containers, sending more up into the air like a juggler but not with the intent of catching them. Instead it launched the large metal boxes towards them.

"Wicket just stopped!" Dani shouted. "Wicket! Purgatory Arch! Now, dammit! Wicket!"

The silky terrier not only refused to move, he crouched so that he faced them.

"We're about to have company," Ty said. The three demons were almost on them and more came from ahead. Ty wondered if that was why Wicket had stopped.

Their dog wasn't staring at him or Dani or any of the demons. The terrier's gaze fixed on the Kraken. The next volley of containers passed them, and that's when Ty realized what their dog intended.

"Dani!" He shoved his sword into its scabbard and placed a hand over it to keep it in place. Then he mimicked their dog's crouch. "Hold tight to your swords!"

As Dani shoved her swords into their scabbards on her hips, the dead center of one of the red containers collided with their rope bridge up ahead. The bridge shifted under that weight, stretching on that point like a rubber band. For a split second, the bridge felt as if it might split, but then the container tumbled away and the bridge snapped back. Ty, Dani, Wicket, and the fish demons all flew off the rope bridge towards the Kraken.

The wave of dizziness Ty had felt the last time he'd gone airborne hammered into him again. Even having realized what might happen, he screamed as he tumbled head over ass.

One of the Kraken's massive, diamond-shaped eyes narrowed on them. Then the world went impossibly bright as their path led straight towards one of the Hell gates. Wicket blinked away into the light with Dani behind him. Ty feared he'd miss the gate, because his path sent him towards its edge. Right before he hit, the Kraken and its sphere of gates shifted. Ty entered the gate at its center, and reality blinked.

PART III

THE SLIPPERY SLOPE

Chapter 26

Five Years Earlier

A month before the wedding, Ty got "The Text."

Dani and Ty were standing next to the front door of their new loft apartment, ready to go out. She snatched Ty's cell phone from him and scowled at the message from Zuma. "That is bullshit. I thought Madison was next." Even though Dani didn't add it, Ty could tell she suspected her mom changed the order to ruin their plans for tonight.

Ty didn't voice his irritation. Dani didn't need fuel added to her temper, a lesson he'd learned a long ways back.

They were dressed up for dinner at a fancy wine bar within walking distance of their apartment. One of Dani's friends had raved about it on social media. They wanted to celebrate their wedding being one month away. Dani wore a long, dark red velvet, strapless dress with a slit up the side that had Ty fantasizing about sex later with her still wearing it, or rather barely wearing it.

He loosened his tie while reading the text again.

'Be at work in less than thirty minutes for your first exorcism.'

This was the last hurdle in their training, and it wasn't the sort of thing you could plan ahead of time or reschedule.

Ty considered texting Zuma to fuck off, but he wanted to get this over with. They'd spent weeks going over their role in exorcisms, and if he screwed this up badly enough, they'd cut him loose. Dani had assured him that rarely happened. Still, the news of their engagement last month hadn't gone over half as well with Dani's mother as they'd expected. Up until that night, her mom/his boss had gotten along fine with Ty. Now, she'd turned into a massive ice bitch.

"I'll call the restaurant to reschedule for tomorrow night, if they have any openings." He wondered if they charged customers for changing their reservations at the last minute.

"I'm going to break Zuma's legs," Dani said before launching into a list of curses in both English and Spanish. After she'd started to repeat herself, she tossed out ideas for appropriate punishments, suggesting someone should fuck Zuma with a cactus.

She was still fuming when he came out of the bedroom in blue jeans and a black turtleneck. By now, she'd lounged on their purple sofa with her legs resting on the coffee table as she munched her way through a bag of cashews and washed it down with a bottle of hard cider. When she saw him, her eyebrows lifted in obvious approval. "You do look really good like that."

"Glad you approve." He laughed and then felt his throat go dry as she shifted one of her legs to rest a foot on the edge of the coffee table. The split of her dress shifted to reveal a lot of leg. Any doubt he had whether she was doing that on purpose ended as he noticed her smirk. "That's cruel."

She crooked a finger for him to come closer and kissed him, long and hard. That kind of kiss included an invitation for far more. When she broke the kiss, her teeth lightly raked his lower lip and pulled a moan out of him.

"Some incentive for you to get home in one piece."

They kissed one more time and kept it brief, because another kiss like that first one wouldn't end anytime soon.

Unlike Ty's old apartment, their new one only required a five block walk to the Rigney Building. He strolled down the sidewalk as he carried his bag with his hunting gear. The long, slender bag hid his sword from any passersby. The shadows of the office buildings had grown long, leaving half of the city in early night. The traffic on the road fought in both directions, half hitting downtown to start the partying early on a Friday night while some of the stragglers from work headed home, having missed the worst congestion of the evening commute.

By the time he strolled out of the elevator onto the twelfth floor of the Rigney Building, Ty had fallen into a right sour mood. He still felt the tingle of Dani's teeth on his lower lip, and if Zuma ended up telling him to never mind, that he'd been summoned by mistake, he'd have sprinted home.

Ty found Zuma in the small office space carved out for the handful of people who performed the more mundane duties of running the place. He stood with his broad back to Ty and appeared oblivious to his arrival.

"Zuma, if you had any idea the dress I left Dani standing in to come here, you'd be"—

Zuma turned to look at Ty and the only reason the man's smirk didn't piss him off was because all of Ty's focus shifted to the person standing behind him.

"By all means, Mr. Faison, do go on about my daughter's dress." The thin, hard line of Maria Cortez's lips made it clear Ty really shouldn't keep talking about Dani or the dress.

"She looked damn good." He slid his bag off his shoulder and dropped it on the floor. He hadn't planned to scrap when he got here, but now that the opportunity presented itself, he decided why the heck not? "Madison was supposed to be next. Why the hell am I here?"

"These summonses aren't the sorts of things we schedule well in advance." Zuma stood with his arms crossed, almost daring Ty to attack him. "If you find this unacceptable, then perhaps you should consider a different career."

Ty hadn't dealt much with Zuma since he and Dani had finished their official training. As much as Dani had made it clear she wanted Zuma proved wrong about him, she'd left out how much the old codger resented being proven wrong about him. The guy must have loved that Maria had turned on Ty since the engagement.

"If you wish to argue the matter," Maria said as she walked into the open door of her office and picked up her sword bag, "then you can take it up after the exorcism. The priest and doctor are already waiting there."

Ty didn't respond right away. His brain skipped as he realized his future mother-in-law planned to go as his mentor for this exorcism. Once upon a time, he'd have preferred going with her instead of Zuma. He didn't bother with another objection. Instead, he picked up his bag. "So where are we going?"

"You're in luck," Zuma said as he sat on the edge of the desk that belonged to Maria's secretary. "This one is local."

That wasn't all that shocking. The Purgatory Arch Maria had taken him to when she'd recruited him made this city a hot spot for possessions, part of why the Order of the Emerald Blades based their East Coast operations here. Didn't stop Ty from doing an internal happy dance, since it meant he'd get home to Dani that much sooner and limit his time with his future "Mommy-in-Law Dearest."

Chapter 27

Five Years Earlier

Maria drove them to their destination in her Mini Cooper. The competing voices of men and women singing in Latin filled the silence between them. The LED display identified the music as "Angus Dei" from John Rutter's "Requiem," instead of her usual selections of classic rock. He supposed she listened to this when she wanted to get psyched up for an exorcism. Ty couldn't say it did anything for him.

After they'd left the lights of downtown and traveled into the dark on I-64 West, the requiem shifted to "The Lord is My Shepherd."

"You will not strike with your sword until I order it." Maria didn't take her eye from the road as she issued her instructions. "Don't speak with the demon, not even to taunt it. Most of all, we do not say each others' names."

The bit about names wasn't something he'd ever heard Zuma bring up, nor the stuffed-shirt of a priest who'd lectured them on the exorcism process.

"Why is that? Is this something about names having power?"

Even without her turning to look at him, Ty found Maria's eye roll impossible to miss. "No, it's about social media. If the demon gets loose and returns to Hell, then it can share what it's learned. A demon who'd possessed someone in London hunted down one of our swords there. We eventually learned the demon had figured out where to find the sword by stalking them on Facebook."

"And if I need to get your attention?"

She grunted with what sounded like approval of the question. "We address each other by title. You will simply call me Sword."

"We're both swords for this, though?"

She shrugged.

They pulled off the interstate into the heavy traffic nightmare of Short Pump. Dani refused to come to this part of the metro area's West End. This stretch of West Broad Street turned into a multi-lane, cluttered mess of large malls and shopping centers. At night, the entire area transformed into a chaotic mess of light, especially with the addition of all the headlights and brake lights on the road. Ty preferred Maria driving, because he could barely make out the white dashes that defined their lane.

When they eventually got out of Short Pump, he knew they'd reached the farthest western suburban hell of the Richmond metro area. The GPS on Maria's phone brought them to an address on Claremont Court. Wherever they were, Ty knew they'd found the money. A long driveway of cement ended next to a three-door garage, attached to a red brick house that could qualify as a mansion, given its size. Maria's car tripped a pair of motion-activated lights attached to the outer wall of the garage.

"How many bedrooms you think this place has?" Ty asked as they got out of the car. Two other cars were parked outside. One was a shiny, newer model Lexus and the other a tan Toyota Rav4 that had seen better days judging from the damage to the paint job.

"Don't know. Don't care." Maria took in their surroundings and nodded with approval. "Now, I see why they said we could do this here."

Thick rows of trees and bushes barely hid a tall brick fence that defined the borders of the sizable estate. The glow of light from the rear windows of the house revealed a large pool in the back yard. According to their classes, things could get loud during an exorcism, so this place provided plenty of isolation for what they needed to do. When they needed someplace more private than the victim's home provided, they used warehouses that belonged to the Order.

"Bout time you got here, cyclops." A middle-aged man in a black priest's shirt, complete with the white tab collar, appeared from around the front of the house. His deep voice didn't mesh with his short stature. A thin pair of glasses with rectangular lenses and a well-trimmed set of mutton chops framed his face. He tapped off the ash from a cigarette between his fingers before pulling it to his lips to take in another drag that produced an orange glow on its tip.

"Thought you quit smoking." Maria popped open the trunk and pulled out her sword, still in its scabbard. She belted it around her waist, letting the sword rest on her left hip.

"Aw, fuck that." The priest paused to blow out some smoke, all the more pronounced from the winter air. "Let a man have his vices, will ya? Besides, steadies my nerves."

"I thought nicotine was a stimulant." Ty belted on his sword. Like Maria, he wore his sword on his left hip.

The priest pointed at Ty with the black-wrapped cigarette in his hand. "Who's the tall stick in the mud?"

"Rookie." She walked up to the priest and gestured with a pair of fingers for him to share his smoke. He held the black stick up to her lips to take a drag. Her eyes closed for a moment as she savored the smoke drifting out of her lips. "Nice. You know if you spent half as much money on your car as you did your cigarettes, you wouldn't be driving that piece of shit."

Ty figured that meant the beat-up Rav4 belonged to him.

"Cars are overrated. I'm proud enough of my dick that I don't need to drive in one."

The priest took a long, last pull on the cigarette before dropping it onto the driveway. He squashed the still smoking butt beneath the heel of his shiny, black shoe.

"So, Sword," he said the title with a hint of a taunt, "what are we calling the rookie?" The priest blew into the palms of his hands and then rubbed them together to fight the chill.

"For tonight, call him Hollywood." Maria didn't bother to hide her amusement at the improvised nickname.

"Really?" Ty took that as further confirmation she came tonight for the singular benefit of busting his balls.

"Oh." The priest dragged out that sound with a hint of a laugh behind it and leaned back a bit as he looked Ty up and down. "So you're the future son-in-law. God be with you." The priest made the sign of the cross to him.

"And also with you." Ty mimicked the sign of the cross but with his hand flipping the bird.

The priest barked out a laugh as he clapped his hands together. "Oh, I like this one."

"So what's the story inside?" Maria asked, clearly not happy to see the priest take a liking to Ty.

He canted his head towards the house. "Doc is checking the guy's vitals. I already took his confession."

"Think he meant it?" Ty asked.

While taking the possessed person's confession wasn't required for an exorcism, the priest who'd lectured Ty and Dani's group had made it clear that a sincere confession could grease the wheels for pulling out the demon.

The priest shrugged. "That's between him and God, but since you ask, I think he's more sorry he fucked up enough to go to jail."

Now that they were here, Ty realized Maria hadn't offered any insights into the victim beforehand. "What'd he do?"

"Put his soon-to-be ex-wife in the hospital," the priest said with the appropriate level of disdain.

"Charming."

"His trial is next week. His daughter is in there, too. She's the one who requested all of this."

Ty didn't bother to ask if this was wishful thinking on the daughter's part. Who could blame her for wanting to find something to explain her father beating up her mom? Ty would probably feel the same. Thankfully, his mom and dad enjoyed a healthy relationship that set the bar high enough to scare him, because he wanted to do right by Dani the way his parents had for each other.

"Mind you, the guy feels guilty about it, that and plenty more. Pretty sure that's how the demon got its hooks into him."

That also fit what Ty had learned in the lecture weeks ago. Guilt, the kind that left a person desperately wishing the bad things they'd done belonged in someone else's ledger, created an easy "in" for a demon. Maybe the guy cheated on his wife or embezzled money from wherever he worked to buy this McMansion. Whatever the reason, it opened the door for the demon to take the blame and then things escalated from there. Being able to pass off the burden of guilt provided a spiritual high of sorts, not unlike the way getting drunk turned off a person's normal filters.

"Very well." Maria strolled towards the front door with a hand resting on the hilt of her sword. "Let's get this over with."

Chapter 28

Five Years Earlier

The inside of the McMansion had that look-but-don't-touch museum quality that left Ty ready to break out in hives. How anyone could live in a place like this baffled him.

The stain to the hardwood floor straddled the fine line between brown and black. The walls were painted all white, as if color were a sin. The thought forced Ty to bury a nervous laugh at the private joke.

A set of stairs in the foyer led to the second floor. The dining room sat open to their left with the living room to the right. A large, white rug covered most of the floor of the living room. The daughter, Ty assumed, sat on a black velvet sofa in front of the fire. She'd pulled her black hair up into a loose bun held together by a black clip. He smelled her freshly brewed coffee, the steam wafting from the large white mug held in both of her hands. The daughter stared at them with a hopeful expression until her gaze settled on the swords Ty and Maria wore. Her eyebrows pushed towards one another, and he could almost hear her internal debate of whether she wanted to know why they brought the weapons.

The priest walked over to her and spoke in a hushed voice. "Are you sure you won't leave? We can call you when it's finished."

She shook her head. Even though she directed the answer to the priest, the daughter's gaze stayed fixed on Ty and Maria.

The priest placed a hand on her shoulder. "I take it you spoke with him already?"

That brought her attention back to him. Her face tightened, but whatever fire the priest had kicked up in her with the question vanished. When she nodded, she didn't meet the priest's eyes, as if ashamed.

Maria leaned close to whisper to Ty. "We encourage loved ones to say their goodbyes, just in case. Most refuse to."

"Since you're electing to stay, please understand it's vital you not interfere," the priest told the daughter. "What's going to happen downstairs will not be pleasant. No matter what you hear, do not come down there until we're finished."

They left the daughter there and were met by the doctor as she emerged from the door that connected the kitchen to the basement. The doctor stood half a head taller than Ty, and that wasn't counting her locks which she wore pulled up into a high bun. She shut the door behind her and shook her head.

"This one is a piece of work."

The priest snorted. "Is that your professional opinion, Doctor?"

She rolled her eyes towards him with an obvious "Really?" in her expression. "He told that girl how glad he was that he and his wife had stayed together, even though they only did it for her."

The priest grunted. "The man himself isn't the most charming shit I've met, but I think it's safe to say the demon is running the show in that head right now."

Ty nodded, realizing what the priest meant. The same way it used the man's guilt to get into him, he intended to soften up the daughter for the same. Wouldn't be difficult for her to connect him staying with his wife this long and eventually beating her up as the daughter's fault.

"First time?" The doctor offered her hand to Ty, which he shook.

"Yeah."

"Feel free to make this demon suffer a bit before you cut it up."

The priest tapped on the door. "Let's go meet the catch of the day."

Ty followed all of them down into the cellar. He expected an ephemeral disturbance to the air in the room, given it now hosted a demon. Nothing felt out of sorts, though. Four light fixtures hung from the ceiling with one of the bulbs burned out. Some folded tables and chairs were propped up against one of the brick walls. Another wall had an honest-to-God wine rack, loaded with enough dust-coated bottles to kill someone from alcohol poisoning a dozen times over. Boxes piled like a game of 3-D Tetris covered the third wall and the space beneath the wooden stairs he and the others were descending.

It all looked and felt perfectly normal except for the heavyset, balding man sitting on a metal folding chair in the middle of the cellar's concrete floor. The pleasant smile he extended to them didn't fit with the way his wrists were zip tied to the back of the chair and his ankles to the front legs.

"I've had some time to consider this," he said, as if changing the agenda of a board meeting, "and I'm thinking we should go out for dinner first."

Maria knelt in front of the man to bring herself eye level with him. "Aren't you the witty one?"

He leaned towards her as much as his bindings permitted. "Aren't you hungry? I know I am." His voice then dropped an octave, giving his next words a rumble. "I'm positively starving."

Maria stepped aside for the priest. He crossed his arms as he stared down at the man. "I offer you the chance to leave this man and return home without conflict."

The man—no, the demon—chuckled. "Oh, where's the fun in that? Besides, doing this the hard way improves my chances of taking home a morsel. As you can see, I've been fattening up this one."

Maria pulled out her sword in a languid motion that produced a scrape from the blade sliding up and out of its wooden scabbard. "The hard way ends with your head and heart turned to ash."

"Honestly, Heathcliff here hasn't proven worth the trouble. He's so eager for all the personal vices—wine and sex—but none of the really good stuff. Tried to get him to buy a small arsenal and shoot up a school, send a few young souls to Hell. It's not like you humans don't have them to spare."

"Glad to know Mr. Martin is still in there." The priest's brows pushed towards one another.

Ty drew his sword and stood on the demon's left, opposite from Maria.

The demon rolled his head in the direction of Ty's sword. "Ah, a little piece of home. How I love the smell."

Ty didn't care for the way this demon looked at him through Heathcliff's eyes. It wasn't that he wanted to run screaming from this place, but the demon's gaze unsettled him, a queasiness that threatened to send him praying into a toilet.

"Your souls glow, and the brighter they shine, the better they feed us." He leaned towards Ty, almost threatening to tip his chair and himself over. "No, not you. You're not in charge here."

The demon swiveled his head and body the opposite way to Maria. "Now, you—you definitely have that boss bitch air about you. I'm flattered to make the acquaintance."

Maria smirked at him. "Priest, let's get on with this."

"No!" The demon sat up. "Before you do, I've a message from my Lord Revol to deliver to the Order of the Emerald Blades."

Maria stepped back as if she'd been slapped.

"That's right. We're getting closer to finding you. Our patience with you and the rest of humanity nears its limit. In the past, your souls made for an endless feast—fields of delicious light—but you keep living longer and multiplying. When billions of you walk this world, you leave Hell to famine. Your science continues to lengthen your lives and that forces more of my kind to seek refuge here in your filthy flesh while our siblings fight over the scraps left in our home. We only do what we must to survive, and yet you dare to enter our realm and end our existence to extend yours even longer?" He slowly turned his head to look at each of them. Ty shivered as that demon's glare landed on him. "Your order declares war on our survival, and we will repay that unkindness in full. Your end is dawning."

Unlike the rest of them, the priest stepped close to the demon.

"I've heard enough." He looked over to Maria. "If you and Hollywood are ready?"

She nodded.

"Oh, and here comes the chanting." The demon rolled his eyes.

"You've watched too many movies. I don't require some eloquent chain of Latin phrases to expel you. All I need are two words."

The priest stepped back with a swagger that made it clear he wasn't retreating. He made room for what came next.

"Get. Out."

The demon smirked, but that vanished into wide-eyed panic as the demon's lips pressed tight to hold in what resembled a croak—a cough fighting for release. His throat worked to fight down whatever threatened to come out. Eyes shut and his face contorted with disgust as a belch forced his lips open. His body convulsed with revulsion, threatening to topple him and the chair he was zip tied to. Even six feet away, Ty caught the stench of bile and something burnt polluting the air of the room.

Heathcliff's body shook forward and back in time with his rapid, desperate breaths. The doctor walked up behind him and placed a foot on the horizontal bar that connected the rear legs of the chair to keep him from tilting over. Then a trickle of blood spilled out the corner of his mouth and down his chin in a dark red line. He glared up at the priest—a look that wished a dreadful murder upon him. Then he coughed. A spray of blood misted out onto the cement floor, forming a red Rorschach. Another belch shook his body, and the dam broke.

Ty used to think he had a strong constitution, but watching the blood covered chunks slapping onto the floor along with the pain-heaving grunts from Heathcliff tested his limits. Being close enough to smell the foulness spilling out of Heathcliff only made it worse. Ty feared he might vomit, as well, until something in the bloody pile distracted him. A slender digit bent and straightened. The pointed fingertip hit the floor and slid into place on the end of the finger. His training warned him an exorcism caused a person to vomit up a demon. That didn't prepare him for watching the creature reassemble itself, covered in a mucus-like layer of blood. He'd worked on the set of a horror movie called *Three Devils After Midnight* a few years ago that leaned into the gore. This made that production look like a G-rated film.

The finger quickly turned into a hand. Then what Heathcliff expelled slid into place to form internal organs and other body parts.

Ty raised his sword.

"Hold that blade, boy!" Maria's voice as good as reached across the room to slap sense into him.

A reflex in him wanted to snap back at Dani's mother, tired of receiving her disdain, but the way she gave her sword a little spin and her gaze stayed focused on the demon forming before them made it clear she was all business now. They needed to incinerate all of the demon's heart and head in order to end it, and if they struck down the demon too soon, they'd get it before its body had finished pulling itself together and miss part of those two vital pieces. That didn't prevent the demon from lashing out at them before it finished assembling itself.

"A whiter?" Ty asked.

Maria nodded.

Ty wiped the sweat from his brow. He hated how obvious to the others his building sense of panic must be.

A black eyeball with a red iris and the slimy, worm-like nerve attached to it launched out of Heathcliff's mouth and rolled across the floor. That, more than anything else thus far, pushed Ty's gag reflex to its limit.

"You're looking like the color of your sword over there, Hollywood." The priest played with his lighter, flipping its top open and snapping it shut. "Hold it together, and I'll buy you a drink after this."

Up until this moment, Ty hadn't questioned his ability to pass this test. As the shape of the demon writhing on the floor in bits and pieces assembled in grotesque slaps of flesh and cracks of reformed bones, the doubts he'd held in check started to cut into his thoughts. The room wasn't too cramped to keep him from using his sword, but with four extra people in here, he needed to control his attacks to avoid hurting any of them.

As the demon's lower half reached a point where most of its satyr-like legs had reformed, Maria slashed at one of the lower legs. Her sword slid through it like a knife through warm honey. The leg didn't come apart, though. The body, still assembling itself, simply held together as if a liquid in a leg-shaped vessel.

"Still too soon," Maria said.

Only once the demon reached a point where they could hack off its limbs would it be ready for them to cut out its heart and behead it.

As Heathcliff continued to spew forth the demon bits like a faucet left running, he grew paler. The doctor held down the folding chair, leaning all of her weight onto it to keep Heathcliff from falling forward.

The demon's throat assembled from the inside out, screaming a strangled note of agony that gained definition as the mouth, with its fanged teeth, formed.

The legs shifted so that the demon only rested on one knee, the other leg's taloned foot stood flat on the floor as if ready to pounce. The demon's left shoulder and upper arm had come together with the radius sticking out the end of it. The other pieces of the lower arm and hand writhed in many pieces on the floor struggling to come together separate from the rest of the demon's body. The right arm, fully restored, swung blindly.

Maria stayed out of the arm's reach. The priest did the same, moving as far away as the room allowed. He still fidgeted with his lighter, but his playfulness vanished as he whispered, "And here we go."

Chapter 29

Five Years Earlier

The black eyeball on the floor shivered and then launched up to the writhing head forming atop the demon. As soon as the optic nerve embedded itself into the demon's brain, the whiter lunged at Maria and slashed at her throat with the hand on his only fully-formed arm.

Instead of attacking with her sword, Maria ducked beneath the attack. She kicked the demon in the back, sending it into the two tables propped up against the wall behind her. The collision knocked the tables flat onto the floor. The demon landed atop the tables with a sound similar to rotten tomatoes splatting against a hard surface. The not-yet-solid demon peeled itself off with a sucking sound and pursued Maria.

Ty jumped over the puddle of blood and not-yet-assembled bits of demon on the floor. He refused to let Maria get in the way of proving himself. The demon was still pulling together its head and left arm. The unattached forearm flopped on the floor as if to seek its two missing fingers and patches of skin. Ty ran up behind the demon and grabbed for the throat with his free hand. He meant to fling the demon at the brick wall, but getting a grip on the throat felt like squeezing wet clay.

The demon kicked behind itself at Ty. Unlike the neck, the taloned foot landed solid against Ty's stomach and sent him falling onto his ass.

"Focus on its legs!" Maria snapped at him as she planted a kick on one of the demon's knees. That sent it to the floor with a shriek.

Ty cursed at himself, because he'd known the part of the demon's body that assembled the earliest would be the most solid while the rest of the body pulled itself together. He hadn't expected the demon to be that difficult to grab, though.

The sounds of Heathcliff vomiting had stopped. The doctor shouted, "Priest, get over here and help! He's not breathing!"

The demon grinned. As Ty got upright, the demon jumped feet-first at the brick wall and kicked off of it to fly in Ty's direction. Ty ducked but too slow to avoid the demon's talon as his nails scraped across the top of his head. Ty swung at the demon's legs but missed as it leaped up to perch atop the stairs.

Maria ran to Ty and grabbed his sword arm by the wrist. "He's not going anywhere yet, not while part of him is still on the floor."

The demon's second eye flew up past Ty's head and slid into its socket. It shrieked in pain and then growled at them.

The priest and doctor, over by the wine racks, cut Heathcliff's body free of the chair and placed him on his back. The doctor repeatedly counted to four under her breath as she performed chest compressions.

Ty sheathed his sword. It wasn't doing him any good until the demon finished playing LEGO with its body. A pointed ear flew up onto the demon's head as Ty ran up the stairs. The demon crouched as more pieces of its body shot up off the floor to return home.

Ty wiped his forehead. When he pulled his hand away, he realized blood, not sweat, was dripping down towards his eyes.

A robotic warble tone sounded from an AED that the doctor and priest had attached to Heathcliff. A recorded voice from the yellow box then said, "Administer shock."

Each time a small piece of his body slapped into place, the demon twitched. The second ear flew into place, and Ty attacked during that split second of distraction. He grabbed the demon's right leg by the thigh and hoisted it up off-balance, sending it tumbling down to the floor at Maria's feet. She slammed the pommel of her sword's hilt down on the demon's knee.

The demon screamed and slashed at Maria, forcing her back. Ty jumped down while the demon focused on her and dropped all of his weight onto the demon's stomach. The demon gasped as its torso caved beneath Ty's legs. The sensation reminded Ty of a trampoline, even as the demon's body expanded like a balloon to shove him off.

The demon slashed at Ty's throat, but Ty grabbed the demon's wrist, stopping it short of his neck. Ty used the demon's momentum against it, twisting the arm behind it. Then Ty slammed the demon face down in the pile of bloody muck Heathcliff had vomited up. The limb didn't collapse or bend so easily now, making it near impossible for the demon to free itself from Ty's grip. That meant the demon was almost ready for the kill, and keeping it that close to the rest of its scattered body bits sped up the process.

"I need to get him out of here and to a hospital!" the doctor said as the priest took over the compressions to give her a break.

"Almost there," Maria said.

Ty struggled to keep the demon pinned, his weight pressing down on its back. The demon struggled, but Ty had it pinned tight. Felt like riding on a mechanical bull set to "expert level."

"You have a plan for cutting off his head?" Maria asked.

He hit her with a look demanding if she was too dense to realize she held a sword, but then she pointed at him. Of course. He needed to make the kill himself, or he wouldn't pass the test.

"You are really ruining my night," Ty said to the demon as he grabbed the back of the demon's head. He repeatedly slammed its face against the cement floor until the fight went out of the demon for a moment.

In a fluid motion, Ty released the demon, stood, and drew his sword. Then he slammed the blade down on the demon's neck.

Chapter 30

Five Years Earlier

While they moved Heathcliff to a bathroom—which the doctor didn't recommend—the daughter called an ambulance for him. She told the paramedics she'd found him vomiting blood, which wasn't a total lie.

The doctor left as soon as the ambulance pulled off with the daughter following in her own car. Heathcliff's odds of making it through the night, according to the doctor, were fifty-fifty. The blood loss from vomiting up a demon often killed the victim, but they'd gotten Heathcliff's heart going again. Given he'd likely end up in jail for beating up his wife, the kinder of the two fates remained open for debate.

Ty, Maria, and the priest started cleaning up. Ty sawed open the demon's chest and pulled out the heart under the critical eye and shaking head of Maria Cortez. The demon's head and heart went into a duffel bag. They stuffed the rest of the demon's corpse into a black body bag.

The ride to their next stop offered Ty some welcome solitude. He drove the priest's tan Rav4 with the body bag in the back. He didn't dare speed given his "precious cargo." The priest rode with Maria in her Mini Cooper with the small duffel bag. They didn't have to transport the heart and head in a separate car from the body, but rumor suggested demons pulled themselves together if all of their pieces were left too close. No one had recorded an instance of that in the past two centuries, suggesting the notion was more myth than fact. Supposedly, a few exorcists had tested the theory, but the demon involved never showed any signs of reviving.

Ty followed Maria's car onto the Downtown Expressway and then the exit to Idlewood Avenue at Hollywood Cemetery. At this time of night, the cemetery passed by him as nothing but a blur of trees and shadows, but ever since Ty's first visit into the Purgatory Arch, that place made his body tingle with nerves. He and his peers went on a more thorough tour of the cemetery during training, including the infamous Sherrilyn Austin grave where the grass would never grow over it, because the soil kept getting turned as if she climbed out and then crawled back into her grave at night.

A few blocks later, they pulled into the alley behind an Episcopal Church. The Gothic building shared its block along Idlewood with a private school. The buildings looked out of place, surrounded by row houses with vinyl siding.

A red door with a small window in the top half of it, protected by metal bars, allowed entrance into the rear of the church. A large lock box attached to the door handle contained keys for the church, not that Ty knew the combination. "You get that once you've grown up." The priest smirked.

"This your parish?" Ty asked.

"Nah. Given my skill set, the church keeps me moving around a lot."

The light from the street offered enough to see what they were doing without making it easy for anyone across the street to notice as Ty and the priest pulled the demon's body out of the Rav4.

"Watch yourself." The priest took the demon by the feet and led them inside the church. A bump of his elbow against the inside wall turned on some lights. "The stairs in here are kind of narrow."

He wasn't wrong. They practically had to hold the demon's headless body upright to get him around the turn and down into the undercroft.

Maria came in behind them, carrying the duffel bag with the demon's head and heart. She closed the door to the alley and locked it.

The undercroft didn't live up to the Gothic exterior of the church above. The walls were painted white and the cement floor blue grey. Exposed pipes obscured the ceiling. Doors to the right led to the bathrooms. Halfway along the left side of the undercroft, a door blended into the white wall, only noticeable because of the door knob and the black seam that defined the door's borders. Maria went ahead of them and pulled out her keys to unlock the door that led to another set of stairs leading to another sub-level. Ty silently joked to himself that they were descending into the "under-undercroft."

Maria flipped a light switch inside the second set of narrow stairs. What must have been a sixty watt light bulb on the landing below lit their way. This part of the undercroft lived up to the Gothic brickwork of the church above with red, brick walls and exposed wooden beams. Apparently, no one felt the need to add any drywall or insulation.

The stairs ended in a round room with a tall ceiling and a fire of blue flames dancing in a round hole in the black marble floor of the room. Much like the Purgatory Arch in Hollywood Cemetery, the borders of the hole were lined with bones. These bones belonged to a single creature that resembled a serpent biting down on its own tail. The head looked less like a snake and more like a fanged horse head. A few feet back from the head were a pair of wings. The wing on the outside reached up to the ceiling. The blue flames obscured the inner wing.

Ty would have expected the room to be sweltering. Only, this so-called Eternal Flame chilled the space. At its center, the fire reached as high as Ty's waist.

Maria dropped the duffel bag next to the skull. "You two get the demon cooking, and I'll get the party favors."

As she strolled to the stairs leading out of the "under-undercroft," the priest watched her over his shoulder until she disappeared from view.

Ty leaned towards the priest and whispered to him. "Were you checking out her ass?"

The priest chuckled. "Well, yeah. She has a mighty fine one."

Ty cringed with all the appropriate melodrama. "Ew. What kind of priest are you?"

The priest offered Ty his hand to shake. "Sebastian Shannon."

Ty took the offered hand, relieved his shake wasn't like Maria's, the hand-crushing-for-dominance kind. "Take it you and she go a ways back."

"Hoping to go a long way with her again tonight, too."

"Augh! You're killing me, man." He cringed again. "Anyway, I'm Ty Faison."

"Oh, I know all about you. Maria's given me an earful, ever since you and her only child got serious."

Ty groaned, glancing towards the stairs for fear his future mother-in-law would already be there.

Before Ty could say anything, Sebastian held up a hand to stop him. "I know you feel like she hates you—and she thinks she does—but I know better." He crossed his arms. "She sees you stealing the only family she's got. If you'd blown it tonight, she was petrified that wherever you went next, her girl would pull up stakes and go with you, leaving her behind."

"I'm not 'stealing' her daughter. If she wasn't such a controlling pain in the ass, she wouldn't need to worry at all. Her stunt tonight, jumping me to the front of the line for this final test—she wanted to ruin the date Dani and I had planned."

"She wasn't sure you'd get your chance before the wedding if she waited for your turn in line. You stand there and tell me it's not a load off your mind that you've passed this before the ring is on your finger. Just try selling me that horse shit."

Ty walked over to the duffel bag, which turned his back to Sebastian. That hid the involuntary lip curl that screamed Ty knew the priest was right on all counts. He'd been stressing for weeks over what would happen if he failed this test. He knelt and zipped open the duffel bag. "Let's give our friend his bath."

Sebastian dragged the body bag closer to the fire and unzipped it. The stench of rot hit Ty hard enough that he doubled over, fighting the need to vomit.

"I thought that thing smelled bad when the guy spit it out."

Sebastian waved a hand in front of his face, but he acted less taken aback by this. "They decompose faster on the mortal plane." That he meant as opposed to in Hell went without saying. "Give me a hand tossing gruesome here into the fire."

"Meant to ask," Ty said as he grabbed the headless demon by its armpits, "how'd you excise the demon by just telling it to get out?"

"Together now." Sebastian grabbed the ankles and then nodded a cue to Ty. They lifted the demon together. Swinging the body back and forth for momentum, Sebastian gave a three count and then they tossed the demon into the flames.

The blue flames turned purple and red as the body disintegrated into ash and then vanished.

Sebastian pointed to the opened duffel bag. "You do the honors."

Ty tossed the head and heart into the fire. The red and purple flames surged with what sounded like a scream.

"So, how'd you do it without all the fancy Latin words?" Ty asked again.

"I used to do it that way. Most priests do, but after I saw priests from other faiths pull out demons without using the same recitation we do, I realized it isn't about the words or the way I pronounce them. It all comes down to faith."

Ty laughed. "You just believe more, and that's it?"

The sober expression on Sebastian's face as he nodded wiped the smirk off Ty's face. "There are still nights I need the fancy wind-up, because faith isn't a straight, ascending line. Even the best priests harbor doubts. Sometimes, the ones who preach the prettiest sermons struggle with the most crippling questions, and the answers don't always come at a convenient time. I was a decent rector. I can write an adequate sermon, kept my church's bank account out of the red...well, barely." He stared into the fire as the last of the red and purple flames vanished. "First time I assisted another priest in an exorcism, I realized that's what the Almighty meant for me to do."

"Elizabeth always had good instincts about that sort of thing," Maria said as she walked into the room, followed by Dani.

Ty couldn't restrain a grin at the sight of his fiancée. Dani no longer wore the red velvet dress, having traded it in for a black scoop neck shirt and a leather jacket with red and gold dragons running down the sleeves. She walked straight up to Ty and kissed him.

"Congratulations," she whispered.

"You did well tonight." Maria smiled, but Ty thought it looked forced. "A little sloppy, but you got it done."

"Thanks."

Dani's leather jacket creaked as she slid an arm around his back, allowing him to put his arm across her shoulders.

Sebastian made a show of looking at the watch on his right wrist. "Well, look at that. I do believe it's Guinness O'clock. What say we hit Siné and celebrate?"

"A priest drinking in an Irish pub." Maria shook her head, but it didn't hide her amusement. "Sometimes, you are walking cliché."

While Ty didn't relish the idea of a double date with his future mother-in-law as part of the other couple, he and Dani enjoyed their evening at the pub listening to Sebastian's stories, most of which had nothing to do with being a priest and more about his days as a young hellion. Maria and Sebastian only stayed long enough for two rounds of stout. Dani and Ty stayed for a couple more rounds and celebrated late into the night.

PART IV

WAIST DEEP

Chapter 31

The chill air stabbed into Ty's lungs as soon as he flew out of the Hell gate. He landed on his ass, skidding down a soft pile of what resembled snow. Friction burned against his back as he slid down a hill. Most of the terrain blurred past him, offering glimpses of distant mountains and hills of snow with no hint of trees.

Ty grabbed at anything to slow himself but only latched onto more snow until his body collided with something solid.

A few seconds passed while his brain made sense of where he was. Strange icy formations sticking three to four feet up out of the ground covered the hill. He shouted for Dani, but before he could finish her name, another body slammed into one of the icy formations protruding from the snow off to the left. The snow erupted as the fish demon leaped to its feet. The demon looked around them and issued a loud series of panicked clicks until its eyes landed on Ty.

Ty rolled away and jumped to his feet as the demon's claws bit down into the patch of snow Ty had vacated. Using the icy protrusions that dotted the hillside as a protective barrier, Ty drew his sword before the demon caught up to him. He swung at the demon, but their claws deflected his attack. The two of them parried sword and claws as they danced around the ice formations reaching up from the ground at the sky. Snow floated on the wind and into Ty's eyes, but he couldn't decide if it was a fresh snowfall or the wind kicking up the snow on the ground.

Despite the overcast sky, Ty could see the fish demon more clearly than he had within the previous realm. The demon took deep breaths, and gills flared open and then shut along his throat.

Ty kept the protrusions between them, and during a pause in the fight, he discerned what the icy things sticking up out of the ground were. They were demons and souls. They were buried waist-deep in the snow and encased in ice. The one between him and the fish demon confirmed what he saw. The demon in the ice—a whiter—resembled a deformed pitchfork with its arms and head trapped in the moment it had fought and failed to climb up out of the ground. The whiter's eyes blinked at Ty.

Then the fish demon launched at Ty, pushing aside the questions about the nature of this realm and how and why these half-buried beings were trapped in ice. Ty retreated from the fish demon's attack. He swung at its claws, keeping either from biting him. He'd suffered that punishment enough on the aircraft carrier.

Ty tried to take the offensive, slamming down with his sword. The blade aimed for the demon's head. The monster's two claws bit onto the green blade, scraping against the metal as the demon tried to rip it from Ty's hands. They fought until Ty kicked the demon in the stomach, sending it through the air and onto its back.

The fish demon got up onto its knees ready to leap at Ty when a small, furry blur zipped between them. Just as Ty realized the furry blur had been Wicket, Dani raced past them and shouted, "Run!"

Ty and the fish demon turned their heads in the direction from which Wicket and Dani had come.

At first glance, Ty mistook it for an avalanche, but it rolled uphill. Then the individual shapes became clear. Dozens of white-furred rodents the size of large rabbits leaped up across the snow, some bounding over the tops of the frozen demons and souls. They reminded Ty of round Koosh balls but with long narrow snouts, round ears, and legs like kangaroos. Ty didn't see anything horrifying about them until one of them opened its mouth, which yawned wide with fangs.

The fish demon and Ty ran in the direction Wicket and Dani had fled. They struggled to keep ahead of the Koosh horde. The beings trapped waist-deep in the ground created constant obstacles for them to navigate, and the murderous tribbles leaped over them with ease.

"Cliff!" Dani shouted from ahead.

She kept moving, though. Even though the snow in the air partially obscured her from view, Ty saw her skipping around as if walking on air.

Pillars reached up from the ravine and provided a way to skip across, assuming the snow hadn't frozen to ice or their balance failed them.

"This is probably a bad time to mention I sucked at hopscotch in kindergarten!" Ty stepped onto the closest pillar.

The fish demon looked back and forth between Ty and the approaching horde before committing to the same path.

Some of the pillars provided enough room for one foot. Wicket jumped across the field of pillars without any pause or apparent fear. Didn't take long for Ty to realize keeping moving without stopping in order to maintain his momentum for each leap worked better. He cursed incessantly as the need to watch his steps made it impossible not to constantly see how insanely high he was.

Tiny shrieks erupted behind him as the Kooshes reached the cliff and most of them fell into the white abyss. The rest of the killer Kooshes crossed the path of pillars with the same ease as Wicket.

Ty muttered to himself random things like "Keep moving!" or "Must go faster!" He added in the occasional "Go! Go! Go!" like he was cheering on some beat poet. More curses flew between all his various mantras. The field of pillars felt like they went on forever, and he feared that instead of simply running out, these narrow pillars might occupy the rest of this realm. If so, they'd fall to their deaths at some point, either because of slipping on the snow or losing their balance.

Loud clicks sounded and faded into oblivion as the Kooshes tackled the fish demon. Both the demon and the Kooshes feasting on him fell into the ravine. Many of the Kooshes plunged after the demon, hoping to get a bite before their hordemates polished off their meal. Ty suspected the fall wouldn't kill these critters.

The Kooshes not plunging after the demon set their sights on the next closest meal: Ty. He tried to go faster, but exhaustion and stress were setting in hard. His legs burned, still suffering from the wounds caused by the fish demons' claws on the aircraft carrier.

The field of pillars narrowed. On the upside, he didn't need to think as hard about where to place his feet, but that also meant avoiding the Kooshes got harder as they closed in on him.

"Land ho!" Dani shouted.

"About damn time!" The Kooshes had dwindled from a horde to a large pack. Considering only two or three could fit onto most of the pillars, many bounced into each other and knocked themselves into the ravine.

Dani came into view on the edge of the next cliff. Wicket crouched at her feet and barked at the Kooshes in what probably translated from dog speak into "Fuck off!"

As Ty neared the cliff, Dani drew her swords and gave each one a spin. "Batter up!"

Ty still had his sword in his hand, having never had a chance to slide it into its scabbard after his fight with the fish demon. When he leaped over to the cliff, he nearly slipped onto his butt, but saved himself. Dani's swords attacked the Kooshes. As soon as Ty had his balance back, he joined her. They used the flats of their green blades to swat the Kooshes into the ravine, plunging away in an ever-fading series of shrieks and croaks.

Wicket went ballistic when one of the Kooshes made it past Ty's sword. Wicket chased after it, bit one of its feet and flung it into the ravine.

When the last of the Koosh horde plummeted away, Wicket ran up to the edge of the cliff and barked one last time. Dani dropped to one knee. Ty lowered himself down to sit in the snow, trying to not aggravate the wounds in his leg any more than he already had.

Dani looked over at him as she wiped the sweat and melted snow from her brow. "So how's your day been?"

They laughed for a bit, taking turns at petting Wicket, who happily hopped through the snow.

"You already give him the command for the next gate?" Ty asked.

Dani shook her head. "I'm hoping that when we do, he doesn't make us hop back to the other side."

Ty groaned. "I think at that point, I might quit."

"Nope. Can't do that." Dani stood and offered a hand to help Ty to his feet. "Let's keep moving."

Wicket, realizing they were leaving, ran back to stand between them.

Ty brushed the snow off of his jeans. "Shall we?"

Dani nodded and then knelt to stroke the fur on Wicket's head. "All right, baby. Seek Purgatory."

Wicket yapped and then hopped out onto the pillars, taking them back across the ravine.

Ty hung his head and groaned.

Interlude 5

While Char had made himself a visible and determined presence among the demons around the Purgatory Arch, he spent most of his time in the tent. He'd wasted hours studying maps of the various realms and their gates. Nothing he'd found had changed his strategy. He knew it wouldn't, but he needed something to keep him occupied as he waited to make his next move.

He was searching the many gate routes through the Triangle Realm when Nera pulled open the flap to his tent and entered.

"The raven you sent to the mortal realm has returned." She stayed by the tent flap as it closed, out of his reach. She crossed her arms and scowled.

Char straightened and curled up the map as best he could without ripping it in his claws. "How many?"

"Ten."

That pulled a growl out of him. He'd hoped for twice that, but they'd make do with what fate provided. "Very well. Ten it is." He picked up a list of names and scratched out the bottom half of the list before he handed it to her. "Assemble these nine I've picked to take with me."

She took a tentative step closer to take the list from him. The stench of rage hit him within seconds, that bitter mix of sweat and oak that numbed the senses.

"I'm not on this list."

Char pulled up to his full height, his ears brushing against the top of the tent. "I don't trust you for this, because I sometimes think you miss too much the delights of your mortal life."

She slammed her fist on his desk. "I chose Hell! When other mortals pray to a fucking uninterested deity to save them from this place, I entered this realm and claimed my right to dictate my destiny!"

He lowered himself enough to meet her at eye level and smiled to her. "Then I want to know the means and the reason for it. Convince me this wasn't some divine punishment forced on you. Why should I believe a mortal would abandon her natural cycle when she covets the secrets of that matter so dearly?"

The charred flesh of Nera's face tightened as she seemed to debate the right move to counter him. Char realized she'd expected him to strike her, and he'd come close to it.

When he thought she might storm out, she crossed her arms again.

"I did it for love and hate."

"That's not an answer." He mirrored her pose, crossing his arms. "Surrender your truth now, or hold your tongue with me forevermore."

Her lips curled back as her teeth gritted tightly enough to make a piece of the charred flesh on her upper lip flake off onto the desk between them.

"I was married but unsatisfied with my life. Quentin provided a logical match. He earned enough to make me comfortable, loved me, and even made an adequate lover. But I could never find the happiness everyone expected me to. I often crawled into my bath, the water hot enough to scald, and then cut myself just enough to watch the blood drip and diffuse into my private sea of tears."

He smelled the truth of her words, but even if he couldn't recognize the unpleasantly stale scent, Char would have known it by the distant look in her eyes as she stood in her memories.

"Then a demon possessed Quentin." Her eyes shut, and her breath shuddered out of her as she licked her lips. "I didn't know what had changed—not at first—but I knew we weren't the same. Everything in my life tasted better, including him." She grinned up at Char then with a knowing and almost accusing look. "That's what love does. Wouldn't you agree?"

She didn't wait for his answer. Instead, Nera continued. "I only learned the truth of my joy when a priest and a man with a green sword took it from me. Those two saved Quentin and ruined me.

"I refused to accept that fate, though. I sought out others possessed by demons and learned how to enter Hell. Once here, I searched for the one who stole my heart."

Once more, her gaze turned distant, but this time, she snarled. "I found him, and he rejected me. By then, I'd learned too much of what eternity means for a mortal soul: a time spent scrambling through the world for meaning only to have that knowledge die, leaving one as another mindless soul for the demons of this place to feast upon until they cycle into another pointless life. I cursed the god—if one even exists—for damning me to such an existence. I followed the river of blood to its source, high in the mountains of this realm, and found the great dragon Metheum chained there. The shackles cut into her legs. The more she struggles, the more the blood flows to form the river that sustains all the demons who live here. She recognized my wish and my need better than I did. So she jerked on her chains and held her talon high as her divine blood rained on me. Then she reared, opened her mouth wide, and bathed me in her blue flames."

Char smiled, not so much at her tale, but at Nera's awe from the memory of that encounter.

He smirked as he finally spoke again. "That had to hurt."

"It was exquisite."

Char leaned forward with both his claws placed flat on the table between them. "And the demon?"

Judging from the way she canted her head and shook it, she recognized the hint of an accusation behind his question. "Save your whimsy for conspiracies. It wasn't Malum. The demon's name doesn't matter, because he no longer exists. I cut out his heart and ripped off his head, then offered them as a sacrifice to Metheum's eternal flames."

Char felt the hunger for her then, as he so often did, because the way Nera declared that demon's destruction exposed her for the fellow predator she was. If the time had permitted, he'd have taken her to the ground then and there. Instead, Char stood tall and took a deep breath to bring his desire into check.

"Very well." He pointed to the list in her hand. "Strike the last name. You will take their place."

She bowed her head to him.

"Gather those eight now," he said. "I want to leave as soon as possible."

"Of course." She then slipped out of the tent.

For all the doubts her secrets had begat, he valued her sword above all others. He'd dreaded going to the mortal realm without her at his side. For one born as a mortal, she fought more viciously than most of his demons.

Char had finally pried free her hidden truths, though. Now, more than ever, he knew he could trust her.

Chapter 32

While Wicket always enjoyed when it snowed in Richmond, which usually only happened once or twice a year, this realm tested even his limits. Didn't help that the depth of the snow forced him to hop the entire way. By the time night fell, he stopped hopping and lowered into a crouch.

Dani lifted the dog into her arms and hugged him close. Wicket's patience for being held usually only lasted for half a minute, but when he squirmed within her grip, he drew closer to her chest and not away from her. Dani kissed the top of his head.

"He needs a break," she said

"So do we. I'll see if I can find anything to build a fire."

Ty rubbed at his forehead, which ached from a lack of sleep. Didn't help that his legs were probably bleeding again, having aggravated his wounds in escaping the Kraken and then the Koosh hoard.

He looked at their surroundings, which had changed little since they'd gotten here. Thankfully, they hadn't run into anymore ravines with pillars for them to hop across. Instead, they walked up and down hills lined with half-buried demons and souls in ice. That it resembled walking through a cemetery crowded with headstones didn't encourage him. No shelter existed, not that they'd seen, not even a cave.

Ty's eyes settled on a demon in the ground—another whiter. Its eyes pleaded up at them for release. One of its arms rested on the ground. No telling what snapped it off from the rest of its body. Ty thought it looked bitten off. Perhaps the demon had struggled before getting fully trapped in the ice and the arm had broken off from the effort. Regardless of the reason for it, the severed arm gave Ty an idea.

"Dig away as much snow as you can," he said to Dani. "I'm gonna get us something to burn."

Ty offered the demon missing an arm a look of apology before he hacked off the other arm with his sword. He cut off a few more demon arms from the others frozen in place. Using his sword, he chipped off the ice around the arms as much as possible. He tossed the six demon arms he'd cut off into the space Dani had cleared.

Dani used her lighter to set the limbs on fire, which took a while. Once the first arm caught fire, though, the flames quickly spread to the others. Ty mainly suggested the fire to see better and less for the cold.

"Is it me," Dani said as she rested her head on Ty's shoulder, "or is it too warm for all of this snow and ice?"

"Yes, which seems suspiciously considerate for a realm in Hell."

"I keep wondering what the catch is."

Ty looked around them. Hell gained its reputation as a place for people to avoid for a reason, so a snowy field that wasn't frigid made no sense.

"Do you think that's what all of the land here is like?" Dani tapped her foot on the rocky ground exposed by the fire.

"Even if it's not, I gotta think dirt here would be as hard as rock." Ty kissed the top of Dani's head. Wicket crouched between their feet, getting as close as possible to the fire as he dared.

"I'm not sure what to make of all these demons." The tone to her voice conveyed an uneasiness that he felt as the unasked question became obvious. For the first time, Ty wondered if these beings were even buried.

Had something ripped off their legs, leaving their torsos here to freeze? If so, then how were some still living?

"Let's hope we don't find out firsthand." He decided against digging up the snow from around one of the buried demons to determine the truth.

"What I would really like to know," Ty said, choosing to change the subject, "is how Wicket got us to that Hell gate to come here."

Dani quirked a brow at him. "That's what dogs do. They sniff out the gates for us."

"Yeah, but that gate—the one that brought us here—moves with the Kraken. I mean, we've always assumed that dogs somehow smell out the gates, but maybe it's more intuition than smell."

Dani shrugged. "Does it really matter?"

"I don't know. I just think it might be useful to better understand how he does it. Somehow, Wicket knew the exact spot to stop us on that rope bridge for the Kraken to fling one of those cargo containers at it, causing it to launch us through the air and into the correct gate. The Kraken even had to move for the gate to line up right for me after you went into it, because I almost hit the edge. If the gate hadn't moved in time, I might have bounced off the edge of it or it might have cut me in half."

Dani went wide-eyed at that part. "You didn't tell me that almost happened."

"We've been a little busy since we got here."

Dani turned her attention to the fire, staring into it. "Well, that would explain how dogs don't get distracted by gates that have collapsed. We know some close and new ones spawn in different locations. I've never heard of a dog leading someone to a gate that's no longer open."

"Yeah, and who knows? Maybe Wicket is just special."

Dani reached down and gently stroked the fur on the back of Wicket's neck. The silky terrier turned his big, black eyes to look up at her, and there was no denying the love he had for her. "He's always been special," Dani whispered as she lifted up their dog to hug him. "He found us, you know. Not the other way around."

"Yeah." Ty scratched Wicket's chin, and Wicket licked the back of his hand. "Can't imagine our lives without him."

Chapter 33

Five Years Earlier

Ty and Dani climbed into their car, and the unspoken feeling of failure crowded the interior of their white Toyota Corolla. The absence of a dog frustrated them.

Of all the things that becoming an exorcist's sword meant he had to do, Ty hated this the most: finding a dog.

Dani placed a hand on his arm. "They weren't right for us."

Ty could tell by all the things she didn't say that she sensed he was troubled, even if she didn't get why.

"No, they weren't right for us."

When they'd gotten here, they'd parked in front of the Richmond SPCA, a red brick building in the northern part of the city. They'd gone inside optimistic about their chances of finding a dog. Most of the exorcist's swords had come here for their dogs. Ty and Dani had first looked at a pale brown pit bull who'd mostly strolled around the room sniffing at everything and ignored them. The other dog, a black lab, had run wild through the room, but for all of its excitement, the dog hadn't shown any interest in the humans sharing the space with him.

Dani rubbed his arm. "Not that this isn't a big deal, but for a guy who always loves to pet our neighbors' dogs, you act like this is torture."

He took her hand into his. "I had a dog growing up. Mocha was this sweet, sixty pound mutt. I think she had some golden retriever in her, but no guessing what went into her DNA. Wasn't the brightest dog, but a lot of fun. When my friends and I would play superheroes in my backyard, I'd put a cape on her, so she could be my sidekick."

Dani covered her mouth, but failed to hold in her snort laugh. "That is ridiculously adorable and about the dopiest thing you've ever admitted to me. I'll bet you two were insanely cute."

He laughed. "I was a cute kid. I even had a girlfriend when I was three."

"Oh, really?" She pulled back at that, giving him The Look. "Who is this girl I gotta go kill now?"

Ty raised his hands, pretending to hold her back. "Susie. I think. Couldn't guess her last name if I tried, so good luck finding her."

"Oh, I will find her."

"I don't doubt it." He grinned and gave her a peck on the lips. "Look. The point is that Mocha died after I went away to college." He stopped there, because he could feel the tears threatening to come out as if it happened last week.

She placed her fingertips on Ty's mouth. "I understand, and if you're not ready for this today, then we wait. At some point, we have to do this, though. We can't navigate Hell without a dog."

He kissed her fingers. "I know."

"Those two dogs were wrong for us, though. If we're doing this, we aren't going to settle. They have to be the perfect dog for the Cortez-Faison Dream Team."

They were the only members from their group who'd yet to find their dog. Madison had gotten a Great Pyrenees and named her Cinto.

That stooge Nelson had gotten a Rottweiler and named it Hercules. Others had gotten Dobermans and German Shepherds.

He looked out the window at the dog shelter. "You said we might check another place?"

"There's a shelter south of the river in Chesterfield."

"Then let's go now." He let out a long breath. "Let's just do it."

She leaned her head against his shoulder for a moment and then kissed him on the cheek.

There weren't many people in the lot as Ty and Dani pulled up to the grey brick, single-story building. The shelter was located on a street behind a shopping center. After telling the staff they were there to get a dog, they followed one of the shelter workers into the room where the dogs were kept in their cages. The space here looked more cramped than the other dog shelter. The dogs barked, and it was hard to tell which were barking at Ty and Dani and which ones were simply barking at the other dogs because they were barking.

He exchanged smiles with Dani, but he felt sick to his stomach. Memories of Mocha, of not being there when she passed, were bad enough. What they required of a dog went beyond dangerous, and part of him wondered if they even had a right to do that to an animal. All that was true, but in the end, he didn't want to have to eventually lose another dog.

The tall cages on this row housed the larger breeds. He noticed a hyper husky barking and then spinning in circles, possibly chasing its own tail. A tan and black dog with pointy ears like an Australian Cattle Dog growled as Ty passed her.

"Ty!"

Dani's shout drew him to the row over where the cages were smaller and stacked on top of each other. She stood next to the shelter worker, a woman with long brown hair and round glasses.

"Look at him," Dani pointed to the cage on the top row next to her. "He looks like a small Benji dog!"

"Benji?"

"The dog from the movies? How do you not know Benji?" She pointed to the small fluff ball of light and dark brown fur in the cage. Big, round black eyes stared out at Ty. The dog's head tilted a bit to the left as he silently studied this human.

"Well, he's definitely one of the quieter dogs," Ty said, "but he's kind of small, isn't he?"

A part of him couldn't stand the idea of the other exorcist's swords mocking them if they showed up with this tiny fluff nugget.

"What kind of dog is he?" Ty asked the shelter worker.

"We believe he's a silky terrier mix." She had this knowing smile, as if amused that he wanted to "pretend" to hesitate about this dog. If she had any clue why they were getting a dog, she'd probably have called Dani nuts and sent them both over to the larger dogs. No, this animal loving lady would probably send them packing and curse them out into the parking lot for wanting to take any innocent creature into the bowels of Hell.

The shelter worker cleared her throat and pointed at the cage. "Would you like to meet him in our back room?"

"Yes!" Dani answered before Ty could insist they weren't interested.

He held in his sigh as the shelter worker led them into the back. The previous place had several rooms with glass doors that were tidy with benches to sit on. This room had brick walls painted yellow with a sofa and two comfy chairs that had the trademark look of second-hand donations victimized by one-too-many cat claws and dog bites. Ty and Dani sat in the comfy chairs, and once they were alone, Ty finally spoke up.

"This is a bad idea."

"Tell me that's not the cutest dog you've ever seen."

He leaned towards her and lowered his voice. "We're supposed to be getting a dog that can guide us through the horrors of Hell, not a tiny decoration for our apartment."

The scowl she fixed him with made it clear she wasn't taking any shit from him on this. "Fine, then let's talk serious. Every dog in there is barking like an idiot, but that clever little boy kept quiet. Did you not see those come-hither eyes he was hitting me with? That dog is smart, and I'd rather have a clever guide than an attack dog whose best bite won't amount to a pinprick against a demon."

Thankfully, the shelter worker returned before Ty was forced to respond with a counterargument he didn't have. The shelter worker led in the dog on a thin, blue leash. The dog pranced in there as if he owned the place and then stood in the center of the room while the shelter worker sat on the sofa.

"If you like," she said, still sporting that knowing smile, "we can let him wander around a bit."

"Sure," Dani said.

As soon as the worker unhooked the leash, the dog walked over to Ty's chair and hopped up into his lap, making himself right at home. Reflex kicked in, and Ty petted the dog's silky fur. When the dog glanced over at Dani, Ty could tell there was a satisfied look on the furball's face, as if he was the one making the decision here.

Dani's face lit up at the sight of them together, and that was it. That icy dread that had plagued Ty from the start of this exercise finally cracked.

He smiled over at Dani and nodded his surrender.

Their dog had found them.

Chapter 34

Wicket's barks woke Ty to get more demon arms whenever the fire got too low. Wasn't the most pleasant sleep he'd ever gotten, but it did the job. One arm woke him without Wicket needing to bark. The arm cracked open and large pellets rolled out. Each one popped like a balloon as the flames consumed them.

Dani and Ty set out at sunup, not that they could see a sun. The sky turned more white than grey. Wicket must have gotten enough rest, because he'd regained his snow-hopping momentum.

"We might have to burn these clothes." Dani waved a hand in front of her face to dispel the unpleasant stench. "I don't think there's any way we'll ever get the stink of burned demon carcass out of them."

"Are you kidding? Like that blood swamp alone wasn't the death knell for these outfits?"

They'd gotten halfway down a hill when they spotted an oddly shaped pile of snow that pulsed. It sat on the edge of a cluster of waist-deep bodies. If they had any doubts as to the nature of the thing, Wicket's growls as they drew closer confirmed they needed to give it a wide berth. He led them far off to the right of the thing before taking them in the direction he'd originally been hopping.

"I don't think that was snow." Dani kept looking over her shoulder, as if she expected it to chase after them. "Looked like a giant egg covered in white fur."

"Yeah, the way it kept expanding and contracting, I think it was breathing. Maybe it's the granddaddy to those killer Kooshes we had to get away from yesterday."

Ty couldn't deny his relief that they'd avoided more of those tiny monsters. The pulsing furry egg was the only other sign of real life they'd encountered since arriving in this realm, assuming they didn't count the beings trapped in ice.

His feet hurt from having walked for more than a week. Little doubt he'd gotten a few blisters out of this. All their previous trips to Hell had helped them build up plenty of calluses, but they'd never done this much walking.

Ty checked his watch. The countdown left them with a little less than two days. He debated on telling Dani, but then he saw the deep lines on her face. She knew, and if she didn't, then she'd guessed it.

The hours flowed like an hourglass filled with sand soaked in molasses. The wind hammered them as they descended a path along the side of a steep hill. While the realm didn't freeze them, the chill still made them uncomfortable when the wind joined in. Wicket stopped with each gust, crouching down as if to dig his paws into the land. Ty and Dani clung to the side of the hill, praying the wind didn't cause an avalanche to fall on them.

Then a blue sun in a red sky shone through a gap in the fast-moving clouds.

"Look down there," Dani pointed into the valley. A Hell gate shimmered there. "Think that might be the one Wicket is leading us to?"

"Given our luck, probably." The initial joy Ty had felt at the sight of the Hell gate vanished when he took in all that surrounded it. The most half-buried demons and souls he'd seen in this realm crowded the valley. Even worse, eight of the giant furry, breathing eggs ringed the gate.

"Whatever those things are," Dani said, "they're predators taking advantage of a choke point."

Ty agreed. Anything entering this realm from the gate would get attacked before they even had a chance to take in their surroundings. They might not have the element of surprise for anyone trying to escape this realm through the gate, but their numbers and formation made it impossible to get past them without a fight.

"They've got to be the reason for all of the bodies buried up to their waists." Ty pointed to the crowd of trapped beings. "Seems like that would explain why there are so many of them down there."

"I'm starting to lean towards the idea they aren't buried in the ground," Dani said with an undertone of revulsion.

"What? You think the big furry eggs eat the legs and then freeze what's left to the ground? That much trauma should kill the demons and make them regenerate in their home realm."

Dani looked at him like he'd lost his mind. "You're telling me that getting buried in ice and solid rock isn't traumatic? Either way, it doesn't make sense, and I don't care to find out the hard way which of us is right. Thank you, no!"

Wicket, oblivious to the content of their argument, ran behind them, because they'd stopped walking. He growled his impatience and turned his body to the side as if to shove them onward, same as he did at home when he decided they needed to go to bed. For a fifteen-pound scrap of a dog, Wicket possessed all the herding power of a hundred pound sheepdog.

They continued down the hill, silent for a while as they considered how to avoid getting surrounded by the predators at the gate.

Chapter 35

One Year Earlier

Ty and Dani drove their white Corolla past the expensive brick houses with vast lawns until they reached her mom's house. Maria's two-story, white brick house with a purple front door sat on a corner lot of Monument Avenue in Richmond's West End. As soon as Ty parked the car on the side of the road, the front door opened and Pastor Sebastian strolled out, already dressed in his priest clothes: black shirt with the collar and black pants.

He climbed into the back seat of the Corolla, the smell of smoke strong on him, even though he didn't have a cigarette lit. "Thanks for picking me up for this one. My Rav is in the shop."

They'd gotten the call yesterday afternoon for an exorcism out in Powhatan. This one wasn't getting the usual vetting that a request for an exorcism might, because the victim was a six-year-old. Demons rarely possessed children, because the bond between a demon and their host normally lasted for the host's entire remaining life span. Possession allowed demons to sustain themselves off of a single soul for an extended period of time, but most demons didn't want to get trapped in a human for that long, especially given the way modern medicine prolonged lives. Sure the demon could push the host to kill themselves, but that wasn't as easy to accomplish as it sounded, and the demon suffered the pain of their host's body. Demons could vacate a host prior to death, but doing it without the death of the host sometimes killed the demon. In situations like this, when the victim was this young, the Order performed the evaluation and the exorcism on the same day.

"I thought you already got your car fixed?" Dani asked as Ty swung their car around to drive towards the Monument Avenue ramp merging onto the Powhite Parkway.

Sebastian grunted. "Your mother is pressuring me to take my car out to the country and set it on fire to collect the insurance."

"Yep!" Ty laughed. "That sounds like Maria and another woman I know." He hit Dani with a bit of good-humored side-eye.

Dani answered with a middle finger salute. "She's not wrong, though."

Sebastian groaned, his head bobbing around with his frustration. "I'm trying to save my money for other things right now."

Ty sensed he and Dani were being baited into asking. That wasn't usually Sebastian's style, but that's also why it worked enough to make Dani ask, "Such as?"

"Well, that depends a little on you, Daniella." Sebastian leaned forward his elbow resting on the back of Ty's seat.

Dani and Ty exchanged a look before she shifted her focus to Sebastian. "Do tell."

"Would you grant me your blessing to have me as your stepfather? Because I'd like to get your mother a diamond ri"—He stop short as Dani punched him in the arm. "Ow!"

"What the fuck has taken you this long, you insufferable ass?"

Sebastian leaned back into his seat, rubbing his wounded arm. "Ty, you care translate that for the Dani-impaired?"

Ty snort laughed. "That's Dani-speak for 'Yes.' You have her blessing."

"Good to know. To answer your question, Dani, I'd have asked her years ago, but Maria always goes on about how she has no interest in ever getting married again."

"Ugh." Dani rolled her eyes. "How dense are you? Have you not noticed that she's the one who is always finding ways to bring that up with you around?"

The car fell silent as Sebastian and Ty both processed that. "Huh," Ty eventually mused. "The apple didn't fall far from the tree on that one."

He felt Dani's scowl but opted not to look her way to confirm it. Thankfully, she spared his arm from any punches as she returned her focus to Sebastian.

"In my defense," Sebastian said, "I'd have to be around your mom when I'm not around your mom in order to know she only brings that up when I'm around her." He moved a finger through the air as if to copyedit what he'd said and then appeared to nod to himself that he'd said it right.

"Not an excuse." Dani sighed. "If you want my advice, don't plan out anything fancy. Don't take her to a restaurant or some romantic setting. Propose to her at home over a bottle of wine. She'll say, 'No.' Then you argue with her about it until she twists it around to make it where the idea to get married is hers and then you tell her 'Yes'. You should have sex somewhere in there, probably during the argument. Sex afterwards is probably also a good idea, so take your vitamins beforehand."

"Ew." Ty shook in revulsion as he drove them south on Powhite Parkway. "I did not need those details."

"Yes, but he obviously does."

Ty saw in his review mirror as Sebastian shrugged. "She's right."

"I didn't think priests could get married," Ty said.

"That's Catholic priests," Sebastian said. "We Episcopalians are Catholic-lite: all the ceremony without the guilt. Well, some of the guilt, just not all of it."

Sebastian's plans for a successful proposal occupied most of the drive until they made it out into the rural portions of Powhatan County, southwest of Richmond.

"From what I've been told, these people are some serious fish out of water," Sebastian said from the back seat where he'd started to get visibly twitchy from the need for a hit of nicotine. "They moved out here a little less than a year ago, when the problems with the daughter started. The parents were hoping that getting her out of the city and into a place with more conservative values would help."

Ty didn't see Sebastian's face, but he didn't miss the added emphasis he placed on "conservative values." They'd heard his rant enough times about what a load of hypocritical bullshit went along with so-called conservative ideals.

"Bet you tonight's first round of Guinness that the parents are the real problem that got this kid in this predicament."

"We're not about to let you buy the drinks tonight, because you've got a ring to save up for," Dani said as they turned onto a dirt road leading up to a large, two-story house of white brick and a bright red pair of front doors. The front of the house even had a deck with four white, wooden pillars that went all the way up to the roof of the house.

"Who lives here?" Ty asked. "The President?"

Sebastian leaned forward for a better look and growled. "Well, this probably also explains how this one got rushed. Money talks, even in the church. Let's get in there and find out how bad things really are."

Chapter 36

One Year Earlier

Walking up the front steps, Sebastian shivered. This wasn't a little shake, but a full-body shimmy of discomfort.

"Jesus, this place fucking reeks," he said.

Ty didn't pick up on the bad vibes, but he'd come to trust Sebastian on these things. "Well, at least we didn't waste our time making a trip to the middle of nowhere." He patted the hilt of the sword on his hip.

"Be ready, you two," Sebastian said. "This one is gonna be bad. Always is when it's a child."

The door to the right cracked open and a man who looked to be in his late forties with disheveled salt-and-pepper hair stared out at them. To Ty's surprise, he looked less disturbed as he took in Ty and Dani with their swords than when his gaze settled on Sebastian.

Sebastian stepped forward and held out his hand. "Mr. Kincaid, despite the circumstances, a pleasure to meet you."

The man raised a hand to beg off shaking. "Sorry," he said with a sniffle, "I've had a cold. Wouldn't want to get you sick, too."

"Of course."

Mr. Kincaid pulled the door open for them. The place reminded Ty of the mansion where he and Sebastian first met; although, this place put Heathcliff's home to shame. A set of stairs, shaped like a giant horseshoe, led upstairs, and the open doors on the first floor, beneath the landing led into several other rooms. Ty wondered how far back this house went.

"Let me get my wife." Mr. Kincaid called out towards the second floor. "Karen, they're here!"

Karen appeared on the upstairs landing and descended on the right to meet with them. She looked much younger than her husband, twenty-five at the most. She'd dyed her long hair bleach blonde and wore bright red lipstick. Her white blouse and khaki pants suggested she'd dressed to match her husband, who also wore a white shirt with khaki pants.

The wife slipped her arm through her husband's as she stood beside him. "We're so grateful you're here. Gavin and I really do hope you can help our little Claire."

Ty fought down the urge to grab his sword when another person appeared from one of the side rooms.

"Oh!" Mr. Kincaid pointed to the young man who might have been close to fifteen, which had Ty suspecting Karen was his stepmother. "This is our son, Alan."

Alan greeted them with a sloppy two-finger salute and a wiggle of his blonde eyebrows. He sported a buzz cut and, like his parents, wore a white shirt with khaki pants.

"Has the doctor gotten here yet?" Sebastian glanced around as if he expected to see her.

Karen shook her head and placed her free hand to her chest. "Goodness, no. Was she supposed to get here first?"

"I suppose she's running behind," Sebastian said. "Why don't I give you a little bit of an idea what to expect. First of all, we won't offer you our names. It's important for what we do that we remain anonymous. You may simply refer to me as Priest or Pastor and this young man and woman each as Sword. He-Sword or She-Sword works, too," he said, making it clear by his tone he intended that as a bit of levity. None of the Kincaids laughed much less looked like they caught he'd made a joke.

As Sebastian launched into a speech that Ty had heard him deliver dozens of times, Dani leaned over to whisper into Ty's ear. "We would have totally lost that bet."

He nodded his agreement. These three could pass as extras from a Southern knock-off version of *The Stepford Wives*. No wonder their girl was so fucked up.

After Sebastian finished his routine and took a few of their questions, he asked a question of his own.

"So, where is Claire?"

Mr. Kincaid and his wife exchanged an uncomfortable look. They directed their eyes to the floor as if ashamed to meet anyone's gaze.

Karen answered for them. "She's in her room upstairs." She closed her eyes and buried her face against her husband's shoulder. "We had to tie her down to keep her from hurting herself." Her voice broke on the last few words.

"Please don't judge us. We didn't know what else to do." Mr. Kincaid kissed the top of Karen's head. "I can take you to her."

Sebastian shook his head. "It's best if you wait here so we can meet with her alone to make our evaluation. While it might not seem a comforting thought, with any luck, we'll determine if it's a mental health issue better handled by a doctor."

Ty knew Sebastian well enough after all these years to recognize the priest didn't believe that. He knew this was the real deal before they'd come in the front door. If Ty were to place a wager, he'd bet Sebastian knew it even before he left Maria's house.

"Go to the right when you get upstairs," Mr. Kincaid said as Karen clung to him and sobbed. "Her door is the only one that's closed."

Sebastian nodded to the Kincaids and then gestured for Ty and Dani to follow him.

Once they got upstairs and out of ear shot, Dani whispered, "In terms of creepy, the Addams Family has nothing on these people. Yikes."

Ty opted against voicing his agreement that there were realms in Hell less disturbing than the clothing-coordinated Kincaids.

Their footsteps echoed along the wood panel floors. The closed door waited at the end of the hall.

"Let me do the talking," Sebastian said before he opened the door.

Ty went in last and closed the door behind them. The room embodied "textbook suburban white girl" with pink walls, a white four-poster bed with pink, gauzy canopy curtains. The room even included a Taylor Swift poster over a white desk by the windows. Lots of throw pillows and stuffed animals covered the bed.

Claire sat in the middle of the room. She'd missed the family's dress code memo, wearing an orange t-shirt with a cartoon image of a porcupine on it and blue jeans. She looked small for a six-year-old. As the Kincaids warned them, Claire sat tied to a dark brown wooden chair too big for her and looked like her parents had borrowed it from another room. The stench of urine choked the air enough to make Ty want to gag. The poor kid had peed on herself, probably multiple times, and the parents had left out that they'd gagged the poor thing. She didn't look up at them, and her head drooped forward so that her brown hair obscured most of her face.

Sebastian knelt in front of Claire and carefully pulled the linen gag down so that it hung around her throat like a necklace.

"Hello, Claire." Sebastian placed a hand on her left forearm. "We're here to help you."

She coughed as she tried to speak. Even as the coughing subsided, she struggled to talk. The words came out in a croak, suggesting it had been some time since she'd last had anything to drink.

Ty stood to Sebastian's left and Dani took his right.

"Your parents think you're troubled, Claire. Can you tell me a little about what's been happening with you?"

The words came out muffled. Her eyes were wide and reminded Ty of an animal caught in a trap.

"I'm sorry, Claire, but I can't understand what you're saying."

She closed her eyes tight and swallowed several times. When she opened her eyes again, they looked straight ahead at Sebastian. No child should have to wear an expression that hard. Lord, no child should have to endure any of this.

"It's not me."

"I know." Sebastian squeezed her arm, trying to give her what comfort he could. "You can't help it. We understand that."

"It's them."

"Them?" Sebastian jerked back as if he'd cut his hand by touching her. "There's more than one? How many are there?"

Ty looked over at Dani to see if her shock mirrored his, because this wasn't normal. Even though legends existed about people being possessed by more than one demon, the Order of the Emerald Blades had never documented any occurrences of that. One demon for one person—that's how it worked. Dani didn't look shocked, though. She stared off into space, seemingly distracted by something else.

"How many are there?" Sebastian asked again.

"All of them!" She had regained her voice, and there was no missing the frustration and anger behind her words. "It's not me! It's them!"

Sebastian looked confused, and took a moment before he could form his next question. "Claire, can you tell me how many voices you've been hearing?"

"No! It's them!"

Before Sebastian could try a different question, Dani grabbed his shoulder.

"They knew the doctor meeting us is a woman." She shook her head and looked ready to jump out the window. "They couldn't have known that."

Claire shook her chair. "It's not me! It's them!"

Sebastian looked at the girl. His lips quivered. "Oh, God."

"It's them!"

Chapter 37

One Year Earlier

The click clacks of shotguns being armed in the hallway offered the only warning they got.

Ty and Dani ran for the far sides of the room. As the first bullets fired through the bedroom door, Sebastian flipped the girl's chair onto its back and dropped to the floor in front of Claire. He covered his head with his hands.

When the bullets stopped, Ty and Dani moved closer to the door. The hurried clicks of reloading warned another volley was coming. Then the door kicked open. Two barrels, aimed at Sebastian, passed over the threshold of the bedroom.

Ty and Dani moved in unison. Without a spoken word, they grabbed the hot barrels of the shotguns, shoved them up towards the ceiling and yanked as hard as possible.

Karen and her "son" stumbled forward against one another. Karen held onto her rifle by one hand as Dani struggled against her for control of it, but the son lost his gun to Ty.

Ty slammed the butt of the shotgun into the son's face, knocking him senseless. As the son fell to the floor, Mr. Kincaid fired at Ty. The bullet missed Ty and shattered the nearest corner of the four-poster bed.

Ty retreated away from the door before Mr. Kincaid could fire another shot.

On the other side of the room, Karen and Dani fought over the shotgun. When Mr. Kincaid fired again, the bullet nailed Karen in the back of her left shoulder. The woman lost her grip of the gun and spun to the floor.

Claire screamed and shouted, but Ty couldn't make sense of her words.

Dani cocked the shotgun and fired into the hallway at Mr. Kincaid. These weren't innocent victims of some demons. For the demons to have this much control of their hosts and to work together, the hosts were willing victims.

Dani's shot into the hallway didn't hit Mr. Kincaid. He shot at Dani, but only shattered a window along the far wall of the bedroom. As he started to reload his pump action shotgun, Dani bolted out of the bedroom, grabbed the barrel of his gun and slammed it up into his face, sending him onto his back.

Karen cursed in pain from where she writhed on the floor. Ty left her alone to focus on the son, who crab crawled on his back away from the bedroom as Ty emerged. The son tried to get to his feet, but Ty pounced on him with his sword. He didn't cut him. Instead, he smashed in the son's face with the sword's pommel. The boy screamed, grabbed a switchblade from his pants pocket and slashed at Ty's leg, catching him on the calf. Ty slammed his sword's blade down through the boy's chest. The boy didn't scream. He eyes stared up in shock, and when Ty ripped the sword free in a spray of blood, the boy gasped his last breath.

Mr. Kincaid bled out onto the floor from his throat with Dani standing over him. Blood dripped off the tips of both her swords.

She glared over her shoulder, her eyes going straight to Ty's leg.

He nodded his reassurance to her. "I'm good."

Karen continued to curse and scream in the bedroom. Dani used Kincaid's pants to wipe his blood off her left hand sword and then slid the blade into its scabbard. She marched past Ty into the bedroom and grabbed Karen by the shirt collar and yanked her up.

The woman—her shoulder a bloody mess—shrieked in pain. She spat at Dani but the effort missed the mark, landing mostly on her own shirt.

Off to the side, Claire had stopped screaming, her cries reduced to whimpers.

"Lord Revol sends his best." Karen laughed as pain-filled tears ran down her cheeks.

Dani pressed her sword's tip against Karen's throat. "If you're his best, then I'm not impressed."

"We will slay you all, same as your priest." Karen grabbed Dani's arm and then shoved the sword into her own throat.

Ty looked over at Sebastian and Claire. The priest hadn't moved since the start of the attack.

"Sebastian?" Ty ran over to him. Blood soaked the back of his black shirt. When he touched the wound, Sebastian shook.

"Hurts." The word bubbled out of Sebastian's mouth without any of his usual bravado.

Ty rolled him over, holding him in his lap. Dani ran over to them. "Is he all right?"

"Been," he paused to cough, blood spilling out over his chin, "better."

He reached up and grabbed Dani's hand. His eyes fluttered as he struggled to speak and choked on the words. His hand slipped and then reached up to grab her forearm.

"Tell...love her."

The air rattled out of him as all the tension left his body.

Chapter 38

One Year Earlier

The rest of that day turned into a long blur that Ty couldn't fully remember and would never forget. Dani performed CPR while Ty tried to call for an ambulance with his cell, only to discover there was no service. His search through the mansion for a landline led him to phones with their cords cut and the doctor's body in the basement.

Sebastian had saved the girl, though. They cut her loose from the chair, and threw her into their car to drive until they reached a place with cell service.

Ty made the call. Dani didn't speak and just stared out the passenger window.

"Zuma, we need a clean up crew."

"Why are you calling me? You should be contacting Maria."

Ty's throat clenched. He couldn't breathe as he struggled to force out the words and couldn't.

"Are you there?" Zuma's irritated voice gave Ty the emotional kick in the gut to find his words again.

"Pastor Shannon and the doctor are dead."

Dani's hands rested in her lap with Sebastian's dried blood on them. Her fingers curled into fists.

Ty heard Zuma whisper a curse. "Is Dani?"—

"We weren't hurt, and there's a six-year-old girl here who's gonna need a lot of help. The demons were holding her captive." Ty had gotten enough out of her to learn the demons holding her weren't even possessing members of her actual family. They'd abducted her from her home in Illinois before bringing her here and had kept her tied up in that place for days. Hopefully, her real family was still alive, and the Order could reunite them. She hadn't said anything to suggest the demons hurt her loved ones when they kidnapped her.

Ty drove them back to the mansion, much to Claire's horror, despite Ty's reassurances. They washed off what blood they could as they waited for the clean-up crew to arrive to get rid of the bodies and remove any blood stains. Ty wasn't sure if they'd go so far as to repair the damage from the gunshots, but that wasn't his problem. Zuma arrived with the clean-up crew. As much as Ty despised the jerk, he'd always be grateful for the way he handled himself that day, looking out for the girl and for them.

Sitting in the mansion's living room, Ty told Zuma everything that happened, how the demons had set up the ambush and how they'd survived it and why Sebastian and the doctor hadn't. The real salt in the wound was that all three of the demons got away. They'd only killed the hosts, freeing the demons to go back to Hell or find new hosts.

"I haven't told Maria yet," Zuma said.

"I'll do it." They were the only words Dani had spoken since they'd left Sebastian's body to call for help.

"I don't think that's a good idea," Zuma said.

She glared up at him, and he relented.

Ty and Dani drove straight to Maria's house in silence. Ty had considered putting on some music, but he couldn't think of anything to play that wouldn't forever be tainted by the memory of Sebastian's death.

By the time they pulled into the same place they'd parked earlier that day in front of Maria's house, the sun had long since set. Dani wouldn't let Ty go inside with her. She insisted on doing this alone, and he didn't argue. He would've done it, if she'd wanted, but he'd be a liar to claim he wanted to be there in the moment Maria Cortez found out she'd lost her heart.

He sat there for three hours.

When Dani walked out, she climbed into the passenger seat without looking at him. Her body heaved, and she held it together as she gritted her teeth, not letting the tears out. She slammed her fists on the dash board again and again until she cracked it and then pressed her fists as hard as she could against her temples.

When she pulled her fists away, she gasped for breath until she could speak. Her rage was a cold thing that he'd never seen from her and hoped he'd never see again.

"We are going home," she said each word as if forging a blade with the heat of her voice. "We are getting Wicket and our gear, and we are going into Hell tonight to find this demon and kill him."

He kissed her, and then they did exactly what she'd said.

Interlude 6

One Year Earlier

Char and Malum rode their dovras down the Arch Highway with only moonlight to guide them. Premier Revol had sent them to check the rumors that of a pair of exorcists had entered the realm, searching for him.

A half-dozen whiters were dispatched with them, all traveling on their own dovras. Char trusted Malum, but he got the uneasy feeling that these soldiers were sent to spy on them or betray them, rather than provide extra swords for a fight. Revol was a whiter and tended to prefer dealing with his own kind. That Char was a wolf and Malum a steed meant that the rest of Revol's lieutenants either saw this as a fool's errand or suicide.

As the Arch Highway led them through a forest of petrified trees, Char caught the scent of death, rot, and brimstone.

"Up ahead." Char pointed to a shadow swaying beneath a petrified tree on the side of the road. "A body."

As they neared the tree, the moonlight provided enough light to make out the details. Someone had cut off a whiter's head and ripped out its heart and then placed them in the road. The body hung upside down by a rope, directly above its excised parts, from a bare tree branch.

The black blood, having drained out of the demon's neck, covered the head and heart.

Malum chuckled as he halted his dovra at the edge of the blood-stained dirt. "Charming."

Char dismounted his dovra and knelt close enough to sniff the head and heart. Through the stench of decay, he caught something else. "Humans."

Malum snorted his amusement as he clapped his taloned hands together. "Seems the rumors are true."

"But they left the head and heart here?" One of the whiters said, his nose wrinkled in offense at the stench.

"Yes," Malum said, loud enough for his words to carry to anyone hiding in the woods. "It's a message that they know how to kill our kind."

Char walked over to Malum. He lowered his voice. "It's a trap to distract us."

Malum took Char by the arm and pulled him closer as he whispered. "Do you catch their scent?"

Char sniffed again and shook his head. "If they're here, they're keeping downwind."

"Oh, they're here." Malum's long chin rested against his upper chest as he considered that. When he looked up, his red eyes shifted from one side of the road to the other. He went towards the whiters and pointed to the most muscular of the group.

"You, with me and Char. We'll search the woods on this side. The rest of you search the other."

Malum didn't wait for an acknowledgment from the others. He drew his sword and stalked into the woods on the side that the wind came from and would certainly not contain the humans.

The whiters took their time to move until Char growled at them. They might not respect him or Malum, but they feared them.

"Stay close to me, fool!" Malum snapped at the whiter following him.

Char stayed a few steps behind the whiter. He drew his sword, holding it ready, not to fight the exorcists but to defend Malum if this whiter tried anything.

When the first scream came from the other side of the road, the whiter turned his back to Malum to run for the fight. He didn't make it two steps before Malum beheaded him.

Malum scratched the long bridge of his nose and then strolled to the edge of the woods. Another whiter cried out from the other side of the road, followed by several shrieks.

Before Char could march out to join the fight, Malum placed a hand on his chest to stop him. They stayed hidden in the shadows.

A whiter, missing his right forearm, limped out of the woods from the opposite side of the road. A man with a black beard emerged from the shadows, behind the whiter, and slashed his head off with a single swing of his sword. He wiped the demon's black blood from his blade with a cloth hanging from his belt.

As Malum walked out of the woods, he made a show of putting his sword into the scabbard on his hip. "I take it that's the last of my whiters?" Malum asked the human.

Char kept his sword ready to strike, but Malum reached over to block him. "Put it away."

Despite his respect for Malum, Char kept his sword in his hand, but he did lower it.

The human also kept his sword ready. He looked around, probably suspecting Malum wanted to distract him while other demons might attack from a different direction.

"It's just these two left." The voice belonged to a woman with long, black hair who emerged from the same side of the road where Malum and Char had been. She held two swords. A small hound strolled out of the woods behind her and growled at the two demons.

Char raised his sword again even as he wondered how this woman had managed to get this close without him smelling her. Malum glared at him. "I said to put that away."

"What?" The male sounded amused. He moved to stand beside the woman. "You two plan to offer your necks instead of fighting?"

Malum walked towards the humans with his arms held out to show he had no intention of drawing his own sword.

"I think it unlikely my head is the one you want."

"We want Revol." The woman shook with half-controlled rage. Malum grinned at the sight of her bloodlust.

Char stayed put, ready to fight. What game was his friend playing?

Malum pointed down the Arch Highway in the direction from which they'd traveled. "You'll find him in the city of Vel, but you will not take his head and heart so easily as this one." He pointed to the body they'd strung up.

"We're aware of that." The man spun his sword. "We want to know how we get around his defenses."

"Give us what we want to know, and we'll make this quick." She tapped her sword blades together to make her point, offering an efficient and temporary death in return for the information.

Char growled his opinion, but Malum's condescending look silenced him.

Malum approached the exorcists with no sign of concern.

"You think you can simply invade our realm and eliminate the one who rules it all, and that will be the end of it?" Malum shook his head, causing his red mane to shake in a wave down his back.

"Something like that." The woman sounded as eager for a fight as Char.

"Then you are either a fool or woefully naive."

"He started this. We're here to finish it."

"Revol's war with you exorcists is simply his way of appeasing his followers." Malum stopped within reach of the exorcists but crossed his arms without any sign of concern. "Strike him down, and the one who replaces him will only push back all the harder."

The woman moved to attack, but her partner grabbed her by the shoulder to stop her. Char raised his sword. Malum could order him to put it away all he liked. So long as his friend stood threatened by these humans, Char intended to defend him.

"If you have a point," the male said, his free hand still resting on the woman's shoulder to keep her from striking, "then get to it."

"To stop Revol's war, you need to destroy him and the ones who support it." Malum snickered as he turned his back to them and walked over to Char. "And you must kill them all in one night."

"This sounds like horse shit to me," the woman said with a hate-filled smile at her pun.

Char lowered his voice so only Malum heard him. "You cannot bargain with rabid animals."

Malum whispered to him. "On the contrary, they are the most negotiable."

"Care to share with the rest of the class?" The man removed his hand from the woman's shoulder. He also gave his sword another spin, eager for things to turn to bloodshed.

"My companion believes I am foolish to bargain with you."

"We're not here to bargain," the woman said. "We want Revol. That's it."

"Then you will return soon after for his successor when they take another life you value. Revol has six lieutenants, so you will need to make this same trip five more times. Each time, you will find them more prepared for you. How soon before your desire to burn heads and hearts gets you killed?"

"If there are six lieutenants serving Revol, then why would we only have to come back five times?" The way the man asked the question left little doubt he'd already guessed.

"When I made my oath to Revol, I swore to protect his realm. I never promised to protect him. The other five lieutenants desire your order wiped out."

The woman rolled her eyes. "And we're supposed to believe you don't want to kill us?"

"Oh, I'd love to, but I respect the natural order of things. You want revenge, and I crave power. As for your deaths, mortal lives are fragile, and I am patient. I see no need to hasten your end. That would benefit neither of us."

Malum approached them.

"I only ask that you exorcists grant me a chance to prove myself. Let us sit and speak of the defenses to Vel, the demons you need to kill, and where to find them."

The man placed himself between Malum and the woman. "And what do you expect in return?"

"A few drops of blood, freely given, but only after I have fulfilled my part of our agreement."

Char realized what his friend wanted: the means to walk in the world of mortals, not as a phantom but as a being of flesh and blood. Blood freely given and painted upon a demon's skin allowed them to walk among the living. That also explained how an excised demon had a physical form. Their host's blood covered them when they emerged.

"Not a chance." The woman shook her head. "We're not fools."

Malum glared at the exorcists, but he feigned the disapproval. Char smelled the satisfaction on him. He knew these humans would refuse him. Char couldn't figure out why that pleased his friend.

The human male canted his head to the side, studying Malum as if he could read him with more ease than Char could. "If we kill Revol and his supporters, that puts you in charge, right?"

Malum held his silence for an uncomfortably long time. He stared across the space between them as he appeared to consider the human male's question. Then he nodded. "I would be raised as the new Premier."

"Seems to me you're already getting plenty out of this deal. You don't need our blood."

"And why should I believe you will not turn your swords on me once you've finished with the others?"

Char suspected Malum didn't consider that a real threat. He didn't share his friend's confidence.

The woman placed a hand on her partner's upper arm, giving him a nudge to move out of her way. "All we want is Revol's head and heart. If we have to take five more to get to him, then I'm willing to deal, but no blood and no names."

The man whispered to the woman. Char couldn't make out the words over the growls of their puny hound.

Char tightened his grip on his sword, expecting these exorcists to attack them. When Malum walked over to him, Char whispered, "You can't trust them."

"I have lived for hundreds of their lifetimes," Malum whispered. "The hearts and wills of these humans offer as little mystery to me as a simple yes or no. Love and rage cloud them both; they will honor our agreement so long as they get Revol."

"What if they fail and Revol realizes what we've done?"

Malum glared at him. "We have little time before Revol turns on us. We either strike now, or he will take his sword to us both."

"And it's only a matter of time before these humans turn on you."

Malum shook his head in frustration and snorted. "Of course, but tell me whose swords you fear more, Revol's or these blood-hungry humans?"

Char hated this bargain, but as foolish as he considered Malum's reasoning, even he couldn't argue against this point. They'd both known that as Malum's success increased and his position advanced, Revol and his other lieutenants would eventually cut him down. If Char hadn't already spoken his ironclad oath to Malum, he might have turned on him before now to protect himself from the unwanted attention he shared from his friend's ambition.

"If we plan this with them, then we can know exactly when to place a demon outside the Purgatory Arch they take to get here. A demon in their mortal world will be an invisible phantom to track them, and they will give us all we need to know. About them. About the Order. And when we accomplish what Revol and his followers could not, it will shore up my position of power within the Blood Realm forever."

Chapter 39

By the time they reached the valley of the Hell gate, the sun dropped near the horizon. The snow had kicked up again but light enough to see for a good distance. That didn't stop the snow from getting in their eyes. Not good for a fight.

"What do you think the chances are that those giant furry eggs might be hibernating, and we can walk right past them?" Dani asked.

Ty barked out one, sarcastic laugh. He knew Dani thought the same.

They stood at the edge of the cluster of half-buried bodies. Wicket danced along that edge, growling softly without stopping.

Kneeling down, Ty scratched Wicket's back. "He's eager for a good fight."

Dani grinned down at the terrier. "Aren't we all?"

Ty studied the field of frozen bodies. It reminded him of a previous venture into Hell. He and Dani had stumbled upon a cave realm with lots of stalagmites and stalactites biting up and down. They'd fought a gang of whiters there. Avoiding tripping or impaling themselves on some of those rocky points made for sloppy fighting. At least the demons had also struggled with the cave's protrusions. He suspected these furry eggs, once they decided to make their move, could somehow navigate this terrain more easily than they. He couldn't guess how, but a successful predator didn't set a trap in a place that left them at a disadvantage.

Ty pointed towards an opening in the bodies off to their left. "That's the clearest path that I can see."

"There's no way it's that simple, but if we need to run away, at least we can do it without tripping on anything." Dani drew both of her swords. Ty followed her lead.

"All right, Wicket." Dani mussed up the fur on his head. He grumbled at her, as if to complain that he didn't want to look cute in front of the big mean, furry eggs. "Let's go."

Wicket went quiet when he entered the path.

The snow stopped pelting down and floated on a light wind that came up behind them. A chill ran through Ty's back. The wind sent their scents up towards the predators.

Yes, they were walking into a trap, but sometimes that was the only way to figure out how the trap worked.

As they drew closer, the actual size of these furry eggs sent another chill through Ty's body, and that had nothing to do with the weather. Each one stood about fifteen feet tall. Nothing changed in the eggs, pulsing as if to breathe.

Among the half-buried bodies, a raven missing one of its wings watched Ty, Dani, and Wicket as they passed. Its shifting eyes followed their movements and seemed to scream they were fools to approach these predators.

They came within twenty feet of the giant eggs. This close, they heard the breath rushing in and out of the creatures in deep notes.

Then the breathing ceased.

Wicket stopped in his tracks.

Well, Ty thought to himself, so much for these things hibernating.

The closest pair of eggs at the end of their path split open along a jagged seam running top to bottom that the fur had hidden. Thousands of razor-sharp teeth ringed the slimy, pale blue insides of these creatures. A random corner of Ty's mind wondered if any monster in Hell had any other kind of teeth, with molars a woefully neglected piece of evolutionary design.

Ty and Dani retreated down the clear path the way they used to get here, but Wicket took off into the thick of the half-buried bodies.

"Wicket!" Dani shouted after him.

The giant eggs shrieked as they lumbered after Ty and Dani, and it dawned on Ty how odd it was that these things could catch anything moving like that.

The frozen bodies on the far edge of the field burst apart. Dozens of the killer Kooshes flew out of the shattered torsos and hopped up the clear path towards Ty and Dani, blocking their escape. Ty remembered when he'd used the demon arms for timber and how one arm had split open, spilling out burning pellets. The Kooshes used the half-buried bodies as incubators.

Ty and Dani followed Wicket's lead and ran into the bodies closer to the giant eggs in the hopes that their dog knew what he was doing. Possibly, the Koosh pods in these frozen bodies weren't ready to burst free to attack, and Wicket could sense it. His barks let them know where to go. He raced around to the far side of the gate.

The pair of giant eggs that had awakened each sprouted two pairs of long, insect-like legs and waded into the many rows of bodies.

As Ty and Dani followed Wicket's route, more bodies on the edge of the field erupted to free more of the killer Kooshes. Some hopped up and down on the edge, forming a perimeter to trap Ty, Dani, and Wicket within the field of bodies. Other Kooshes pursued them, jumping from frozen body to frozen body.

The direction of their dog's barks changed, heading straight for the gate.

Some of the frozen torsos exploded in the direction Ty and Dani were heading, freeing more of the Kooshes. Although, not all of the freed Kooshes moved. Many collapsed dead on the ground, freed before they'd finished gestating. As Ty swatted away one of the living newborns with his sword, he unintentionally stomped on one of the dead newborn Kooshes that looked like a slimy mass of undefined flesh and toothpick-thin bones.

All eight of the giant eggs had split open now and trudged into the field of frozen torsos. Their long, insect legs lifted their bodies above the frozen torsos, making it easy for them to pursue their prey.

Wicket burst into view at the gate, sprinting past the giant eggs, which shrieked at him.

"Those things sound pissed!" Dani slashed with her swords at a pair of the Kooshes that had leaped at her, slicing one in half. The other squawked as it launched high and away like a pissed-off baseball knocked into the outfield. Its descent collided with some of the other Kooshes, sending them spilling off the frozen bodies and to the ground.

One of the giant eggs leaped high and crashed down where Wicket had been. Its entire maw of a body snapped shut, but missed its prey. The giant egg wobbled in place for a few seconds before splitting open onto its spindly legs. Their dog weaved around the giant eggs, keeping them focused on him while Ty and Dani zigzagged through the frozen bodies. Most of the Kooshes massed together along the outer edge of the field of frozen torsos, more focused on keeping Ty and Dani trapped between them and the giant eggs. That left plenty of other Kooshes chasing after them, though.

Ty smashed into one of the frozen bodies, snapping off an arm when it punched into his gut. To his relief, that didn't release more Kooshes.

Wicket's game of chase frustrated the giant eggs. Several of them bit down at him in vain. Then one of the giant eggs lunged too far as it chomped down at Wicket and bit one of the other giant eggs in half. The other six giant eggs screamed in a mix of despair and rage.

Ty hoped the six might turn on the seventh that killed one of their own, same as the sewer scorpions in the blood swamp had turned on their wounded sibling, but no such luck.

He and Dani kept running as they swung at any of the killer Kooshes that leaped their way. A few overshot, landing in the direction of the gate. Ty feared the Kooshes might go after Wicket, but they seemed more interested in him and Dani.

The eggs' movements grew more frantic as Wicket's circuitous route foiled their attempts to turn him into an appetizer. Two of the eggs collided. Their giant mouths smashed into each other and sent them tumbling down onto the frozen bodies, crushing them and most of the Kooshes that were freed. The surviving Kooshes yelped as they fled in a panic, scared their bigger brothers were turning on them.

"That's our opening!" Dani pointed to where the two open-mouthed eggs struggled against each other to get up, as if engaged in the most perverse french kiss in history and no clue how to break free of it.

Dani slashed at the handful of Kooshes still between them and the gate. One Koosh bit on Ty's boot, but the leather held up against the sharp teeth long enough for Ty to swat it off.

Wicket antagonized the giant eggs, drawing the five still standing to the opposite side of the gate. When they heard Wicket yelp, Ty and Dani sprinted towards him.

The furball didn't bark or yelp as they shouted for him. As Ty and Dani reached the gate, Wicket darted out of the thicket of frozen bodies. Two of the giant eggs leaped after the dog at the same time and bounced off of each other. The two eggs fell onto their backs, their thin legs kicking at the air as they tried to right their bodies.

Wicket ran past Ty and Dani, vanishing into the swirling light of the gate. The few eggs that weren't immobile scrambled after Ty and Dani, but before they could get their teeth into either of them, Ty and Dani dove into the gate.

PART V

THE EDGE OF THE ABYSS

Chapter 40

Ty and Dani landed on their stomachs and scrambled to their feet. Wicket barked his relief to see both of his humans. He danced back and forth on the narrow strip of rock where the Hell gate deposited them.

When neither the killer Kooshes or the giant eggs emerged from the gate, Dani dropped to one knee. Ty leaned over with his hands on his knees, silently thanking God those creatures hadn't chased after them like the glow lizards had. Maybe the creatures found the environment here toxic or feared the gates. For now, Ty cracked his neck and then took in the realm into which they'd fallen.

The rocky path they stood on resembled the skeleton of a mountain. A green sky with no visible sun glowed above them. Wind whistled, as if trying to blow them off the edge of the narrow path. He glanced over the side and stared into a dark abyss.

A light flashed in the sky and plummeted past them and fell into the bottomless space that surrounded them. Before it disappeared into the shadows far below, Ty realized the falling light was a soul.

"Wonder if there's a bottom," Ty said.

Dani came up to the edge and stared down into the deep hole. "If there is, it's probably rocky and exactly where we'll end up."

Wicket walked up beside Dani, and she picked him up to check for injuries. His yelp had scared them both.

Ty stroked their dog's back and sighed in relief. "He looks all right."

Dani nodded, then kissed the top of Wicket's head. "Don't scare us like that again, okay?"

Wicket wriggled to get out of Dani's grip. She set him down. He stared up at them, with one of his front paws lifted off the ground, as if preparing to sprint.

The smell of Malum's rotting head and heart fouled the air as Dani peeked inside the leather pouch containing the demon's remains.

Ty checked his watch. They were down to thirty hours. The countdown wasn't ever exact. Malum's head and heart might evaporate a couple hours earlier or later. Judging from the burning odor coming from Dani's pouch, they had less than the time showing on his watch.

"I don't see another gate or Purgatory Arch anywhere near here."

Wicket walked up to the edge of the path. He kicked up a hind leg and relieved himself.

Dani laughed. "Well, I guess we know his opinion of our situation."

Ty answered with a weak smile. Twenty-eight hours likely remained for them to return to Richmond and toss Malum into an Eternal Flame. He wished he could ask Wicket how much further they needed to go to reach the nearest Purgatory Arch.

They got Wicket going again. Their path left only two options to start, either going around the gate to go downhill or the other way uphill. The answer turned out to be the latter. The tiny dog adopted a sassy trot. If Wicket didn't always walk around like he owned the entire universe, Ty might have thought their dog took pride in getting past the snow creatures from the previous realm.

"We need to have a conversation about Wicket." Ty had put this off as long as he thought he could.

"Do we?" She didn't look at Ty, but her tone left little doubt she knew exactly what he wanted to talk about.

"You and I both know what's next, after we get back. Doesn't matter whether we make it in time to end Malum or not."

Dani didn't answer. She kept her focus straight ahead.

"Dani, come on."

She stopped and turned to face him. "We're not discussing this."

Ty chewed on his bottom lip to keep his tongue in check. He settled on responding with a shrug.

She knew damn well they needed to figure out what to do about Wicket.

Literature portrayed deals with the devil as a spiritual crime for a reason. The Order placed deals with demons on a short list of unforgivable sins. That their deal with Malum got dozens of people killed left little doubt what the Order would do with them or with Wicket.

Chapter 41

Four Months Earlier

Heavy rains pelted Richmond this evening, so Ty and Dani decided to drive their new Hyundai Elantra to the Rigney Building instead of walking there. They'd reserved the training room for a practice session that night at eight o'clock.

The south side of the building sat lower than the rest of it, which was why the entrance to the parking garage was located there. Dani hated navigating the narrow structure, so Ty got the honors of driving them down to the third, lowest level where the Order had reserved spaces.

"Guess we'll have to behave," Ty said, thinking fondly of the night they'd first kissed. Judging from all the cars parked in the Order's spaces, a lot of people were working tonight.

"My mom's car is here?"

Maria's red Mini Cooper sat in her reserved space. Since Sebastian's death ten months earlier, Maria had opted to work from home most days. Zuma had started running most of the day-to-day operations of the office.

"Looks like we've got visitors, too." Ty pointed to a pair of cars that had out-of-state license plates, a blue Ford Fusion with New York plates and a dark red Toyota Prius with Washington, DC plates. "Is there something going on tonight I forgot about?"

"Not that I know of."

The repeated "thud-thud" of a car driving over seams in the floor of the parking garage warned that someone else was heading down to their level. As Ty and Dani unloaded their gear from the trunk, a pair of headlights appeared on the ramp leading down to them. The shiny, dark green Jeep Gladiator pulled into the empty space next to their car. Before the driver got out of the small pickup or turned it off, a giant white dog riding in the back hopped out and padded over to Ty and licked the hand Ty wasn't using to pat the big beast on the head.

"What is it with you?" Dani teased him as she walked around the hundred-pound Great Pyrenees to meet Madison as she climbed out of the pickup. They hugged and exchanged surprised expressions.

"What are you doing here?" Madison asked before Dani could ask the same of her.

"Ty and I reserved the training room to spar. We haven't double-booked it, have we?"

Madison shook her head and scowled at her dog when she hopped up onto her hind legs to place her paws on Ty's shoulders. "Cinto, get down."

The large dog obeyed Madison with a low grumble of token protest. Ty and Madison hugged one another. Despite being one of the shorter exorcist's swords, she was built like a tank. She leaned against the rear of her truck. "I got called in for a meeting." She shrugged. "Asked me to bring along Cinto and my gear, too. No clue why."

"Lord help us." Ty noticed the white Honda Accord parked next to Maria's Mini Cooper. "Zuma's here, too. Heard him talking the other day about doing surprise training drills for everyone. Maria didn't sound on board with it, though."

Madison, her eyebrows pinching in towards one another, looked at Dani. "How is your mom?"

"She's well. We had lunch with her after church Sunday." Dani put on her poker face. Even if Ty hadn't seen Maria the other day, he'd have seen through his wife's bluff. Maria's black hair had turned mostly grey. She'd also taken to smoking and drinking more. He hadn't said anything to Dani about it, but he felt certain Maria had shown up to church with a buzz. By the end of lunch and two shots of tequila later, Maria had gotten too drunk to drive herself home and stumbled most of the way to their new car. Maria was doing better, though. The initial fallout had been much worse, to the point that Dani had stayed over at her mom's for a week at one point to help her pull things together. That happened after one night when Maria had gotten so puke drunk and dehydrated that Dani had threatened to call for an ambulance.

Ty couldn't tell if Madison recognized Dani had held back. She pulled out her own bag of gear. Ty and Dani grabbed their stuff, and they all walked to the elevator.

Madison absently scratched behind Cinto's fluffy ears as they rode up to the offices on the twelfth floor. "All I know is that if Zuma thinks he can make me jump through hoops with what little pay they give us, he can kiss my ass."

"I hear that." Ty had hated getting a new car. Even though their car payments weren't big, they'd gotten used to not having that monthly expense. After they'd destroyed Revol and his lieutenants nine months ago, their old Corolla reminded them about Sebastian's death every time they got into it and saw the crack in the dashboard from Dani beating on it. Dani never offered that as a reason to get a new car, but Ty never argued against it because of that.

When the elevator door slid open into the outer lobby, they were startled to find Zuma standing there. He looked just as surprised.

"What are you two doing here?" He clearly meant the question for Ty and Dani.

"We have the training room reserved." Dani's tone warned Zuma that he better not try to pull rank and cancel their sparring session.

Zuma's eyes narrowed on them. "You reserved it for six."

"No, we reserved it for eight, like we always do," Dani said.

"The schedule showed it was six."

"Then the secretary got it wrong. I'd offer to show you the email, but that seems pretty damn stupid when the room is available." She pointed towards the doors to the training room. Even though the frosted glass made it impossible to see any details inside, no lights were on in there.

"Very well," Zuma said. "Just stay out of the offices for now."

"What is this all about?" Madison asked. Her dog grumbled, as if to voice her own objection to being summoned.

"You'll have to ask Maria." A shift of Zuma's eyes directed Madison to the right towards the office space. "You can leave your dog with me for now. Where's her leash?"

"My voice is her leash, so treat her nice until I get back." She turned to her dog and pointed down. "Cinto, sit. Good. Now, stay."

Cinto whimpered but remained sitting as Madison disappeared through the double glass doors to the offices. For such an intimidatingly large breed of dog, Cinto often acted like a big baby.

Neither Dani nor Ty made a move towards the training room to their left.

Dani dropped her pack on the floor and crossed her arms. "Zuma, what's going on?"

Zuma stared at her. "Either train or leave."

They went into the training room, but they didn't spar. Dani stopped in the middle of the room and put her bag down again. Ty picked up on what she wanted and walked over to her so they could whisper.

Dani watched the doors of frosted glass as she spoke. "He wanted us gone."

Ty nodded. "Realized he couldn't make it happen without saying why, and I got the feeling he wanted that even less."

They fell silent for a moment as they considered that. Ty kept thinking about Zuma's insistence they not go into the offices. Dani said what they were both thinking.

"Any chance this has to do with what we did to take down Revol?"

No one but Dani's mom knew knew they fed Revol and his lieutenants to the Eternal Flame. Even then, they didn't let Maria know the deal they'd made with Malum.

"Your mother wouldn't have mentioned it to anyone." Ty felt the urge to grab his gear and march the pair of them to their car. "Would she?"

Dani hesitated, but then she shook her head. "No, she knows better."

Ty decided against pointing out that the way Maria had been drinking since Sebastian's death, she could have easily loosened her lips around the wrong person. Maria had never accused them of crossing any lines, but all the things she hadn't said suggested she suspected what they'd done.

Cinto barked, a deep guttural warning for someone to back off. Ty and Dani ran out into the lobby. They'd expected Zuma, who was still there, but not the pasty pale man shoved up against the elevator door with one very pissed off Great Pyrenees snarling at him.

A man in a black suit and tie whom Ty didn't recognize ran out of the office doors with a gun drawn. Shouts came from the offices in the brief moment the door opened for the gunman to run out into the elevator lobby. Before the office doors closed, Ty glimpsed a woman in a red fedora and a black trench coat staring down someone, apparently unfazed by the drama with Cinto in the lobby.

"What do you think you're doing with my friend's dog?" Dani placed herself between the pale man and Cinto. The pale man wore a tan shirt and blue jeans and held a leash and collar.

"The Order sent me to retrieve it."

"Dani, step aside." Zuma's tone left no doubt he expected her to obey his command. "This man is one of the Order's canine handlers."

"I don't care if he's a hemorrhoid on God's ass, this pendejo better keep his hands off my friend's dog."

Ty positioned himself between Dani and the guy with the gun. "And who's the Secret Service reject?"

The man with the gun didn't bite at Ty's insult. Instead, he put his gun into a holster on his right hip. Zuma answered for him. "They are both employed by the Order and here on official business."

Dani stayed in front of Cinto. "This dog belongs to Madison. If you want Cinto, then you take it up with her owner first."

"Dani, stand down." The command didn't come from Zuma. Maria entered through the office door. The yelling from the office wasn't as loud this time.

Cinto growled as she crouched. She looked ready to charge through the office doors to get to Madison.

Ty walked over to Cinto and placed a hand on her back. "It's okay, girl."

"You Swords kill me getting these monster dogs," the dog handler muttered.

Dani punched him in the stomach. He dropped to his knees.

"Daniella!" Maria charged over and grabbed her by the arm. "That is enough. As for you," she snapped at the dog handler struggling to stand, "you knew how big this dog was going to be. You didn't think to bring another handler to help you?"

"Most dogs behave better than this beast."

Maria sighed. "Ty, can you assist him with Cinto?"

As much as things had improved between him and Maria in recent years, he didn't hesitate in his one-word reply. "No."

"Both of you," Maria said as she walked to the training room, "with me."

Dani pointed a warning finger at the handler. "This dog better be here when I get back."

Maria held open one of the frosted glass doors until Dani and Ty had gone inside.

The room remained half-lit since they hadn't even started their training session. Despite all the shadows in the room, Ty saw how tired Maria looked. She rubbed at her forehead as if nursing a migraine.

"The Order is taking Madison into custody. They're confiscating her sword and her dog."

"Into custody?" Ty looked over at Dani when Maria didn't explain that.

"There's a private prison for exorcists who go rogue. Its location is kept secret."

Maria nodded. "Even I don't know where it is."

Ty felt like he should be wearing a hat made from tin foil. "What did she do, though?"

"This doesn't leave this room, but she was making deals with demons. The Order discovered she was using insider information to buy and sell stocks."

"That sounds like more of a problem for the regular police." Ty wasn't tracking this, and he wanted to go into the offices and smash in some heads.

Maria watched the doors as she whispered to them. "They're certain demons were feeding her the information that they obtained from people they've possessed, and part of the money she made went into other bank accounts. God only knows what these demons are doing with that money."

Ty had wondered how the demons who killed Sebastian had gotten their hands on that mansion in Powhatan County. He originally assumed they killed the original owners, but being able to buy the property would have made it much easier for them to set up their covers and prepare their trap.

"For how long?" he asked, suddenly nauseous at the idea that the money Madison made might have paid to set up that ambush.

"I don't know. They aren't required to show me their evidence, but what they confronted her with in there," Maria didn't finish the thought, and she didn't need to. They'd convinced Maria, and that was enough.

"But Cinto?" Dani looked ready to grab Madison's Great Pyrenees and make a break with her.

"They aren't going to hurt the dog." Maria sounded exasperated. She threw her hands up in the air. "The dog has proven a capable navigator, so the Order won't waste a resource like that."

"A resource?" Dani shouted. "Are you fucking kidding me? They consider her a resource?"

"Enough!" Maria included Ty in her glare. If the Order thought for one minute that Cinto would simply partner with another random person, then they were out of their minds. That large ball of fluff loved Madison, and no one would replace her in Cinto's world.

"Both of you, go home. We can argue about this later." Then she leaned in close and motioned as if to yank them to her. She lowered her voice. "You hold your tongues and keep your secrets to yourselves. I will spill all the blood in the world for you two, but I'd prefer not to find myself with a reason to do it."

She stormed out of the training room without a look back. The door shut behind her, muffling her orders to Zuma and the others in the lobby.

Ty and Dani didn't speak. They shared a look, and Ty recognized the same throat-crushing panic he felt in the way she looked at him.

They picked up their gear and got on the elevator to go down. Cinto stared up at Ty with her big brown eyes. She was prone on the floor, and the handler held her leash. Ty remembered his dog Mocha, wondering if she'd looked like that when he left for college, and closed his eyes for most of the ride down to the parking garage.

Dani touched his arm, already recognizing where his mind was. "You okay to drive?"

"I'll be fine."

Her soft smile and the way she squeezed his arm let him know she recognized the lie.

They said little else as they drove home and parked in their apartment complex's garage. The rainstorm had stopped, so they immediately took Wicket for a walk. They'd meant to only go around the block, but they made it all the way down to Brown's Island instead.

Wicket, oblivious to their mood, happily pranced along the sidewalk that ran around a large grassy field. He sniffed his way along and occasionally kicked up a hind leg to engage in a little doggie social media.

Ty wasn't indulging their dog because of the break in the rain. He'd brought them down here, because what they'd just seen had spooked him enough to worry if their apartment and car might be bugged.

This time of night, the small park area on Brown's Island was all but deserted with only the occasional car passing overhead on the Manchester Bridge to the south side of the city, so Ty decided it safe to speak.

"We need to make a plan for Wicket."

Chapter 42

The sky transitioned from green to yellow and then a brownish-orange. Ty assumed this meant they'd entered what passed for night in this realm. They'd only walked for four hours, but the exhaustion of pushing themselves for so many days was taking its toll.

This realm had only offered two kindnesses to them. One, they didn't need to think about where they were going, because the path they were on intersected very few other paths. And two, nothing seemed to live in this realm that wanted to attack them. No birds occupied the sky. No foul gas disturbed their ability to breathe or threatened to poison them. Nothing lived in the ground, not even grass. The only consistent companions this place offered was the wind above and the darkness below.

When they neared a summit, Wicket stopped. He walked in a circle and then lowered himself to his stomach and met them with those big black eyes of his.

"Looks like we're taking a break." Dani knelt beside their dog to stroke his back and kiss him on the top of his head.

Ty looked at the countdown on his watch, a little less than 26 hours now. "I can carry him, if you want to keep going."

Dani answered with an exhausted sigh that left her shoulders drooping.

"Thank God." Ty joined her and Wicket on the ground.

He stroked Wicket's back. The dog then rolled over for some tummy rubs from both of them. The shameless display had both of them laughing.

"When should we set our alarm?" Ty pulled up the display on his watch.

"Can we set it for two years from now?"

"I think that might be a bit much."

Dani answered with a lazy grin as she rested on the ground with her eyes closed.

He took a deep breath and opened his mouth to bring up the subject they'd been avoiding ever since the night the Order took Cinto, because he couldn't sleep until they'd settled this.

"No." Dani opened her eyes and fixed him with a look that wouldn't abide an argument. "We aren't discussing this."

"I was thinking maybe Kristi and Adam. Them or Katharine and Rob." He couldn't offer more suggestions, because they barely knew anyone else outside of the Order. Those two couples were the only friends at their church with dogs that they would hang out with.

"Even if I was willing to discuss this, they already have dogs bigger than Wicket. All of them, and Wicket hates dogs bigger than him."

"I think Kristi and Adam could get him used to Bowie."

Dani sat up. When she did, he reached over to stroke her left cheek. She melted into his touch. He ran his thumb over her lips, and she answered his touch with a kiss. She pulled his fingers away from her face but held onto his hand as if scared to let go.

"You weren't part of my plan. Have I ever told you that?"

He shook his head, not sure what she meant. He kept silent for her to keep going.

"I wanted to be like Mom. She'd never needed a man. She kicked my cheating ass father to the curb when I was three. She was this secret warrior that owned any space she occupied, and dear God, I wanted to be like that. Sure I dated, but I didn't need a ring on my finger. I wouldn't make the mistake my mother did. I'd cut straight to the finish line. Then you showed up, and the first day I saw you in the training room, my heart pulled out a red pen and crossed out everything I'd had on my to-do list and started a new one with you at the top of it.

"At first, I assumed that after I'd gotten you in the bed, that would be enough. Either you'd lose interest or I'd have my fun and then ball you up like a tissue and toss you away. Only, that wasn't enough, and deep down I'd known we were meant to be more than that. You are everything I'd never known I wanted and needed."

She grinned over at Wicket, who'd curled up on his tummy again and closed his eyes. "And as crazy as it sounds, this little ball of fluff was like that, too. I knew I'd have a dog for this job, but I didn't expect to love him as much as I do. That wasn't the plan."

"You've never struck me as a woman who worries about making a plan."

She placed her head on his shoulder.

"No one takes you or Wicket away from me. You two are all I have left, and you're all I will ever need. I get you're terrified about the Order taking him from us, but I'm not. If they try to break up our family, I'll cut them down like I would any demon. I know we'll have to run after this is finished, but no matter how difficult taking him along might make things, Wicket stays with us."

A long list of good reasons to find a new home for Wicket came to mind, but Ty ignored them. He supposed he'd known the moment that dog hopped into his lap back in the shelter that Wicket would stay with them for the rest of his life.

And Dani... yeah, he'd never expected anyone to want him the way she did or that he could ever need someone this much. He'd expected to live his life alone, but after sharing the air with her, he never wanted to take another breath without her by his side.

He kissed her, and the ache they'd carried since their world fell apart a week ago screamed for more. They answered it. They pulled at each other's clothes until they were naked and made love on the edge of the abyss.

Chapter 43

Something brushing against Ty's face woke him. He found Wicket walking in a circle between him and Dani until he plopped down, curled up like a croissant.

"Decided it was finally safe to come over here, huh?" Ty muttered, still not fully awake.

"He's been here a while," Dani said in a dreamy voice without opening her eyes. "Just decided to shift."

The sky had faded to its daytime green. Ty checked is watch. Eight hours had passed.

"Do I want to know?" Dani asked.

"We've got eighteen hours left, and that's being kind at the rate Malum is decomposing."

Ty forced himself to sit up.

Dani didn't move, even though her eyes were open. She stroked Wicket's fur. "We're not going to make it, are we?"

Ty shook his head. "I don't know, and I'm sorry."

"For what?"

He stared up at the summit. "I should have never talked you into doing this. I thought we could pull it off. We could have gone on the run from the Order a week ago and taken more time to plan a better attack on Malum."

Dani sat up then. The expression on her face didn't fit with what he'd expected. He thought maybe she'd comfort him or rightly scold him for putting them in this position. Instead, she looked perplexed.

"This was my idea," she said.

"What?"

"I'm the one who said we should do this."

He blinked as he tried to remember if it had really been that way. "Wait." He said that one word many times until his head managed to put together a complete sentence. "Are you telling me that this whole time we've both been feeling guilty about talking the other into doing this?"

"No, that's just you. I knew this was the right thing to do all along."

She leaned over and kissed him. Wicket grumbled at having his comfy spot disrupted.

They got up and dressed. Wicket stretched with his front legs straight out, his head low to the ground, and his butt high in the air. Moments like this, Ty suspected their dog might be part cat.

Ty stared over the edge of the path into the void while Wicket relieved himself into the abyss. Ty kept looking down after Wicket had finished.

"What are you doing?" Dani asked.

"Seeing if it stares back."

"You've been waiting this whole time for me to ask so you could say that, haven't you?"

"Yep."

They walked up to the summit. The path split off in a half-dozen directions. Far in the distance, Hell gates glowed along almost every trail.

"Ty!" Dani grabbed his arm and pointed to the left. "It's there!"

He narrowed his eyes, trying to make out the shape of the gate she pointed to, and unlike the other gates that had the hint of yellow from the lightning dancing along their edges, this one glowed silver. It also didn't shift. Unlike the Hell gates, a Purgatory Arch in Hell was an actual door made from the same metal as their swords, only the doors glowed.

"How long do you think it'll take us to reach it?" she asked.

"A few hours."

A shadow coming up from the abyss caused the Purgatory Arch to vanish behind it and then reappear. Wicket growled.

Ty squinted, trying to bring things into better focus. Dani's eyes made it out much faster.

"Ravens," she said. "Dozens of them."

The flock vanished into the abyss and then reappeared moments later.

"That's why Wicket stopped us last night," Ty said. "He must have known this was our last place to stop and rest before the ravens might see us."

"Up until that business with the gate at the Kraken, I'd have called you nuts for suggesting that. Pretty certain you're right, though." She knelt and patted Wicket on the head. "Good boy."

"They must have figured out the closest gates we could go to and took the short way through Purgatory to reach them before us."

Dani groaned, leaning her head back and staring up at the sky. "Please tell me we didn't take the long way for nothing."

"Well, it's only ravens." He pointed towards the Purgatory Arch. "I don't see any demons on the ground. They've split up their forces for this. Guess they couldn't reach this gate on foot."

"That's still an awful lot of ravens."

Ty squinted. "I can't tell exactly how many."

"They're moving around too much, but I'd say it's at least three dozen."

"More than enough to pick us off."

"If we were in an open field, picking them off one-by-one would be easier. These narrow land bridges only give us two directions to run: forward and back." Dani shook her head as she considered the trap ahead of them. "If they come at us the right way, they'll cut us down or knock us into the abyss."

He scratched at the beard hair that had filled in beneath his chin, where he usually shaved it off when shaping his beard. He'd reached the point where the beard hair was getting itchy. "So what do we do?"

"We get moving and figure out our strategy on the way."

Chapter 44

Ty expected the ravens to make their move sooner. Instead, the birds lingered close to the Purgatory Arch. Wicket led the way, growling his irritation with the flock spiraling through the air around their destination.

When they were less than two miles from the arch, one of the ravens broke off from the others and flew in their direction. The raven landed a safe distance from them, not that Wicket cared one bit for it. The dog barked and growled.

"That's enough, Wicket." Ty said.

Wicket didn't stop, though. He kept barking, same as he would at a large dog when he came across them in the parking lot of their apartment complex. They'd nicknamed him Sir Barks-a-Lot for a reason.

The raven blocking their path started to speak but stopped when she realized Wicket wouldn't shut up to let her say anything.

"Dude, seriously." Ty tried to pick up Wicket, but the furball wasn't having that.

"I've come to"— The raven, her voice a hideous screech, tried to talk over the barking. "Can you not shut up that raving creature?"

Ty held up a hand. "Give us a minute."

Dani finally scooped up their dog and moved behind Ty to hide the raven from Wicket's view, not that it helped much. Wicket growled at what he knew was still there.

Ty shrugged to the raven. "Sorry, I think this is as good as it's going to get. He gets this way around other animals, so you should probably go ahead."

"Can you not snap its neck?" the raven said.

"Bitch, I know you did not just say that!" Dani sounded more pissed than Wicket now.

"If you'd like to offer us your surrender," Ty said, "we'll accept it and be on our way."

"Why would I?"— The raven stopped short in her question and flapped her wings in frustration, probably realizing Ty was taunting her. "I am Kene, a lieutenant to Premier Malum. I will let you and your hound," she placed an added emphasis of disgust at the mention of Wicket, "pass through the Purgatory Arch without conflict, if you hand over Malum's head and heart."

Wicket barked and growled more, probably irritated by the hideous voice of the raven.

"Did you understand our dog's answer?" Ty asked.

Kene's head jerked to the side as if to look around Ty at Wicket. "No, I did not."

"Well, he said 'Fuck you!'"

"And this hound speaks for you?"

Dani stepped forward with Wicket still in her arms. "My sword is gonna speak its way up your ass!"

The raven's head jerked around some more as she took a few steps back. "So be it." She then leaped off the edge of the path and flew towards her fellow ravens.

Dani kissed the top of Wicket's head and then set him down. "Good boy." Their dog ran down the path barking at the retreating raven.

"She's lucky Malum's head is so big, because if I had room in this bag, I'd toss her head and heart into an Eternal Flame with him. Snap our dog's neck, my ass!"

Ty couldn't contain his grin. He loved it when Dani got like this. Well, at least when her rant wasn't directed at him.

She drew her swords from the scabbards on her hips. "Let's go dissect some birds."

Ty drew his sword, and they kicked up their pace to a jog. Wicket ran back and forth growling for them to hurry up and then took off running as they caught up to him. Much as Ty and Dani would have gladly sprinted the remaining distance, they needed to save their strength for what came next.

When Kene rejoined the other ravens, they changed their flight path to fly towards their prey. Halfway to Ty and Dani, the ravens split up with half going to the left while the others went to the right. Each group launched high into the sky and adopted reverse V formations.

"This could be a problem," Ty said. They'd considered the ravens might employ this strategy, coming at them in a reverse V formation. If the ravens trapped them inside that formation, the demons might cut them down or knock them off into the abyss. Dani had cooked up a counterstrategy for dealing with one reverse V formation, but not for two.

"They can't attack at the same time," Dani said. "They'd crash into each other, if they did."

"Doesn't mean they can't come at us one right after the other in opposite directions." Even from this distance, the group on the left seemed to be falling a little behind the right group.

"Then we react faster."

The group on the right swooped high, but the formation on the left dropped down into the abyss. Ty definitely hadn't expected that move. He assumed both groups of ravens would start their attack from high up to let gravity add to their momentum.

"Right group is coming in first!" Ty shouted. They stopped jogging and took a position near the left edge of the path. From there, he could see the group on the left curving around below them for their own run. The group on the right hurtled towards them from above.

"I'll call the right," Dani said. "You keep your eyes on the left."

They had to time this right. He supposed the ravens had to as well, but even if the demons killed each other in a collision, they'd most likely revive five days later. Ty and Dani didn't come with the same kind of cosmic do-over. Their soul might get another shot at life, but they'd be different people and God only knew when and if that would happen.

"High!" Dani shouted.

Ty turned and picked his target. As Dani predicted, the ravens came at them chest-high. At the last moment, Ty and Dani dropped to their backs with their swords held tight. The tips of their swords were pointed up and in the direction the ravens were flying. They didn't want to spear the ravens, because at the speed they were flying, any impaled raven would probably rip the swords right out of their hands. If this worked, the ravens would cut themselves on the edges of the swords as they flew past.

The raven that hit Ty's sword swooped right at the last second, trying to dodge the blade. The sword still caught it on the torso. Black blood sprayed out as the raven shrieked and spiraled out of control. They slammed into the raven next to them in the formation and they tumbled over the edge of the path.

Dani's sword sliced off one of the wings on her raven. The demonic bird slammed down against the rocky path and bounced off into the abyss. Dani cursed.

There was no time to check on each other, though. Ty rolled over as the second wave of ravens swooped up over the edge of the path.

"Incoming!" The ravens came at them before they could reset for the same attack. Ty rolled again, trying to avoid a demon who tilted to their right to slash at Ty with their wing. The attack caught Ty's back as he rolled away and sliced through his jacket and into his shoulder blade. If he'd been a fraction slower, Ty might have lost his arm. As it was, they did more damage to his jacket than anything else.

Ty struggled to get on his feet. Dani made it to her knees with a hand pressing down on the right side of her shoulder.

"Raven wing?" he asked.

She shook her head. "My sword. The demon slammed it against my chest when they collided with me."

Wicket ran to position himself behind them and barked as he did that sideways herding move. "Working on it, dude," Ty said.

He grabbed Dani by the left arm and pulled her up, aggravating their injuries. They both cursed from the pain.

The ravens circled back for another run, maintaining their reverse V formations.

"Bet you they go low this time," Dani said as she sprinted after their dog who had run ahead of them again. Wicket barked for them to catch up and ran in impatient circles.

"Hope so, because they won't fall for that trick again." Blood ran down Ty's back.

The ravens squawked at each other, and their formations shifted to make up for their losses during their first run. The two attacks looked like they might time out farther apart this time.

"We gotta make them hurt on this one," Dani shouted.

They tried in vain to get ahead of the ravens. "Here!" Ty shouted, and they stopped. They stood ready with their swords.

The ravens swooped in low, as Dani predicted. This time, Ty and Dani stayed upright. As soon as the ravens reached them, they didn't try to position themselves between the ravens. The flying demons could close the gaps to slice them up with their wings. Ty and Dani leaped up and stabbed down with their swords. Ty missed his raven, and he dropped onto the rocky surface, landing on his stomach. Pain shot through his chest and knocked the air out of him.

Dani's leap and strike timed out so that she sliced into the back of her raven, but the demon's momentum caused her to spin in midair. She landed on her back, sliding towards the edge but stopping halfway. The raven tumbled off the side.

Ty scrambled to his feet as the next wave came at them. Dani didn't have a chance to move. He positioned himself in front of her and lined up with the approaching raven. He swung his sword up like a club at the raven's head. The raven's torso split open, down from its left shoulder and into its waist. The demon collided with Ty and knocked them both to the ground. They slid towards the far edge of the path. Thankfully, the surface wasn't smooth and helped Ty stop before he could tumble off into the abyss, but the unforgiving rock made the cut to his back worse than it already was.

"We can't take much more of this." Dani winced as she stood. "We need to change our strategy."

They ran for the Purgatory Arch, trying to get ahead of the ravens.

"Picking them off isn't what we need to do. We gotta do this like that old video game *Frogger*. We ditch fighting with our swords and dodge these bastards like a frog crossing a busy highway."

They returned their swords to their scabbards and focused on running. If they could make it into the cramped space of Purgatory, they'd have a better chance against these ravens.

Wicket had run far ahead of them. He stopped every few feet to bark at them, as if they weren't already running as fast as they could.

Another wave swooped in on their left, coming at them waist-high. At the last second, they ducked under the attack and popped up as soon as the ravens passed them. The wave from the right went for their feet. They leaped over the ravens. One of the wings clipped Ty's boot. The wing didn't cut him, but it knocked him off balance. He crashed down onto the path again.

He managed not to hit his head. That didn't stop the rush of pain from blinding him for a split second with everything fading into a blue haze. He got up and ran, trying to catch up to Dani and Wicket.

They fared better with the next few rounds of attack. The ravens squawked at each other as if arguing amongst themselves as Ty and Dani made it within less than a mile of the Purgatory Arch. The neatly formed V of the ravens collapsed into a chaotic swarm.

"They're getting ready to change it up!" Dani sounded almost finished. Running long distances had never been her strength.

Some of the ravens dove for the Purgatory Arch, landing on the path to block their escape. The rest of the demons flew towards Ty and Dani. They didn't form up into any fancy pattern. The ravens came at them in random attacks, like a hail storm of razor-sharp feathers.

Ty and Dani drew their swords again. The ravens couldn't risk flying as fast as they had in the V formation, otherwise they might collide with each other.

"Here they come again," Dani said in a singsong voice.

Ty gave his sword a spin. "Batter up."

Some might see this swarm of demons flying at them and think their best strategy finesse, some pithy bit about flowing like water around their enemy. At this moment, Ty and Dani needed speed and brute force.

The ravens swooped in from all directions. Ty and Dani's swords punished them for each incursion. Their green blades ripped the demons apart. A couple dodged their swings at the last second only to collide into other ravens. Blood and feathers piled onto the rocky ground. The entire time, Dani and Ty advanced. They moved at a slow walk, but they drew closer to the Purgatory Arch.

The handful of ravens that survived long enough to learn their lesson flew back to rejoin the group guarding the way out of Hell.

Wicket led the way. As they came within a hundred feet of the gate, Wicket slowed to a cocky trot. He growled, building up into several threatening barks.

Some of the ravens unfurled their wings, croaking their protests.

As Ty, Dani, and Wicket charged the Purgatory Arch, half of the ravens leaped off the edge of the path. For a brief moment, Ty hoped these ravens had thought better about sacrificing themselves for Malum, but demons didn't think like humans. If Malum survived this, failing to fight for him would have consequences. The half that flew off regrouped on the path, landing behind Ty and Dani. The ravens opted to face them on the ground and surround them.

Ty and Dani ran all the harder towards the ravens at the Purgatory Arch. Some of the ravens behind them ran while others leaped through the air.

Wicket dove into the mess of ravens in front of them. He barked and nipped at the bird demons' talons, forcing them to scatter to avoid his bite. Some of the demons stomped after Wicket, but judging from their frustrated croaks, they repeatedly missed the small dog.

The furry distraction left several of the ravens vulnerable to Ty and Dani's attack. Some leaped into the air while others swung with their wings, hoping to cut into Ty and Dani or at least block their swords. The ravens coming from behind caught up to them. Ty took the group at their backs.

Ty battered the ravens with his sword. Wicket bolted out from the raven group closer to the arch and zipped around his humans to pester the rear group of demons.

"Oh, I see how it's gonna be," Dani said with a laugh to her voice as she slit open the throat of a raven in a spray of blood and feathers, "go help Daddy and leave Mommy all on her own."

Ty slashed off the wing of a raven as they launched into the air, sending them tumbling off into the abyss with a loud shriek. "Please, like that dog doesn't love the ground you walk on."

Dani and Ty tore their way through the ravens. By the time only a handful remained standing, the surviving ravens decided the pain wasn't worth it and flew away.

Kene didn't retreat with the others. Dani had pinned her to the ground with one of her swords shoved through the demon's right shoulder and into the rock.

Ty walked over to Kene and stared down at her. "Bet you wish you had opposable thumbs right now."

The raven flapped her wings, but she couldn't shake herself free. Dani stomped on Kene's left wing to keep the demon from cutting her. Ty planted his foot on the right wing.

Kene filled their words with pain and rage. "You will never reach an Eternal Flame."

"Shut up and listen." Dani rested her other sword across Kene's throat. The implied threat silenced the raven, and her black eyes widened in alarm as Dani slipped off the backpack holding Malum's head and heart to place it on Kene's chest. "If I ever see you again, I'll take your head and heart, because by the end of this day, there's going to be room in this bag for you."

Wicket walked up to the demon and growled at her.

"I'd leave you here like this," Dani said, "but I'm gonna need both of my swords."

Using the sword not pinning Kene, Dani slammed it down on Kene's throat, sending the head spinning away from its torso.

Ty strolled over to the head where it wobbled to a stop. "See you around, Kene, if you're unlucky." He tapped the head with his foot and sent it off the path and into the abyss.

Dani jerked her sword free of the raven's body and wiped the blade clean before she sheathed it. Then she slipped the backpack on again and canted her head towards the pair of green, ornate metal doors. "We ready for this?"

Ty scratched Wicket behind the ear. "Suppose so. Probably a good thing we got the sleep we did."

They held hands as they walked up to the doors and pushed them open. The doors creaked on their non-existent hinges within the arch of skulls and revealed a liquid substance that swam around the space. Waves rippled through the reflective surface, which mirrored only the living on their side of the door while offering a warped vision of Purgatory on the other side. Wobbling versions of Ty, Dani, and Wicket stared back at them but appeared to stand in a distorted version of the large grey brick room that awaited them on the other side.

Dani squeezed Ty's hand, and the three of them entered Purgatory.

PART VI

FOREST OF THE DEPARTED

Chapter 45

One Week Earlier

A sense of wrongness pervaded the loft apartment when Ty woke. Windows ran along the tops of two walls in their bedroom. He felt the warmth of Dani's body in the bed, and the moon shined through the blinds of the windows on the far wall, providing enough light for him to confirm she was still asleep next to him. The artificial crash of waves and thunder played behind him from the white noise app on his cell phone, resting on his bedside table. He wondered if the power went out, because waking to an outage always had a disturbing sense of absence, only that didn't fit this feeling. A twinge of paranoia tickled at the back of his neck, insisting something was here that shouldn't be.

Before he could dismiss his instincts and go back to sleep, Wicket growled at the foot of the bed.

That's when the stench of brimstone hit him.

Wicket jumped up and barked bloody murder.

Ty flung off the covers. He rolled off the bed and onto his feet to see Malum run into their bedroom with his sword raised. The demon slammed his blade down, but Ty dodged the attack.

Ty's sword hung on the wall on his side of the room, a few feet out of reach. He snatched the lamp from his bedside table, jerking it out of its socket, and hurled it at the demon.

As the demon swatted at the lamp with his sword, Ty lunged for his own sword. Dani, now awake, had already drawn her swords from where she hung them on her side of the bedroom.

She charged at the demon. The steed leaped over her attack, landing on their bed. He kicked her in the back, sending her stumbling across the room.

Before the demon could pursue her, Ty swung at the demon's waist. Malum blocked Ty's swing with his own sword. The mattress put Malum off-balance, so when Ty next went for the demon's legs, the demon jumped to the floor.

Dani rushed at Malum as soon as he landed. The demon parried her attacks. The strength behind his swings, sent her stumbling into the bathroom. The door frame blocked Malum's attempt to strike her.

Wicket bit the back of Malum's calf. The demon screamed and raised his sword to swing at the enraged dog. Ty tackled the demon into the wall next to the bathroom door. The drywall shattered from the impact.

The demon's skin felt cold and reptilian where Ty gripped him by the wrist to keep him from swinging his blade. Malum also held onto Ty's sword arm. They struggled to break free of each others' grip. They kicked and jabbed with their knees. Ty caught the stench of blood, but it didn't belong to him, Dani, or Malum. Someone had gifted their blood to the demon. That allowed his physical form to exist in the mortal realm.

Ty heard the shower turn on.

When Malum shoved him, Ty used the bastard's movement to spin him into the bathroom. Ty's sword blocked them from getting through the door, so he dropped it.

Dani grabbed Malum in a choke hold and dragged him into the bathroom. Ty wished she could have cut his head off. They could end the bastard here and now if she did that, but with Ty and Malum so close, she couldn't risk a swing at the demon without potentially injuring or killing Ty, too.

They stumbled into the cramped shower. The hot water burned Ty's neck as he and Dani fought to keep Malum's head in the spray from the showerhead. She must have cranked the water as hot as she could get it in order to get the blood to wash off of Malum as fast as possible.

Wicket stood outside the bathroom door and barked at the demon from there. He stayed put, not getting in the middle of the tangled bodies.

The demon roared as he struggled against their hold on him. He shoved Ty off and down onto the bathmat. Dani kept her hold on his throat from behind. Malum stabbed over his shoulder with his sword. Dani ducked before the sword struck her face. The pointed tip scraped against the shower's ceramic tiles.

Ty scrambled to his feet and grabbed Malum's sword arm. The demon slammed his body backwards, trying to crush Dani against the wall. The tiles shattered as Dani screamed, but she maintained her hold on the demon. Ty stabbed at the demon's eyes with his fingers, taking the fight out of Malum long enough for them to keep him still beneath the showerhead. Malum roared, but the sound faded along with his body. When the demon vanished between them, Ty collapsed on top of Dani.

Wicket continued to bark but had made it into the bathroom and onto the bathmat.

Ty and Dani held onto each other, too tired to crawl out of the shower or turn off the water.

"You all right?" Ty asked.

"I'm fine." She kissed the side of his neck. "You?"

"I'm good." He finally reached up and turned off the water. "Smart thinking."

"I've been known to have a good idea or two."

As they dried off, Ty checked Dani's back to make sure she didn't cut herself on the shattered tiles. Thankfully, she wasn't injured. They changed clothes, brewed some coffee, and sat on their sofa as they watched the sunrise. Wicket lounged like a cat next to Dani on the back of the sofa, not wanting to let her be apart from him.

By this point, Malum's ephemeral form must have fled their apartment. Demons couldn't last long on the mortal plane without possessing a person's body. If he hadn't already reached the Purgatory Arch in Hollywood Cemetery, he'd probably made it halfway there by now. As lovely as the notion was that Malum might die before escaping the mortal plane, neither Ty nor Dani clung to that hope.

"We never should have trusted him," Dani said between sips of coffee.

Ty breathed in the steam from his coffee, his mind struggling to stay awake even as it raced too much for him to entertain going back to bed, not that Malum had left their mattress in any condition to use it. Launching straight from sleep into a fight had drained him.

"What I don't get is why he'd waste it just to kill us." Ty shook his head. "What does killing us even do for him? It's not like that doesn't leave the rest of the Order to come after him."

Dani put her mug down on the table hard enough for coffee to spill out of it. "Where's my phone?"

"What?"

Dani stood and scrambled through their den, checking every surface. "Where did I put my phone?"

He stared at her, wondering why she was panicking. "I remember you had it in the kitchen when I poured the water into the coffee pot. You were checking the temperature outside."

Dani ran behind the counter that divided their den from the kitchen and picked up her phone. She slid her fingers across the phone's screen and then held it to her ear. She slapped the flat of her free hand on the counter.

"Who are you calling?"

"Mom." She slammed her fist on the counter. "It's going to voice mail!"

Ty stood as he realized what she was thinking.

"Mom, it's Daniella. Call me as soon as you get this."

She set the phone down and looked at him.

"It's early," he said. "There's a good chance she's not even awake to know you called."

She paced in the kitchen and then ran for their bedroom. Ty and Wicket followed.

Dani slipped on her hunting jacket. Ty geared up, too.

At first, they weren't going to bring Wicket, but after what happened—a demon getting into their home—they weren't about to let him out of their sight.

Wicket sat in Dani's lap as Ty drove them to her mom's house. Dani lowered the window for the dog to stick his head out into the wind. He didn't get to ride in the car often, but he loved every chance he got. He kept looking inside the car at them, more often than he usually did, suggesting he sensed their mood.

When they pulled up in front of Maria's house, nothing looked wrong from the outside. Even though the gifted blood allowed Malum to make himself solid on the mortal plane, he could still transition to pass through walls, which is exactly how he would have gotten into their apartment without making any noise. Each time he did that, though, some of the blood would come off. Given how quickly the blood came off in the shower, that made it all too likely that might have happened.

They ran up to the front door with Wicket on their heels. Dani banged on the door, not bothering with the lion head knocker on it. She didn't even give it fifteen seconds. At a quarter to eight, her mom would be awake. She pulled out her keys to find the one for her mom's house.

Ty's instincts twitched and he reached past her to turn the door knob. The door wasn't locked and slid open. Maria never left her door unlocked.

Dani didn't move. "Ty."

"Maybe you should wait here."

To his surprise, she considered it, but then she shook her head. She pushed open the door the rest of the way and walked into the narrow foyer.

They found Maria off to the left in the dining room. Her body rested on top of the cherry wood table. Her bloodstained, teal nightgown was ripped open above her heart. Her sword rested on the floor and had black blood on it. Even with all the advantages Malum had, Maria had wounded the bastard, which might have helped save their lives when he came after them.

Malum had written a message in blood on the wall behind Maria's body: *Dani and Ty, thank you.*

Dani staggered to her mother's body and dropped to her knees. She rested her head on her arms next to her mother's face and wept.

Wicket laid down next to Dani and waited. Ty stayed silent and went out onto the front porch as if he'd been stabbed. He pulled out his cell phone and called Zuma. The phone rang but went to voice mail.

He tried three more times, trying both Zuma's cell phone and his office phone. From there, he called some of the other exorcist's swords. Each call went unanswered, and with each failed call, he went from numbed to panicked. He grew so desperate, he even tried in vain to call that asshat Nelson. His last attempt, to the front desk secretary of the Order's local offices, met with voice mail.

He returned to the dining room. Dani hadn't moved and neither had Wicket. Ty knelt beside his wife.

"Dani?" Interrupting the silence to say her name felt like an unforgivable sin.

Her head lifted to look at him.

"No one is answering their phones. Not at their homes or the office. No one."

Before Dani could respond, a cell phone vibrated. They checked their phones, but it wasn't them.

"Mom's phone." Dani ran into the kitchen and grabbed the phone off the floor. Dani's mom used this phone only for Order business. Dani answered it before the call went to voice mail and put it on speaker. "Hello?"

"Cortez?" The voice belonged to a man with a British accent and sounded familiar to Ty.

Dani sniffed and wiped the tears from her eyes. "This is her daughter."

"What is your identification code?"

"Sword 52695."

A long pause followed, and if the screen hadn't shown the call still active, Ty would have thought they'd hung up.

"Confirmed. This is Officer Horwitz with Order Oversight. Where is Maria Cortez?"

Dani didn't answer. Her eyes watered and her throat clenched as she struggled to find her voice. Ty reached over and touched her shoulder.

"This is Tyler Faison, Sword 52698. Maria Cortez is dead. A demon killed her in her home. We just found her body."

Another long pause followed, during which Ty assumed they confirmed his identity.

"Where is the demon?"

"Probably back in Hell by now. He attacked us in our apartment a couple of hours ago," Ty said and then shook his head to stop Dani adding anything. "We called Maria to report what happened, but when she didn't answer, we drove over here. Why are you calling her?"

Another long pause followed. Ty lacked the energy for this verbal chess game. The abrupt awakening from Malum attacking them, finding Maria's body, and the fact no one in their local branch of the Order was answering their phones had him wanting to drop Maria's phone in a sink full of water and run for it.

"We received a panic activation from her phone at 3:57 am, eastern time. We've been trying to reach her ever since. We were also unable to contact her subordinate Zuma Lompoc. We were about to call you two."

"We've been unable to reach anyone else here in Richmond."

"No one?" That was the most emotion Officer Horwitz had demonstrated. *"I want both of you to stay right there until our response team arrives. We should be there within the next half hour."*

Ty hesitated, not wanting to commit to it and simply said, "Understood."

The line disconnected as Officer Horwitz hung up.

Dani placed her mother's phone on the kitchen island and pulled out her own phone. Before Ty could ask what she was doing, she cursed.

She handed him her phone with the web browser open to one of the local news station's websites. The headline *"Deadly Home Invasion in North Chesterfield"* sat below a picture of a two-story white house that Ty recognized. The house and the car parked in front of it belonged to one of their fellow swords, Lance Rovelli, and his wife Joanna. The article didn't include any names but said four people were dead, which meant Malum had killed not only Lance and his wife, but their two kids.

Lightheaded and dizzy, Ty stumbled back. He grabbed onto the door frame connecting the kitchen with the dining room, the only reason he hadn't dropped onto his ass. When the world righted itself again, he noticed Dani picking up her phone off the floor. He hadn't realized he'd dropped it.

"Sorry," he whispered.

She gripped his arm. "You okay?"

He shook his head.

"Me neither." With a cant of her head, she directed him to follow her out into the back yard. "Wicket, come."

The terrier hopped onto his paws and padded after them.

The back yard separated the house from the detached garage. Large grey bricks covered most of the yard and formed a labyrinth design that Maria said she walked whenever she needed to make a difficult decision. One Christmas season years ago, all of the swords and staff had gathered for a party, and after getting loosened up from a few drinks, they'd broken out their swords and used the labyrinth as a sparring ring. Maria had been three sheets to the wind, probably four sheets, and she'd still beaten him in less than five moves. She'd literally spanked his ass (and quite a few others) with the flat of her sword that night. He still remembered Dani laughing and teasing her mother that only she got to do that to him.

They stood in the middle of the labyrinth when Dani stopped. Wicket ran around the yard, exploring with his nose while they talked.

"There's no hiding this," she said.

"No."

His thoughts went to the message Malum had scrawled in Maria's blood. There wasn't enough time to clean that, not completely. Even if they did enough to obscure the message, the oversight officers would demand to know what had been there and why they'd tried to hide it.

Dani glanced towards the house. "So if we're going to do anything, it's got to be now."

He knew the smart play meant running: get all of their money out of the bank and head for some remote town on the far end of the country. As long as they didn't go anywhere requiring a passport, avoided using their credit cards, and ditched their cell phones, the Order wouldn't be able to track them. Ty didn't think the Order would threaten his parents, but the idea he couldn't contact them to explain any of this made it difficult to breathe.

Only, going on the run wasn't what he saw in Dani's eyes, and he agreed.

"Malum," he said. "We go after him now before he gets a chance to prepare for us."

"Exactly."

They raced home and packed the food and water they needed to get in and out of the Blood Realm. Less than an hour later, they'd parked their car a few blocks north of the church with the Eternal Flame in its basement. Then they raced for the Purgatory Arch in Hollywood Cemetery. This move all but guaranteed the Order would catch them and toss them into a cell in some foreign country, but they'd make damn sure Malum burned in the Eternal Flame first.

Chapter 46

The sensation of entering Purgatory resembled the ache of returning home after an extended absence, only it filled Ty and Dani with cold dread instead of warm relief.

The spot they appeared in with Wicket had a large space built from dark grey bricks and stone. Polished marble covered the entire floor. Green flames dancing in box-shaped, glass-framed sconces provided the only light. Black, rectangular plaques with silver-plated letters covered the rest of the available space on the walls. Some plaques still showed the entire name of those souls contained within, but most were missing letters, a sign of how far along the soul was in forgetting who they were in the most recent life they lived.

One of the plates off to their left contained only a single letter. Even as they watched, the lone "C" vanished. The wall groaned as seams formed in the cement between the bricks. The grey rectangular bricks floated out from the wall to reveal the prone body of light within. The soul climbed out and walked past them. Wicket sniffed at the heels of the soul up until it reached a round well in the center of the room. The soul stepped into the hole and vanished as it fell into the well's shadows, sending it to one of the many realms in Hell. The rhyme and reason of how the well chose a realm escaped the living's understanding, and if the demons knew the mechanics, they'd never shared that truth. The opening in the wall closed up as the bricks returned to their proper place with the blank plaque awaiting the next soul's name.

Dani let go of Ty's hand and walked around the edges of the room. She searched through the plaques with complete names, most likely looking for her mother, but the odds of finding her place in Purgatory were slim. Demons, those who performed their actual duties, guided the souls of the recently deceased here, the forest of the departed. The souls shed their past lives before Hell consumed them and they were reborn on the mortal plane. Ty supposed some souls made it to Heaven, but if that place actually existed, then it wasn't as easily accessible as the many realms of Hell.

Ty walked to the far end of the room. A stone arch opened into a narrow corridor, illuminated by more of the green firelight. A light wind flowed from the far end, and a musty odor tainted the air.

Dani walked up beside him. "Expected more demons to be waiting here."

"Suspect that wasn't the only Purgatory Arch with demons waiting on us. They can only spread themselves so thin."

Dani let out a long breath. "So they're probably waiting for us somewhere closer to the Richmond Arch."

Ty called Wicket over to them. He shot past them into the corridor, spun around, then crouched and barked as if to tell them to hurry up. The passage felt as if it went on for a mile, but odds favored it was much less than that. Even with the clock ticking away, the race wasn't simply about reaching the Eternal Flame before Malum's head and heart evaporated. The greater danger was Purgatory itself.

Even the demons feared to linger in this place. It didn't simply rob the recently deceased of their past life, but any living being that over-stayed their welcome risked a similar fate. This place purged the mind of memories. That probably also explained why more demons hadn't been waiting right inside Purgatory from the arch they'd used.

The corridor ended in something akin to a grotto. A pool of black water filled the open space. Thick fog drifted over the water and morphed into phantoms of people silently screaming before they faded into the mist. Not every soul made it out of Purgatory. Ty often wondered if these silent screamers in the fog belonged to the living who stayed too long and lost themselves.

He could make out the other green lanterns mounted on the walls of the grotto. The fog obscured any other details. A simple marble platform that rested a few inches above the water served as their dock.

Dani knelt to stare at her reflection in the water. "Suppose it was too much to hope a ride would be waiting here."

Ty looked at his watch. Less than fifteen hours.

Odds favored a boat would pass this way long before their time ran out, but Purgatory offered no guarantees. Even then, they had to float their way to the corridor leading to the Richmond Arch.

Wicket walked up to the edge of the dock next to Dani and laid down on his stomach, his paws sticking out over the water.

"Have you picked a memory?" Dani sounded like her mind had drifted across the water with the fog.

"No." He hated this part of the trip the most. He sat down with his back leaning against the corridor's arch so he could keep an eye out for any demons coming from that direction.

He reached into his jacket and pulled out a small leather-bound notebook from his right breast pocket. The gondoliers of Purgatory demanded a payment to ferry the living. The tradition of placing a coin in the mouths of the dead wasn't because the coin offered the payment. It came from that old saying, "A penny for your thoughts."

Ty flipped through the pages of the dark brown notebook. Their training classes had reinforced the importance of these small journals. The worst thing that could happen was to pick a memory at the last minute. Memories defined a person, and giving up the wrong memory could alter a person in unexpected ways. That's why they wrote down the memories they were willing to sacrifice. Given the number of times he'd gone to Hell during the past five years, Ty had sacrificed plenty of memories. The task of choosing one hadn't proven as difficult in the beginning, but each trip got harder.

Flipping through the pages, Ty came across pages he'd checked off. They disturbed him, because it sometimes read like a different person's journal. One trip, he surrendered the memory of his first kiss. He remembered Isabeau Danvers, that they'd gone on a date to the dollar movies when they were thirteen. According to what he'd written down, they'd kissed during the movie, but even the details of the kiss—the warmth of her lips and the way she smelled like roses—didn't stir up the dust or cobwebs in his mind. The memory simply wasn't there. He couldn't even remember the panic he'd felt. Reading the details of the event came across like a page from a poorly written teen romance novel.

The memories needed to be well-defined, adding to the challenge. He couldn't simply sacrifice the memory of driving down the road somewhere unless he could remember all of the details, and there needed to be emotion tied to it.

In short, the price for passage in Purgatory didn't come cheap.

He'd learned to spot a moment he might sacrifice, and the idea of monetizing the moments that stirred his heart sickened him.

He found a memory from a few weeks ago. They'd been at the grocery store, he and Dani, and while she dug through the poblano peppers for the best ones to use in a family recipe of Maria's for chorizo stuffed peppers, he was struck by how much he loved getting to do this mundane task with Dani. It wasn't that there was anything remarkable about buying food. Hell, Dani hated grocery stores so much that she called them "the Evil Place" (which he found especially funny coming from a woman who frequently visited Hell). The idea that he was the only person on this planet who got to do this with her, though... Yeah, he considered that pretty damn remarkable.

When they'd gotten home, he recognized the moment in the store for what it might be and wrote it into his journal. As soon as he'd finished writing down the memory, he hated himself for turning something so intimate and personal into currency. That Dani did the same offered his only comfort.

His fingers traveled over the words on the page, feeling the tiny dips pressed into the paper. He tried to tell himself he'd probably get to experience that moment again, and it would feel like the first time because he'd surrendered this one to a gondolier. That didn't stop him from silently cursing.

Dani hadn't taken out her journal, though. She sat with her chin resting on her knees and she stroked Wicket's back. His ears twitched from the attention.

Hours ticked by, but they didn't dare sleep. The effects of Purgatory acted more quickly on a mind at rest.

To keep their brains active, they played a word game they'd employed on more than one car trip. One of them would think up a word and then the other would need to come up with a word that started with the last letter in the previous word. The trickiest part was that they weren't allowed to repeat a word either of them had used.

"Unorthodox," Dani said with a wicked grin.

"Rude," Ty muttered. She'd managed to trap him with words ending in "x" several times now. He'd already used x-ray and xylophone. "Fine, then xylophones." He put an added emphasis on the "s" making it plural.

She nodded her acceptance, but the mirthful twist of her lips remained. "Sex."

He groaned. "That better be an invitation and not your word."

"It could be both."

They laughed, and Dani rested her head on his shoulder.

Ty checked his watch.

"Do I want to know?" she asked.

"Ten hours," he said, "give or take."

They were at the mercy of the gondoliers. No other way to safely travel existed in Purgatory. The depth of the water didn't threaten them. People could walk in it, but that invited other dangers. Monsters that made piranha look like goldfish swam in the black waters. Even worse, contact with the water sucked memories out of a person that much faster. Drinking it amounted to self-lobotomization.

Dani placed a hand on the bag with Malum's head and heart. "Probably closer to eight."

He agreed but answered with silence.

Nothing guaranteed that if a gondola arrived right now that the trip to the Richmond Gate wouldn't take too long.

If they could, Ty would gladly ask the gondolier to take them to the nearest gate to the mortal world, but then they'd have to find an Eternal Flame in the short time they had left. Sadly, the natural laws of Purgatory didn't work that way. They needed to enter and leave by the same gate. He'd often mused how easy it would be to use Purgatory to travel across the globe. Trip to London or Hong Kong? No problem. Pick a memory to sacrifice. For whatever reason, the gates refused to permit that. Attempting to return to the mortal world through a different arch simply spit a person back out in Purgatory. That the many realms of Hell got a free pass on this made it all the more vexing. Although, the demons apparently had the same issue with coming and going from the mortal plane. If a demon entered Earth by a gate, they had to reenter Purgatory by that same gate.

Dani grabbed Ty by the knee, pulling him from his musings.

"I think I hear a gondola."

Ty closed his eyes as he strained to listen. The unmistakable splash of a paddle came from the passage to their left.

Minutes later, the silhouette of the boat and the gondolier appeared in the fog. A lantern with green flames hung from the front tip of the long, scoop-shaped boat. A figure in a black toga stood on the back scoop. Ty found it difficult to look at her but impossible to look away. Charred, black flesh covered the right side of her body. Two ivory-colored horns stuck out of her head. The horn on the burned side of her body was broken off halfway up and a green flame danced on the broken end. Dark blue scales, like a serpent's, covered the left side of her body. Her mouth split most of her face, and on the charred side, the skin covering her mouth was burned away to reveal rows of sharp, pointed teeth.

A whiter with a soul at their side sat in the middle of the boat. The soul looked like a recent death. The old man was bald with a hint of white peach fuzz for a beard. Age spots covered his naked body. Only his eyes gave away that he no longer counted among the living. The eyes glowed bright yellow with no sign of an iris or pupil in either socket, adding to the vacancy of his stare.

The gondolier stopped the boat at the edge of the dock. Ty and Dani stepped aside to let the demon get off with the collected soul.

Ty wondered if the old man might go into the recently freed up space within the mausoleum at the other end of the passage. The demon's black eyes slid from Dani to Ty with a question he didn't voice. Nothing guaranteed this whiter lived among the demons in the Blood Realm or that he answered to Malum. Ty kept his hand away from the hilt of his sword to avoid antagonizing the whiter.

Dani approached the gondolier, looking up to her from the dock. "We request passage to the Richmond Arch."

The gondolier held out her charred hand, bits of the bones in her fingers visible. The left hand held onto the oar, keeping it buried into the base of the canal to prevent the boat from drifting.

Ty went first and placed his hand in the one offered. They gripped one another, and he focused on the memory of Dani in the grocery store, the way she made him smile as he watched her pick among the poblano peppers. His chest warmed at the memory.

Then his eyes shut as a split second of vertigo struck him.

No matter how many times he'd made this exchange, the experience never got more comfortable. The sensation of having dozed off and awakened reminded him of when he'd been in school and too tired to stay awake. His head jerked up, abruptly alert, and the sensation of having lost his train of thought overwhelmed him, that sense of absence where clear intent had lived. No matter how hard he tried, he couldn't recall what had belonged in the newly vacated room within his mind.

The gondolier released her grip on his hand. A hint of ash stained his palm. He wiped the burned flesh off on his pants. He looked at Dani, and something about seeing her made him pause, a tickle at the back of his mind. He stepped into the boat, which wobbled beneath him. The gondolier prevented the boat from drifting, though.

Wicket hopped from the dock into Ty's lap and then down onto the floor of the gondola to wait for his mommy.

Dani reached out for the gondolier's hand, but the boat's driver pulled her hand away with a hiss. She shook her head.

"I'm offering to pay your fare." Dani's voice came out strained. Ty recognized the stress behind her words. She was close to losing it. He considered getting out of the boat to go to her, but if he climbed out now, he'd have to offer a new memory to get back on board.

The gondolier shook her head and then touched her mouth, pushing up the ends to force her divided face into a gruesome smile.

Dani's jaw clenched and her eyes widened with rage.

Ty spoke, keeping his voice quiet. "I think she's insisting on a happy memory."

"No!" Dani's voice echoed within the grotto. "I've chosen the memory. Now, fucking take it!"

The gondolier snarled and held her fist against her own chest. "Dani"—

"No! I don't want it! Get it out of me!" Her voice cracked on the next word as she whispered. "Please."

That's when Ty knew. She was offering the memory of her mother's death.

The gondolier reached out to Dani and touched her above her heart. She shook her head. The gondolier's yellow slit eyes held no malice. The gaze that met Dani's rage contained only sympathy.

Ty reached up and took Dani's hand into his. "You can't do that. Not yet." He said those last two words, knowing they were partially a lie, because no time could ever exist for Dani to part with that memory. "That's why we're here. You need that to finish this."

Dani reminded him of an animal with her leg in a trap. She didn't say it, but she was barely hanging on. She'd planned to do this all along.

He placed his other hand on top of hers. "Another time."

Dani knew he was offering a false hope. The surrender in her eyes made that clear. She didn't reach into her jacket for her memory journal. For all her fire, Dani must have suspected this would happen. She offered her hand with her head hung low. A tear ran off her cheek to fall into Purgatory's black waters.

She shivered as the gondolier took her hand and claimed whatever happy memory she'd chosen to surrender. Ty helped his wife step into the gondola, the narrow boat rocking beneath them. She sat down on the cushioned seat of black velvet and stared ahead.

Ty sat next to Dani, and Wicket hopped onto her lap. Dani absently stroked their dog's back. Her body jerked forward with a sob. Ty pulled her to him.

They'd been on the run for more than a week with little rest. Every decision they'd made had focused only on surviving and beating the clock to burn Malum's head and heart. The entire time, she'd been running towards this moment, keeping a step ahead of her mother's death, praying she'd rid herself of what she'd seen in her mother's house before she had to face it.

That race was done.

Chapter 47

The gondola floated through Purgatory. While Ty and Dani hadn't voiced the need, their gondolier paddled at a faster pace than normal. They couldn't have protested if their gondolier had chosen to take her time. Same as they needed Wicket to help them navigate Hell, they couldn't hope to find the Richmond Arch in Purgatory without the gondolier.

Centuries ago, the Order sent people here to map out the maze in hope of making sense out of it. Didn't take long to realize the layout constantly changed. One theory suggested that it altered itself based on all of the souls that occupied it at that particular moment in time, those of the living and the departed.

Dani didn't speak during the first hour of their boat ride. Her words came during the second.

"The only thing I remember about my dad is the day he left. Mom kicked him out, but she made damn sure he told me goodbye."

She'd told him that before, when they'd first started dating, when they realized they were going to be something more than a fleeting thing and wanted to learn all there was to know about each other. The pause she gave the story this time added a weight to it, the promise of more to the tale. Ty kept silent and waited for her to continue.

"I've journeyed to Purgatory at least two dozen times, and I've never excised the son of a bitch." She shook her head. "One memory, and he'd be gone."

"Why haven't you done it?"

"It's one of my earliest memories, and if I got rid of it, I don't know who that would make me. I was happy with who I'd become.

"I thought if I could get this one out now, before it changed me..."

He leaned his head against hers.

She let out a long breath, her body shuddering in his arms. "Already too late, isn't it?"

He fought the urge to look back at the gondolier. "I suspect so."

They listened to the paddle hit the water. Ty wondered how soon they might have to fight. Char wouldn't let them out of Purgatory without a challenge, no matter how great the risk of waiting for them in this place might be. No voices sounded from ahead, and the fog hid too much of where they were going for there to be any chance of spotting Char and his demons before it was too late to avoid them. If they could get off the boat and into the corridor leading to the mortal plane fast enough, they could use the space to limit the demons' numbers and give them a fighting chance.

Ty kissed the top of Dani's head. "Did I ever tell you what your mother said to me the day she recruited me? She dressed me down pretty good. I'd gotten bored and sloppy as a swordfighter. I'd lost the passion that made me want to pick up a sword in the first place, and I'll never forget the words she capped off her sales pitch with. She told me she was giving me the chance to find my heart."

Dani laughed.

Her smile filled him with relief.

"I gotta think your mom often wished she could have taken back that one."

"No, as much as you pissed her off some days, she knew you were the right one. Think she figured that out even before I did."

Maria and Ty's love for Dani had turned into a tug-of-war with Dani for the rope. A part of him felt guilty about his relief that the constant battle was finished. They didn't always fight over Dani, though. Strangely, things got better between him and Maria after Sebastian died. He suspected Maria appreciated how far he and Dani had gone to avenge Sebastian and knew they'd done it as much for her as they had for him.

He'd always be grateful to Maria. She made good on her offer. He found his heart because of her, and he'd always regret that he never thanked her for it.

Chapter 48

The voices offered the first warning. Ty couldn't tell how many he heard.

He checked his watch. Three hours to go, but he told himself to accept they'd reached their last hour.

The gondola slowed its pace.

Ty kept his voice to a whisper. "You up for this?"

Dani glared into the fog. He could see her already envisioning her strategy for the fight ahead. "You better believe it."

Ty jolted in his seat when the gondolier sang. He'd never heard one of them speak. She only sang a few words in a language he couldn't decipher, but they shivered their way down his spine, leaving goosebumps in their path. Her voice silenced most of the demons chattering. A part of him feared she was communicating with them, maybe even warning them that Ty and Dani were here.

Then other gondoliers sang from ahead, and the demons that hadn't yet fallen silent now did so. The song didn't resemble a piece of music. They sounded like they were speaking to each other in song. The gondoliers went back and forth with their boat's driver responding to them.

The singing stopped as the fog cleared enough for them to see the approaching dock. The same way the layout of Purgatory changed, so did the places in it. As if the realm had anticipated a horde of demons to greet Ty and Dani, the dock for the Richmond Arch had grown into a long platform of marble. At least fifty whiters, a handful of wolves, and a pair of steeds stood on that wide open space with their swords drawn. Their black and red eyes glared at Ty and Dani with unveiled bloodlust. They looked tired, angry, and eager for the fight.

At least a dozen boats lined the dock which had probably ferried the demons here. Each boat contained a single gondolier. Each of them had that half-burned look, although it alternated which side of their body was charred. The color of their scales varied between blue, green, and red. They all had a pair of horns, but most of them weren't damaged like their boat's gondolier. Some even had an extra pair of stubby horns sticking out of their cheeks. They all stood in their boats with their oars lifted out of the water. Most held the oars by the long wooden handles with the flat, wide blades pointing up towards the stone ceiling. Ty noticed the blades were made of the same green metal as their swords. Didn't take much imagination to see how the gondoliers might hack into him and Dani with those.

Ty and Dani stood in the boat and drew their swords, careful not to cut each other in the narrow vessel. The closest demons stepped back. Even if they were eager for the conflict, none of them wanted to make the first strikes while Dani and Ty were still fresh for the fight. They must have known how the demons in Malum's castle had fared. Sure, they might reanimate days later, but they might not, and getting cut down by Ty and Dani's swords would hurt—a lot.

Wicket crouched on the floor of the boat and growled up at the demons. One whiter twisted his lips into a snarl at their dog. Dani rolled her eyes towards Ty, and he nodded. She'd just called dibs on the idiot.

Ty looked for Char. The wolf probably hid among the rear of the pack, letting the lesser demons wear them out first. Char knew damn well that if they could get his head and heart here, Ty would gladly carry them with his bare hands to the Eternal Flame at the church. This close,

Ty didn't require a special bag to get them there in time to end him for good.

But that wide open space...

Ty felt his gut clench. As soon as they got ten feet onto the dock, the demons would surround them.

One of the wolves closer to them flexed her free hand, popping her knuckles.

The second Dani placed one foot on the dock, the demon who'd snarled at Wicket lunged at her. Dani parried the demon's sword with her left and slashed open his throat with her right.

She waded into the demons, making room for Ty to follow. This close to the water's edge, a single misstep might send them into the black canal.

The demons rushed at them, pressing the advantage of the dock's edge, but their brute force failed against Ty and Dani's finesse. A few demons lunged at them a little too eagerly, and Dani knocked them off course, using their momentum to send them into the black waters.

Ty's back screamed from the wounds taken in the earlier fight with the ravens. Dani's injuries weren't doing her any favors either. She screamed with each swing. Putting all of her effort into the fight aggravated her wounds.

The fight worsened as they pushed deeper into the horde. Wicket barked from where he waited on the boat. Ty was surprised the terrier hadn't joined in, but he was also relieved. He didn't want Wicket hurt.

He'd feared for what to do with Wicket when they finished all this, but now he worried what would become of their dog if he and Dani died in this fight, here and now.

They struggled to keep the demons from surrounding them, but there were too many. They could only hold back the tide for so long. A pair of whiters slipped past the gap between Ty and Dani. Ty answered with a wide sweep of his sword to deter other demons from coming at him from the front but also in the hope of cutting down these two before they could take up a position behind him. He missed both whiters.

A harsh series of musical shrieks and hisses echoed all around them. Ty and Dani went still despite every battle instinct for survival that demanded they not relax in this fight. Fortunately, the demons all stopped, too.

The shrieks came from the gondoliers. From the far end of the dock, demon heads launched into the air as the tall gondoliers attacked with their oars.

The gondolier from their boat sliced through the backs of the two whiters who got past Ty. Wicket stood at her feet, barking at the demons.

Ty and Dani stared gobsmacked. The gondolier pointed with intent at the demons for the two of them to keep fighting.

The eager horde recoiled as the gondolier dove into their ranks like a living scythe. She spun her oar, knocking back the demons, and then thrust with the sharp edge of the metal paddle.

The entire dock fell into chaos. The demons had only expected a pair of weary humans, but now, thirteen of Purgatory's gondoliers had entered the fight against the Blood Realm's minions. Ty and Dani rejoined the battle, staying close enough to their gondolier to fight with her and not get in the way of her oar.

The marble surface of the dock grew slick with black blood as the demons fell. They either fought or fled to the Richmond Arch. A demon could only last so long on the mortal plane without possessing a body, but there was no leaving the dock on a gondola, not when those ships' owners had declared their intention to deny them passage.

Wicket danced around at their backs, cheering them on. He stayed close to their gondolier. He ran past her at one point and tripped up a few of the demons who dared to challenge her. The gondolier snatched the last demon who dared to attack her by the throat, lifting him up off his taloned feet. Her forked tongue snapped out as she hissed at him, then she flung him down on his back and stabbed her oar through his throat, sending his head spinning away.

The smoke of decomposition wafted off the remains of the fallen demons.

The gondoliers didn't cheer or shout. They all looked to the gondolier by Dani and Ty and raised their oars in a salute. Then they returned to their gondolas and pushed away into the fog. Their gondolier walked to the dock's edge and washed the end of her oar in the water. Wicket stood on his hind legs as if he could climb her leg and crawl into her arms. The gondolier knelt and petted him.

When she stood again, she nodded to them.

"Thank you," Dani said.

The gondolier placed her hand over Dani's heart as she had before. She looked over to Ty and nodded before returning to her boat and pushing off into the fog. Wicket cheerfully barked after her until she vanished from sight.

Chapter 49

Ty puzzled over why the gondoliers had sided with them as they had. He supposed it had to do with the fact that Purgatory served as a bridge between humanity and Hell. Malum and his army were disrupting their natural role in the order of things. Seemed the gondoliers didn't approve of that.

"That or she was smitten with Wicket." Dani smiled at their dog, who pranced down the long passage towards the Richmond Arch.

"Wouldn't shock me."

They'd passed the point where the lanterns with green flames existed. The last pair on the walls looked translucent. This far down the passage, he knew they were past the reach of any demons. The nearness of the mortal plane would render them intangible and incapable of attacking them, not without a gift of blood to let them stay solid as Malum had done. At this point, the crystals in their sleeves ceased to work, too. They had to rely on flashlights.

He wished they could go home and drop into their bed after this, but that wasn't going to happen. Once they tossed Malum's head and heart into the Eternal Flame, they needed to take off. Ty's old friend Barry owned a place in the New Mexico desert. Well, he had when Ty last spoke to him a little more than two years ago. They'd go there and rest while figuring out a more long term plan to stay hidden from the Order.

The glow of regular firelight ahead helped them see the arch leading to the mausoleum in Hollywood Cemetery.

"What time is it?" she asked.

"A little after midnight."

She groaned. "Well, that pretty much rules out going somewhere for a real dinner. Humans were not meant to live on protein bars alone. Just saying."

"Right? Why are there no all-night Chinese restaurants in Richmond? I could really go for some teriyaki steak and some fried rice and egg rolls."

Dani hit him on the arm. "Stop it, you evil man! I'm hungry enough as it is without you doing your soliloquy tribute to Chinese food." She sniffed at her underarm and cringed. "Not that any decent restaurant would seat us. I smell worse than a middle-of-nowhere convenience store bathroom."

He blew her a kiss. "Certainly wasn't bothering me the other night."

"You are shameless."

He shrugged. "Yes, but it works for me."

"That it does."

When they got to the arch, Dani stopped and pulled off her backpack to check the bag with Malum's remains. The stench from that dwarfed anything coming off of Ty or Dani. "On the bright side, we've made it with time to spare. Fuck you, Malum." She capped off the insult by flipping the bird at his remains before closing the bag and slipping on the backpack.

"Let's get this over with and hit the road," she said.

Ty pushed open the door, and moonlight split the dark of the mausoleum.

The chill night air hit them with all the best smells of the city. Even the exhaust fumes on the wind tasted welcoming.

As soon as he stepped out, the door shook with a pair of metallic pings. He jumped back into the mausoleum and jerked the door closed. More pings sounded against the door. His first thought was that someone was shooting at them, but as more bullets pounded against the metal door, he realized they faced more than one shooter.

"Char," Dani said in a tone that left no doubt they'd missed something that should have been obvious.

Ty shook his head. "That's why he wasn't saying anything at the demons' last stand in Purgatory. He wasn't there."

Wicket barked as more bullets bounced off the metal doors.

Dani ran her fingers through her hair. "And now we're the idiots who brought swords to a gunfight."

PART VII

THE ETERNAL FLAME

Chapter 50

Ty tried to think through what was happening, but Dani's mind worked faster.

"Any clue how many?" she asked.

"No, I didn't get a decent look. Judging from all the bullets hitting us, gotta be at least five or more."

"There can only be so many of them. They had to possess willing victims to get into them and in control this fast." She had a far off look in her eyes as she worked through the problem aloud. "They're keeping their distance so we can't get them with our swords. And their aim isn't that good, or you'd be dead."

"They're getting close enough."

"We run for it. At least if we're moving targets, we'll be harder to hit. They're also settled in wherever they are like snipers, so getting up and chasing us won't be something they're ready to do, especially since it's cold out there."

She made a good point. It was late fall, and being still out in the cold this long while waiting for Ty and Dani to emerge from Purgatory might make the demons more likely to pull a muscle in their hosts' bodies while chasing after them.

"Well, I know if you're advocating we run, then it's the right call," Ty said. "Because I know how much you hate to run."

She scowled at him.

He couldn't restrain his smirk. "It's true."

"Fine."

Ty glanced down at their agitated Terrier dancing in place, eager to hit the road. "Better to let Wicket run on his own. He'll be faster and less of a target for them than if one of us carries him."

Dani nodded and took in a deep breath before letting it out. "We throw open the door, wait for the first lull in the gunfire, and then we go."

They moved to the sides of the double doors, with Wicket standing behind Dani. They flung open the doors. Gunfire pounded into the mausoleum. Some shots hit the brick walls. Other bullets passed through the Purgatory Arch and echoed their way down the corridor.

When the gunfire lessened, probably because some of the shooters realized they were only hitting bricks or needed to reload, Dani and Ty sprinted out of their hiding spaces. Wicket outpaced them.

Headstones littered the pre-Civil War cemetery with fences surrounding certain sections. That left the roads as the only safe place to run without fear of tripping over something. Initially, that offered Ty and Dani little cover.

More gunshots chased after them, pinging off the asphalt and into headstones. The moon provided the only light in the cemetery, because a place people weren't supposed to be inside of at night didn't require street lights. That added another reason to stick with the roads. The poor light also made it more difficult for the snipers to see them. Some of the great movie myths Ty learned from his stuntwork days focused on sharpshooters. Putting a tiny metal projectile into a person's body from a long distance wasn't easy, even when the target wasn't moving. Sure, sharpshooters existed, but they weren't perfect. The demons controlling these hosts couldn't borrow their hosts' memories or draw on their skills.

Dani cursed. If the demons had wounded her, it wasn't stopping her from running. She struggled to keep up with Ty. That meant little when he'd always been the faster runner. Every instinct in him screamed to not slow down with bullets hissing through the air around them, but he refused to leave his wife in the dust.

Wicket growled as they ran. He'd get way past Dani and Ty, then stop to spin around and make certain his humans were still behind him. Then he'd take off again.

Shouts went up as the gunfire lessened. The demons realized they'd overestimated their ability to hit moving targets. That or they'd expected Dani and Ty to stand their ground and fight.

Dani and Ty struggled to run as fast possible, and they had a lot of things going against them. The Order's mausoleum sat in one of the lowest parts of Hollywood Cemetery and on the opposite end of the property from the exit onto Cherry Street. That translated into running uphill the whole way while trying to cover a little less than a mile.

People lived around the cemetery, but the gunfire didn't guarantee anyone would recognize what they were hearing. Even if they realized people were shooting and not setting off fireworks, they still might not call the police. This was downtown Richmond, after all. The demons shouting and using flashlights in Hollywood Cemetery to track Dani and Ty did more to improve the chances of people calling the police.

The police showing up wouldn't help matters, though. Sure, it might save Ty and Dani from getting shot, but that made their odds of reaching the church in time to toss Malum's head and heart into the Eternal Flame nonexistent. The demons probably realized all that. That's why they weren't bothering with keeping quiet. That and they didn't give a damn what happened to their hosts if they got caught.

More bullets chased after them. None of them sounded that close, though. Certainly not as close as the initial round of gunfire. They also didn't have the same deep, percussive bang as the rifles, suggesting they'd switched to handguns and were shooting while running.

Just as Ty started feeling more confident in their situation, a bullet whizzed between them. He and Dani both ran faster as they realized how close that bullet had gotten.

The demons cursed in the distance behind them. The flashlight of one host illuminated a slightly overweight man with a bushy, unkempt beard. He looked less like a real soldier and more like a military cosplayer from a low budget film production. He'd stopped running, with his hands resting on his knees and gagging for air. Ty hoped the rest of the hosts were as physically unfit as that one. He wasn't going to pin his hopes on that, though.

Ty's legs ached and burned. He envied Wicket's ease to run around in circles without missing a beat.

The gunfire became less frequent, though. Ty assumed some of the demons were running out of steam like their military cosplayer friend. They also didn't have unlimited ammunition. Some might have gotten overeager and run out of bullets. All those things worked in his and Dani's favor. At least, he hoped they would.

The run felt like a year's worth of effort that would only ever end once his chest burst open and spit out his heart and lungs. That's what made the cemetery's grey brick office building on their right and the gatekeeper's house on the left such a glorious sight. The gates were shut, but the fence wasn't that tall.

Ty scooped up Wicket and dropped him on the other side before hopping the fence. Dani hopped over the fence a few seconds behind them. The demons weren't that far off. A few more gunshots confirmed they weren't out of ammo either.

He ran after Dani and Wicket. They'd taken off down the middle of Cherry Street, passing the row houses, most of which were dark at this hour.

"Sidewalk!" Ty shouted. "But watch your step!"

If the demons stayed on the street, the cars parked on the shoulder and the trees would provide cover from any gunfire. He and Dani needed to avoid tripping where the tree roots had broken through the sidewalk made of red bricks. They ran past a house with a white picket fence around its small front yard, and a dog inside the house barked at them. Wicket stopped to bark at the other dog, growled, and then took off again when Ty and Dani passed him.

They reached the corner of the street with the church on it. The traffic lights turned green at the right time for them to run across to the church without any danger of getting hit by a car.

A street light made that bright red door on the back of the church glow like blood. Dani grabbed the lock box turning the numbers to the proper code to open it.

"Dani?" Ty said as the demons turned the corner a half-block away.

"Someone changed the lock box!"

The Order. Had to be.

They knew better than to kick open the door. The bars on the window advertised how unlikely they were to force their way into the church through this entrance.

"Come on!" Dani ran down the sidewalk until they reached the side entrance.

They tossed Wicket over the black, cast iron fence before they hopped over it to join him. They landed in front of a small set of less vibrant red, double doors set beneath a stone arch with the words "Let Us Go Into The House Of The Lord" carved into it. Ty tried to force open the entrance, but he found the doors far less welcoming than the message above them.

Bullets hit the side of the church.

"The front." Dani struggled to get out those two words between breaths. They ran to the front doors which looked identical to the side doors. That didn't bode well, but Ty tried anyway. To his surprise, the doors gave a little on the first try, so he put everything he had left into a second attempt. The doors burst open, and he stumbled over the threshold with Dani and Wicket right behind him.

Ty didn't see anything that might brace the door, so they kept running into the sanctuary and straight up to the altar. Wicket yelped as he slipped on the marble floor once they reached the chancel. Ty and Dani stopped at the door to the room where the choir put on their robes. Wicket got his footing and raced past them into the room. Ty stumbled in the dark against a wooden clothes rack loaded with robes, which tumbled over.

Bullets pelted the altar, knocking one of the brass shields from where the church had mounted it above a pillar and onto the floor with a loud clatter.

How many bullets did these bastards have?

Ty also wondered how well these demons knew the layout of the church. It wasn't like they'd catch on fire if they came onto the property. If he'd been in Char's position, he'd have scoped out the place while still invisible and intangible, before seeking out their hosts.

Ty and Dani had to go up a few steps to get into the back of the church, which led them to the inside of the bright red door they'd first tried to use. They banged against the walls as they careened down the narrow stairs to the undercroft.

They heard the squeak of shoes from the sanctuary, a crash, and a curse. Someone wiped out up there. That also meant Ty and Dani only had a few seconds between reaching the Eternal Flame and the demons catching up to them.

Dani threw on the lights in the undercroft, so they could see where they were going. If they could have left the lights off, they would have, but without those, they'd have been blind down here. Even with the lights on, it might take the demons a moment to figure out their way down. Dani cursed as they reached the door to the Eternal Flame. She pointed in the direction of the back door to the church with the new lock box they couldn't open. "We don't have the keys."

Ty kicked the door. Unlike the doors to the church that opened into the building, this door pulled open. The first kick made a small hole in the door. His second made the hole wide enough to reach inside and open the door from the inside.

Dani shouted Ty's name. Three people appeared from around the corner leading into the undercroft. More redneck military cosplayers, two men and a woman. One of the men, one who looked to be in slightly better shape than the one Ty had seen earlier, raised his gun to shoot. Dani moved faster than Ty and darted down the stairs leading to the Eternal Flame. Ty never got far enough to even think about dodging.

The gun clicked, producing a curse from its owner. He threw the gun to the floor.

Ty laughed. "Yeah, those run out of ammo a lot faster in real life, don't they?"

Wicket, standing at Ty's feet, growled. Ty nudged him with his foot. "Go to your mother." The dog hopped down the stairs and out of sight.

The demons charged at Ty. He drew his sword. The one who'd tossed his gun away pulled out a dagger with a jagged edge to its five-inch blade. He ran with an awkward gate, his knees coming up unnaturally high, and before they collided, Ty realized they probably hadn't yet adjusted going from a leg with two joints to legs with only one knee. The observation distracted him for a second, but he recovered in time to swing his sword.

He didn't hesitate to take a killing strike. This wasn't some unfortunate soul slowly corrupted by a demon's influence. Like the hosts that killed Sebastian a year ago, these people had to have submitted willingly for the demons to get this much control this quickly. As far as Ty was concerned, that made them open game.

Ty's sword slit through the charging man's throat with the same ease as passing through water. Demons were made of tougher stuff, so cutting up a human being with this otherworldly green metal offered no challenge.

That didn't stop the man's body from running into him. The man's dagger missed Ty, but the narrow undercroft prevented Ty from avoiding getting tackled. The impact knocked him back a good ten feet, leaving the door to the Eternal Flame's chamber wide open for the man and woman who were left. Hitting the cement floor knocked Ty senseless for a split second, even though he avoided hitting his head. The cut to his back started to bleed again. The only thing that kept him from getting killed by the other two demons was that they were more interested in rescuing Malum's remains.

Ty shouted to his wife as he shoved the dead demon's host off of him. He whimpered as he struggled to ignore the pain in his back while getting to his feet. He needed to reach Dani. The demons outnumbered her, and her only bargaining chip was Malum's head and heart, assuming she hadn't already tossed them. If she had, then the demons would cut her down for revenge.

Chapter 51

Ty scrambled down the stairs to the Eternal Flame's chamber. He reached the bottom in time to see the female host holding Malum's rotting, horse-shaped head. Her blonde ponytail was coming undone in disarray. Her dark eyes widened at the unexpected sight of him. She'd been ready to run up the steps with Malum's horse head tucked in her arm like a running back with a football.

Dani danced around the Eternal Flame with her swords drawn. The remaining demon, a man who looked less like a military cosplayer and more like the real deal, held a sword of his own. "The heart's already in there!" Dani shouted as she struggled against the other man. "I'll deal with Char. Get the head!"

To Ty's surprise, the woman with Malum's head smiled at him. "So disappointing to see you again." She had a sword in her free hand and stood ready to fight. That's when he recognized her. The posture matched up with his memories of the fallen human, which explained the ease with which she walked in her host body compared to the other demons.

"Nera?" He took his time walking down the steps with his sword pointed at her. "Is that you in there?"

She bowed ever so slightly in answer to his question. "A pity you two didn't run a little faster to another Purgatory Arch." She backed away, her focus shifting between Ty and Dani, who fought the other demon. Nera stayed up against the wall of the round room.

Dani and Char parried swings as Wicket barked at the demon. Their dog kept behind Dani and out from under her feet.

Ty needed to get Malum's head out of Nera's grip and into the Eternal Flame before it vanished. With the head out of the bag and in the mortal realm, it decomposed more quickly, leaving him and Dani with only minutes to end him.

Nera held back during their fight in the blood swamp. They exchanged swings, and her skill at deflecting his attacks and taking her own swipes at him left little doubt how good she really was. She wouldn't hold back this time, not with Char this close to her.

She lunged at Ty, sword tip aiming for his stomach. He pivoted to avoid the sword and punched the right side of her face. She answered with a kick to his calf that sent him stumbling into the curved wall. They slashed and punched one another. She had the advantage of being fresh for the fight, and she had the skill to finish the job.

Nera dropped Malum's head and grabbed Ty by the wrist of his sword arm. She shoved the edge of her sword at his throat, but he grabbed her wrist to stop her short. He spun Nera around and shoved the back of her head against the red brick wall. He expected that to knock her senseless long enough to finish the job, but Nera took the hit without a flinch and kneed him in the lower abdomen.

She tried to shove him away, but his size gave him the advantage. Her demon body gave her superior strength, but while possessing a human, she could only work within her host's limits. Ty slammed her against the wall that much harder, and this time took the fight out of her for a moment. He jerked free of her grip, spun around for a windup, and swung at her waist. She dodged his attack by dropping flat onto her stomach. A bark of pain escaped her as she hit the black marble floor. She grabbed Ty's ankle and squeezed. He jumped out of her grip to avoid her sword. The back of his foot hit something that moved, and for a moment, he thought he might have stepped on Wicket, but then he realized it was Malum's head. He kicked at the head, sending it sliding towards the Eternal Flame behind him.

"No!" Char shouted. He slammed his sword down, trying to block Malum's head from the fire pit but missed.

The head stopped short of the flames, bouncing up against the skull of the serpent-like creature that lined the edge of the fire pit.

Dani took advantage of the opening to swing at Char's exposed torso. He lunged out of the way, but Dani got his sword arm. Her blade hacked through most of the forearm. His sword dropped as he screamed. The now-useless limb dangled by a bit of skin and muscle.

Nera screamed and scrambled to her feet, running to Char's aid.

That distracted Dani long enough for Char to grab her by the throat with his good hand and lift her up off the floor.

Ty grabbed Nera by the back of her shirt. Using her momentum against her, he swung her around and slammed the top of her head into the brick wall. She lost her sword and he pummeled her for it. He kicked and punched her and then slammed his sword down on her legs, digging deep into her left thigh.

"Ty!" Dani croaked. One of her hands, having lost one of her swords, clawed at Char's arm, drawing blood but failing to make him drop her. Her other hand had one of her sword's buried into Char's stomach. She twisted the blade, but that still wasn't enough to make him let go.

"I gave you two every chance to walk away!" Char's voice seethed with rage and pain. "Drop your sword, human, or I toss her into the flames."

The way an Eternal Flame would consume a demon, ending their existence, it could do the same to a human's soul. If Dani went into the fire, that would finish her.

In the silence of Ty's indecision, they all heard the pitter-patter of Wicket's toenails on the marble floor. He scampered up to Malum's head and nudged it with his snout over the serpentine skeleton and into the flames.

Char screamed and flung Dani towards Wicket. Ty dove forward and slammed into his wife's body as he tackled her to the floor, keeping her from going into the flames or crushing Wicket. The flames burned red and purple with the scream of Malum being consumed.

Dani scrambled to her feet as Char grabbed his sword with his good hand. She sliced his wrist open with her sword, causing him to drop the weapon.

Char fell to his knees. "Nera!"

She'd made it up to all fours and glared over at them as she grabbed her own sword.

"Dear Char, I do adore you, but you have never known when to just give it up." She got up on her knees and slit open her host's throat. She collapsed to the floor. Her eyes were wide as the host died, not in shock or pain but in a triumphant glare.

"I'll bleed out soon enough," Char said as his bloody spit slid down his chin.

"Then I'll toss you into the flames before your host dies," Dani said as she grabbed him in a choke hold and slid another arm around his torso to drag him over to the Eternal Flame.

"You'll condemn this human's soul to the flames, too?" Char laughed through the obvious pain he felt. Ty saw the look on Dani's face as she warred over that choice. They didn't have any compunction about killing these willing hosts, but to end their existence forever was another matter.

Char laughed as he spit out blood that hissed into the flames in front of his face. "What a pity. If only you had a priest to draw me out."

"We don't need a priest." Ty noticed the confused look on Dani's face as she struggled to hold Char in place. Judging from the way her eyes assessed him, she wondered if he meant to toss the human in with Char. "A good friend once told me that all it takes is faith and will. Well, I have all the faith in the world in me and my wife to overcome anything, and I have the will to act on it."

Char stared at Ty with an uncertain look that contorted his face. He probably considered Ty's threat absurd, but he also wasn't sure he should dismiss it.

"I have two words for you, Char." Ty walked over and knelt beside him. "Get. Out."

Char laughed at him, but then his host's body heaved forward. His jaw clenched and his eyes widened in disbelief. While Dani maintained her grip on Char's torso, Ty grabbed his head to make certain it faced the flames. The host's body succumbed to his command and vomited up the monster inside him. The waves of demon bits shot out of his mouth and into the Eternal Flame. It took a few minutes, but all of Char's form erupted from his host. The flames turned red and purple as Char's spirit screamed during his last moment.

The host shook in Dani's grip and gaped at Ty. This wasn't Char anymore, just a foolish man who mistook himself as somehow better and worthier than other people. He gasped out one word. "Please." Then his eyes rolled back in his head and the tension fled from his body. Dani released him. He dropped to the floor with a loud slap into a puddle of his own blood.

Dani stood and hugged Ty, careful not to squeeze him too tight.

"Sebastian and my mother would be proud of you," she whispered and then kissed him on the throat beneath his ear. "Almost as much as I am."

They needed a doctor, but there wasn't time for that. Any ER would take one look at them and call the police. Then the Order would find them. For now, they had to get to their car, hopefully still where they parked it a few blocks from here, and get out of Richmond.

Wicket followed them up the stairs as they ascended to the under-croft.

"Don't move!" The threat came from a man with short, curly blonde hair and dressed in a suit and tie. Six others, dressed in a similar fashion, accompanied him, and they all had guns pointed at Ty and Dani. They blocked the path leading out of the undercroft.

The man with the blonde hair tilted his head to stare down the barrel of his gun. "And drop your swords."

"Officer Horwitz?" Dani still held both of her swords.

He nodded, confirming her assumption. "Swords, please." He gestured with his gun for them to drop their weapons.

Ty finally realized why the man had sounded familiar on the phone. He'd heard this voice in the Order's offices on the day they'd taken away Madison.

Wicket growled at the people in front of them.

"We'll put down our swords and go with you, but only if we stay together," Dani said. "And that includes our dog."

"Try to take him," Ty said, "and I guarantee some of you will die for it. Sword or no sword."

Horwitz snorted in disbelief. "You really think you're in any position to dictate terms to the Order after all that's happened?"

"We've been to Hell and back, cut down more demons than I could ever count, and exorcised a demon without a priest." Dani stepped closer to them, drawing all the guns to aim at her. "You're damn right we can dictate terms."

"I don't have an interest in harming any of you, as long as you don't force our hand. We came here for answers." Horwitz lowered his gun and gestured for his partners to do the same. "First, we'll get you patched up—you certainly look like you need it. Then we'll all take a little trip where we can have a very long conversation."

Ty and Dani placed their swords flat on the concrete floor. Some of the Order's oversight officers put their guns away, but not all of them. Dani picked up Wicket and carried him as they followed Horwitz out to the alley behind the church and into the back seat of a waiting grey Mercedes.

Chapter 52

They stopped first at the Order's Richmond offices where a doctor stitched them up and bandaged them. From there, they rode to a small airfield and got on a private jet for a long flight to London. On the flight, they ate some sub sandwiches that their escort picked up for them on the way to the plane, and they tasted glorious after being forced to sustain themselves on protein bars for more than a week. For most of their flight, they slept in the jet with Wicket taking turns sleeping next to Ty and Dani. Anytime one of the four oversight officers on the flight came near them, Wicket would growl and wake them. Ty never got the impression the officers were going to try anything, but he didn't mind Wicket being paranoid on their behalf.

They arrived in London around six in the evening which completely confused Ty's body. Thanks to his brief time as a stuntman, he'd endured his share of international travel, but he hadn't dealt with it much since joining the Order. He'd forgotten the havoc long flights through multiple time zones inflicted on his mind and body. Never mind he was already dealing with the assault on his internal clock from ten days in Hell. No sooner had they landed in London than they were shoved into a van for a two-hour ride down to Canterbury.

They ended up in a bland-looking office building that could have fit into most any city and created the illusion that they hadn't really gone somewhere outside of Richmond or America.

They spent most of that evening in a small meeting room recounting everything to Horwitz and a few other oversight officers. Ty took some satisfaction and amusement out of their reactions to how they got out of the Kraken's realm. They never questioned the idea of a giant kraken floating in an abyss full of ghost ships, but somehow they still scoffed at Wicket's ability to predict exactly where the gate they needed would be, especially since it required using one of the rope bridges like a giant rubber band.

At three in the morning, the oversight officers shuffled Ty, Dani, and Wicket to a hotel where they slept until noon.

When they woke, Horwitz drove them to a café in an uppity-looking shopping center with a glass roof to permit sunlight but keep out any precipitation, not that there was any today. Ty worried they wouldn't be able to keep Wicket with them once they went into the café, and even suspected this might be a trick to separate them. That wasn't an issue, though. The much-needed bath they gave him in the hotel room's sink probably helped. They'd also taken showers and changed into some fresh clothes the oversight officers had picked up from their apartment before leaving Richmond.

The café occupied a long and narrow space with windows looking out on all of the afternoon foot traffic. A few people stared in at them with only mild curiosity. Dani and Ty were the only customers in the café. Apparently, the place had closed for a "special event" for them to meet with someone.

After more than a week tromping their way through Hell, the mortal world seemed the more surreal place.

Classic rock played on the speakers, and Don Henley sang "Desperado" as they sat at a table near the counter. They ordered some drinks and food while they waited for whoever they were here to meet. Horwitz didn't order. He sat stock still in his chair watching the two of them as if he expected them to attack him if he dared to ignore them for even a second.

"Coffee," Dani moaned as she took her first sip and then chugged it. She held up the bowl-shaped mug with a logo of antlers on it and called to their server for more, adding in a "please" as an afterthought.

Horwitz looked scandalized at the way they downed their coffee and devoured their burgers and fries.

"Don't judge, man," Ty said between bites of his burger. "We spent the past two weeks mostly eating energy bars. You have no idea."

Whatever reply Horwitz had planned, he stopped short of saying it and stood as someone entered the café. The Doors' "Riders on the Storm" played as a woman with short black hair crowned with an old, red fedora walked up to them. She took the chair Horwitz had vacated. He walked away, moving over to the door of the business.

Ty couldn't pin down this woman's age. Her features were smooth and porcelain pale. He'd also never seen someone with eyes so black that he couldn't tell where pupil ended and the iris began. Most of all, those eyes had seen a lot of past. He recognized her by the red fedora, more than anything else. He'd glimpsed her in the Richmond offices the night the Order took away Madison and Cinto.

The woman removed her fedora and placed it on the table. "My name's Nevada."

Ty sat up, startled because he'd expected a British accent. "You're American?"

"Yes." She leaned back in her seat with her hands in her lap and glared at him. "And you two have really fucked up. We haven't lost an entire branch of the Order in more than a century."

Dani tapped a finger on the table. "Technically, you still haven't."

"Save it." Nevada shifted her glare to Dani. "The Order has to re-build their entire presence in Richmond, and the Blood Realm would spot you both far too easily. Your apartment—what's left of it—kiss that home goodbye. Your days in the U.S. are done."

"But you're not planning to toss us in a prison." Ty crossed his arms. "Otherwise, why are we meeting in a place like this instead of already sitting in a cell? We might have this café all to ourselves, but anyone passing by can see us in here."

Her black eyes shifted between the two of them, making some kind of assessment. "That story you gave the oversight officers," she paused to glance down at Wicket who sat on the floor next to Dani. He cocked his head to the side, looking up at this pale woman and sniffing her without daring to get closer. His ears perked up as he realized he had her attention. "How much of it was true?"

"We didn't lie about any of it," Dani said. "If we were going to lie, don't you think we'd have left out the deal we made with Malum?"

"You were in the spiritual realms for more than ten days," she said with the appropriate disbelief. "There's no one alive in the Order who's stayed on the other side that long."

"Yeah, we don't recommend it." Ty sipped his coffee. Oh, sweet Jesus! Did this coffee really taste that good or was it because he'd gone so long without any.

"There's also the matter of your dog." As Nevada returned her attention to Wicket, his fluffy ears perked up again. "When I read the transcript of your interrogation, I saw your dog is a fifteen pound terrier. I thought it was the most ludicrous thing I'd ever read."

Dani reached down to scratch behind his ears. "He's a smart boy."

"And possibly one of the most skilled navigators among the dogs in the Order. That's not a resource they want to waste."

Everything in Ty went cold, remembering that exact word being applied to Madison's dog before the Order separated them. He checked Horwitz, but the oversight officer simply stood by the door of the café with his hands at his sides. Ty glanced out the café's windows and didn't see anyone who might be a dog handler.

He exchanged a look with Dani who looked equally pissed and ready to grab the steak knife by her plate.

"Don't." Nevada narrowed her eyes, obviously sensing they were ready to fight. "One, we don't plan to take him from you, so you can relax. And two, I would have you both dead on the floor in seconds."

"We're not so easy to kill," Dani said with only a hint of the hesitation that Ty felt. Nevada's threat lacked any bravado.

"The point is that this world is full of dangers that live in the shadows, and people with your skills are too rare to waste in a prison, no matter how deserved that punishment might be." She placed her hands on the table and leaned forward. "The Order wants to use you to train other exorcist's swords in how to survive Hell."

Dani leaned towards the other woman, their faces uncomfortably close. "I'm curious. What is your position in the Order, because I've never heard of you?"

"I'm not part of the Order. I head what you might call a sister organization."

"Then why are you the one here telling us all this?" Ty kept his arms crossed, opting against getting any closer than necessary.

"The Order's leadership prefers that you not know who they are lest you fuck up again and get them killed as you did your entire branch. I'm here so you can see exactly who will hunt you down and kill you if you two ever step out of line again."

Dani didn't back away. "And if we refuse?"

"Then your dog will be orphaned." She smiled down to him. "And that would be a pity, don't you think?"

"Yes, it would." Ty took another sip of his coffee as he considered their position. "What ever happened to Madison Lin and her dog Cinto?"

"Lin is imprisoned. It's not the harshest of places, but it's cruel enough to be a punishment. The dog has been less than receptive to any of her new owners."

"Then let Madison out and return Cinto to her."

Nevada shook her head. "There's no way the Order would ever reinstate her."

"Not what I'm asking. Free her and reunite her with her dog. You can even give her the same threat you're giving us. She steps out of line, then you hunt her down and kill her. I'm not making this request on Madison's behalf. She earned her punishment. Cinto didn't."

Nevada's lips pressed into a thin line. "I can't promise that, but I'll make your demands to the Order's leadership. They might even agree to it. Is there anything else?"

"Just that we aren't to be separated." Dani reached over and took Ty's hand. "The three of us stay together. We don't ever work apart."

Nevada stood and grinned down at them. "I pity anyone foolish enough to try such a thing." She put on her red fedora. "I'll be in touch soon with your next assignment, but you'll be working out of Canterbury for the foreseeable future. In the meantime, Horwitz will see about returning you to Richmond to get your affairs and belongings in some semblance of order for your move."

On that note, Nevada left the café.

Horwitz didn't rejoin them, not right away. Maybe he felt they deserved the moment to themselves.

Dani squeezed Ty's hand. "Looks like you're officially stuck with me, Mr. Faison."

"Till death do us part, Mrs. Faison-Cortez."

As they kissed, Wicket hopped onto Dani's lap and snatched a fry from her plate.

Acknowledgements

Many people helped me as I wrote this book. The first and most obvious to thank is my wife Sheri. I couldn't ask for a better creative partner, and she saved me from making a big mistake when I started this novel. It might surprise readers to know that I didn't originally plan for this story to take place on Earth. That would have taken away Richmond, the Episcopal Church, and Ty's backstory as a former stuntman in film and TV. Shortly after I started the rough draft, I told Sheri about my original idea to do this as a second-world fantasy. Her immediate response amounted to "Well, where's the fun in that?" As often happens with Sheri, she was right and made this book much better.

This story also wouldn't exist without Sheri, because my journey through life with her has given me reason to believe a story focused on a happily-married couple can still lead to a great adventure. We both came from parents who divorced when we were children. I came across a study that indicates the risk of divorce is 200 percent higher for couples like us. At the time of this book's release, Sheri and I are two months away from our thirtieth wedding anniversary and our thirty-sixth dating anniversary (they're the same day). A nice caveat to the statistic for me is that my parents divorced when I was in high school but remarried a couple of years after Sheri and I married. Mom and Dad got it right the second time around, and I've always been proud of them for that.

I want to thank my beta readers and best friends Katharine Herndon and Phil Hilliker. As always, their feedback helped make this manuscript better. Phil also gets credit for this book's amazing cover.

Thanks to swordfighter Sámhlaoch Swords who allowed me to interview him while writing this book. His insights helped me change my approach to the action scenes and to better develop the personalities for these characters. To any swordfighting professionals, just know the fault for any lack of realism in the many action scenes all belongs to me. I'll be the first to admit to taking liberties in the name of having a good time.

I also want to thank two websites that proved invaluable for Ty's journey through the aircraft carrier. *U.S.S. Yorktown* (http://cv5yorkt own.com/) provided blueprints for the ship. That, coupled with photographs from the U.S. Navy's *Naval History and Heritage Command* website (https://www.history.navy.mil/), helped me map out Ty's journey through the ship, including what obstacles and advantages he might find along the way.

The staff at Fountain Bookstore, including owner Kelly Justice and general manager Andi Richardson, have supported my writing career since my first book was released in 2013. I also want to thank the folks at Abi's Books and Brews where I did a lot of editing for this book.

Thanks to Trudy Hale for her writers retreat, the Porches. I've written there a lot for more than a decade now. I've lost count of the many times I've enjoyed visits there with friends like Sheri, Katharine, Phil, Kristi & Adam Austin, Mike & Shawna Christos, Leila Gaskin, Denise Golinowski, Eric Smith, and many others. These are all friends I've found through my work with James River Writers. So much of my journey as an author and a person is owed to JRW.

Last, but not least, there's Wicket. Sheri and I adopted him in November 2016. He's got a dog bed next to my desk, and he hung out with me as I wrote a lot of this book (he's often with me when I write at home). For those who loved the scene in Chapter 33 where Dani and Ty met their Wicket for the first time, the way their Wicket found them is almost exactly how our Wicket chose Sheri and me.

Earlier that summer, our dog Page passed away. Our family was gutted by Page's death, but when it came to the idea of getting a new dog months later, I was the last holdout in the family. Sheri finally talked me into looking for a new dog in November. That search led us to the Richmond Animal League. I'd wanted another big dog like Page, but Wicket had other plans. When Wicket was allowed to walk freely through the back room at the shelter, he immediately hopped into my lap. Sheri snapped a picture of me and Wicket right at that moment. We've often joked the caption to that picture is "That moment when you weren't getting a dog, and now you are."

About the Author

Bill Blume's love for the written word started in high school with an addiction to comic books that was later hijacked by novels such as *Frankenstein* and *Dragonflight*. His short stories have been published in many fantasy anthologies and ezines. Like the father figure in his *Gidion Keep, Vampire Hunter* series, he's worked as a 911 dispatcher for more than 20 years.

To learn more about Bill and his books, visit his website at www.billblume.net.

Glimmers & Trigger Warnings

For those unfamiliar with "Glimmers," these are some of the things in this story that some people can safely enjoy (I'll get to the Trigger Warnings after this).

- Bizarre Creatures

- Dogs (None Die or are Physically Harmed)

- A Happily Married Couple in a Healthy Relationship Who Work Together as Equals

- Kick-ass Women

- Portals

- Swordfighting

- Strange Settings

Now, for the Trigger Warnings. While I had a lot of fun writing this book and hope you will enjoy reading it, this story does include some dark content. With that in mind, here's a list of some trigger warnings.

- Assault

- Blood

- Child Abduction

- Cursing

- Cutting

- Death

- Decapitation

- Demonic Possession

- Demons

- Dismemberment

- Exorcism

- Gun Violence

- Hell

- Knife and Sword Violence

- Loss of a Close Friend

- Loss of a Parent

- Monstrous Creatures

- Murder

- Profanity

- Purgatory

- Sex

- Smoking

- Suicide

- Vomiting

I've tried to include everything I could think of, so if I've missed anything, please feel free to contact me via my social media and let me know. I keep a mirror list on my website for this book, and will update that with additional items, if needed. If there are future editions of this book, I will update those, as well.

www.ingramcontent.com/pod-product-compliance
Lightning Source LLC
Chambersburg PA
CBHW020244010826

48973CB00006B/1647